CHRISTMAS WITH THE CONDUIT

A DCI MICHAEL YORKE THRILLER BY

WES MARKIN

ABOUT THE AUTHOR

Wes Markin is the bestselling author of the DCI Yorke crime novels set in Salisbury. His latest series, The Yorkshire Murders, stars the compassionate and relentless DCI Emma Gardner. He is also the author of the Jake Pettman thrillers set in New England. Wes lives in Harrogate with his wife and two children, close to the crime scenes in The Yorkshire Murders.

You can find out more at:

www.wesmarkinauthor.com

facebook.com/wesmarkinauthor

PRAISE FOR WES MARKIN

serious crime fan will love it!" – **Owen Mullen, Bestselling Author**

BY WES MARKIN

DCI Yorke Thrillers

One Last Prayer

The Repenting Serpent

The Silence of Severance

Rise of the Rays

Dance with the Reaper

Christmas with the Conduit

Better the Devil

A Lesson in Crime

Jake Pettman Thrillers

The Killing Pit

Fire in Bone

Blue Falls

The Rotten Core

Rock and a Hard Place

The Yorkshire Murders

The Viaduct Killings

The Lonely Lake Killings

The Cave Killings

Details of how to claim your **FREE** DCI Michael Yorke quick read, **A lesson in Crime**, can be found at the end of this book.

Text copyright © 2020 Wes Markin

First published 2020

ISBN: 9798351553467

Imprint: Dark Heart Publishing

Edited by Jay G Arscott

Cover design by Cherie Foxley

For Gill and Derek

1

CHRISTMAS DAY

THE TURKEY WAS wheeled out. It was an absolute monster of a bird. The residents of *Rose Hill* were delighted.

Everyone apart from Bernard Driggs.

He was too busy staring into the eyes of the woman he loved. And, to be honest, he didn't really have much of an appetite these days. He'd lost it when he'd turned seventy-three, and it'd never really come back.

Still, he showed some respect, broke his sacred eye-contact with Louisa and glanced at the mutant bird, which was probably experiencing great relief in being dead, and not having to drag its gigantic body around the farmyard. If it'd indeed been bred in a farmyard rather than a laboratory.

The male carer wheeling in the avian centrepiece for the Christmas lunch looked as if he'd inherited this turkey's steroid supply. Bernard didn't like that he didn't recognise the man, but it was a common occurrence. *Rose Hill* was a nursing care home, not a residential home, which meant most of the people around the hall, currently bobbing their weary heads to *Wizzard's 'I wish it could be Christmas everyday',* were as self-sufficient as this turkey on the platter, and so that required a lot of staff; qualified nurses included. And today, being Christmas Day, meant that there would be agency workers.

The popping of a cracker jerked his attention to an adjacent circular table. Ronnie was looking pleased with himself. He'd taken on Deirdre and won. Surprising really. Until today, Ronnie hadn't been out of bed in over a week. The good old Christmas spirit, eh?

The grating sound of metal on metal jolted his attention back to the large carer. Carving knives.

For as long as he could remember, sudden noise had been a problem for Bernard. He'd been affectionately known as *Flincher* on the golf course a few years back, before the arthritis had twisted up his hands. The truth, though he never liked to talk about it, was that the flinching had worsened since his ten weeks on the Falkland Islands back in 1982—

'Bernard?' Louisa said.

This was a far more welcome pull on his attention, and he accepted it without a flinch. He met her stare again. Her eyes, which although framed by wrinkles, an inevitable weapon of age, were the most youthful eyes in the place. Looking into those eyes, he just couldn't believe that she would be dead by next Christmas.

'You reckon its free-range?' she said. 'You know how Maisie feels.'

Maisie was Louisa's granddaughter. She'd married an ethical farmer. Their animals were raised on grass and were apparently "very happy". Bernard wondered if they were still happy when they got the chop, but he obviously never asked that question.

'Well, you could have gone and had Christmas there?' Bernard said.

'But I wanted to spend it with you. So, the turkey? Free range?'

'I'd like to hope so. Especially since I'm now paying almost a grand a week to live in the luxurious, although rather sleepy, *Rose Hill*.'

She squeezed his hand and smiled. Creases wrapped around her eyes, but the vitality still shone through them. 'Always about the money with you.'

'Let me guess ...' Bernard smiled too. 'You can't take it with you?'

She held up a cracker. 'We live for now.'

'Always,' Bernard said, pulling the cracker. She won. Again.

Lunch was slow, and the Christmas hits playlist was on its third spin. Bernard managed a few mouthfuls of mutant bird, and his taste buds *did* come alive momentarily under the tang of cranberry sauce, but eventually everything turned to sawdust again. Louisa didn't manage a great deal either. As the cancer took greater hold, the medicine regime intensified, and her appetite was the sacrifice. She often joked that she was getting enough calories from the pills anyway.

When *Last Christmas* by *Wham* did the rounds again, Bernard had to wipe a tear from his eye. Louisa took his hand again and leaned over. 'Don't.'

'But next year—' He stopped himself. He'd promised himself he wouldn't do this. Not today.

'*Now*. We live for *now*.'

Bernard nodded.

He looked around the hall again. There must have been eight tables, each with three or four diners. Many of the residents of *Rose Hill* had been taken home by their loved ones to see their grandchildren. Those who remained were the unlucky ones. The ones with no family, or those with a family unwilling to blemish their fairy-tale Christmas Day. Bernard had no family, but he had Louisa and, today, she had him. That made them very lucky.

Also lucky was the fact that they could feed themselves. Over ten residents were being spoon-fed by carers. Some residents were already asleep in their chairs. Being in full control of their faculties, Bernard realised, was an absolute blessing.

And he wanted to use that to their advantage.

He leaned over the table. 'I have some mistletoe in my room.'

'Bernard Driggs!' Louisa said. Her face reddened slightly. He liked it. She'd been looking rather pale of late and that had worried him.

Bernard gestured over his shoulder at Kate, the nearest carer. She had a heart of gold but was an absolute stickler for the rules. 'I'll go first. If I get past the Gestapo, you follow.'

She bit her bottom lip. Bernard felt a rush of adrenaline. He liked it. Christmas Day was now putting a spring in his step too!

'Now, now, Mr Driggs, not eating your vegetables?' Kate said, smiling.

'Please, Ms, can I go to the toilet?'

Kate laughed. 'Knock it off. Are you having fun?' She winked. 'Louisa is quite the catch.'

'Now, you knock it off!'

'Why are you asking me anyway? Communal toilets are that way.' She pointed in the direction he had come from.

'Just going to my room, Kate, if that's alright. I left my

mobile phone in there, and I just want to check if Bryan has written. You know Bryan? My brother who lives overseas. I'm going to ring him.'

'Okay, I'll come with you.'

'I could be a while.'

Kate thought about it for a moment and sighed. 'Okay … I really want to hear *Slade* for the third time, and it's up next, so go on then. Hit the buzzer if you need anything while you're in there.'

Bernard smiled back at Louisa. As he approached the exit to the hall, the carer who'd dismantled the turkey cut him off. He didn't smile. Bernard didn't like patronising carers of which, fortunately, there were few, but he *really* didn't like miserable carers who behaved like they were prison guards.

'Excuse me,' Bernard said.

'Where're you going?'

'No offence, but I've had this conversation already … add to that the fact that I'm not a prisoner.'

He heard someone approaching from behind him. 'I've spoken to Mr Driggs, Roy, thanks.'

Bernard smiled. 'Yes, Roy, she has spoken to me … like an adult.'

As Bernard slipped past, he said to the scowling carer, 'Good work on the turkey, Roy, but try to remember that human beings aren't turkeys.'

On his journey down the corridor, he wondered how on earth Louisa was going to get to his room alone. They were ever so vigilant, and although they only joked about them being like the Gestapo, sometimes it felt like they were giving them a good run for their money.

She'd make it though. Despite the cancer, Louisa was still strong on her feet. She'd pass off a similar excuse. A soul-soothing family phone call needed to keep the Christmas blues away.

When he got into his room, he organised as quickly as he could. He pulled his reading table into the centre of the room, placed a candle on it, and then took some contraband from the bottom of his wardrobe. A lighter. He smiled up at the fire alarm. Although it was highly unlikely that a candle would set it off, he wasn't taking any chances. Following some savvy Google research, he'd pried it open prior to the Christmas festivities and deactivated it. The carers would surely have been alerted to its sudden inactivity, but Bernard had banked on them being too busy with the Christmas preparations to deal with it right away. It seems banking on their incompetence had been a sure bet. And one worth taking now the candle-lit moment with his beloved neared.

After lighting the candle, he glanced at his mobile phone and saw that there was, in fact, a message; not from his fictional brother overseas, but rather a friend he often walked with.

The message said: *Merry Christmas, Bernard. Go easy on that turkey, big man. Make sure you open your present. Take care of your lovely lady, and never, ever, ever forget 1982.*

Bernard slipped the phone into his front shirt pocket, and his heart began to thump.

1982.

He heard the gun shot and flinched. He saw Gavin collapse, clutching his ruined throat. Another gunshot. He flinched again. This time, Bradley took the bullet. His friend scraped at the hole in his chest and fell backwards. They were coming now. It was surely all over for him too—

There was a knock at his door.

'WHY ARE YOU SHAKING?' Louisa said, reaching over and taking one of Bernard's hands.

He looked up at her, struggling to focus, still unable to believe what was actually happening. It was unthinkable ... his beautiful Louisa ... *really?*

He played along with the liar's game. 'You know ... just nervous.'

'Nervous? Aren't we both a bit long in the tooth to be shaky about this?'

He looked up at her. Her face blurred because his eyelids twitched so hard. So real. *She seemed so real.* 'I'll be fine after a glass. Did you bring it?'

She smiled. Those eyes again. Such youth and vitality. *Such deceit.* 'Of course.'

She reached down into her bag. More contraband. A bottle. It read *Rivesaltes* on the label, and underneath: 1960. 'It's from Maisie. We have to go easy though. 17%. That's what keeps it going to a ripe old age, but it will play havoc with our medication. And we want to keep control of ourselves, don't we?' She winked.

Bernard tried to wink back, desperate to maintain the ruse. Her perfection was starting to anger him now.

From her bag, she pulled the two paper crowns that'd fallen from the crackers only minutes earlier. 'And these ...' She put her crown on and handed his over.

He put his on. 'Merry Christmas, Louisa.'

'Merry Christmas, lover.' She leaned across the table, carefully avoiding the candle, and kissed him.

It felt so perfect ... so right ... *so* arousing. *Their* belief in his ignorance, and his stupidity, was infuriating. When she pulled away, a tear ran down his face.

'Are you okay?' She stroked his face.

'Yes ...' he said. 'I just never thought I could be this happy again.' *Oh God, I wish so much that you were really her.* He leaned to his side and picked up his present. He placed it on the table.

'You really didn't have to,' Louisa said.

'It's not for you. It's for me.'

Louisa flinched. 'Sorry.'

'No. I'm sorry.' Bernard said, realising that his sharp tone would break his cover. 'It's just that ... what's in here,' he shook the present, 'is very important.'

'You shouldn't even know what's in there! It's supposed to be a present.' She raised an eyebrow, showing more of her eye. He suddenly felt as if he could see all the way inside of her. It was distressing. Even her inner self seemed wrapped in a disguise. For a second, he wondered if he could be wrong, that the fear and despair that crawled around his entire being was somehow a misunderstanding.

But he'd come too far in this life to deny the obvious. Those bastards from Argentina, who'd executed Bradley and Gavin and plugged Bernard's stomach with two rounds from a FAL battle rifle, were here. They'd finally found him.

'I don't know what's in it,' he lied as he began to unwrap the present. 'It's just the friend who gave it to me is very special indeed so I know it will be important. It was this friend that showed me the truth, Louisa.'

'You're making little sense, Bernie. Are you sure you're okay? Maybe we should lie down for a bit—'

'*After.*' He pulled a shoe box from the Christmas wrapping. *We'll all need a lie down after this. A long lie down.*

He took the lid off the shoe box and looked inside.

Yes, you found me. It may be all over, but don't count your chickens before they hatch Argentinian pigs. Your success comes with a cost. A very high one ...

'Shoes?' Louisa said.

Bernard's hand settled on a tin; he popped the cap and lifted it out.

'Not shoes, I'm afraid.' Bernard said.

'Lighter fluid?' Louisa said. 'You don't smoke—'

He sprayed her. Aiming for the part that had captured his heart. The true source of this whole charade. Her eyes.

She reached up to them, moaning; he could only imagine the burning sensation. He wondered briefly what the pigs had done with the real Louisa. He thought about asking, but decided against it. She'd probably never existed in the first place.

She slipped from the chair onto her knees. He tilted the tin, and poured some more over her head. The fluid dampened her paper crown, her white hair and streamed down over her hands and face.

'This is for the real Louisa, if she ever even existed.'

There was a box of matches in the box, but they were unnecessary. He plucked the candle from the holder and set fire to her head.

He stood and watched the paper crown burn, and then her eyes.

BERNARD CLOSED the door to his room behind him, knowing he didn't have a great deal of time left. He'd just set fire to his bedsheets, and although he'd deactivated the alarm for the candlelit dinner, it would be hardly any time

9

before the smoke crept under the door and sent sleepy *Rose Hill* into pandemonium.

The nerves he was feeling before when Louisa had come to his room were now under control, and he felt steady as a rock. In moments like these, which were few and far between, he couldn't believe that they'd once called him *Flincher*. He marched, rather than walked, something that surprised him considering his seventy-five years. Gaining the upper hand always did that for you. He remembered this all too well from his army days. When you were winning, you were winning. Adrenaline worked with you instead of against you.

Despite the surge in confidence, there'd been a moment of hesitation back in the room. Watching Louisa's eyes burn had almost derailed him. Whenever he'd looked into those eyes, he'd seen a land, a forbidden land almost, in which only the truly blessed could be allowed to roam. And, even before, less than fifteen minutes ago in fact, around that table in the hall, he'd felt that same feeling of being blessed.

All part of the ploy.

It hadn't been real. None of it.

These people were just here to finish what they'd started all those years ago. He looked down at his other Christmas present – the handgun. He bet the bastards hadn't factored this into the equation.

Did they think it would be that easy? That I would just roll over?

Bernard knew his guns.

This was a Smith and Wesson Shield EZ designed for people with arthritis. It chambered for the .380 round rather than traditional 9mm, so it produced less recoil. The slide was a doddle for him to rack back even with his twisted claws.

His friend had been kind to him.

When he reached the hall again, he kept his hands behind his back to hide the weapon from view. It wasn't necessary. Everyone was distracted by the projector screen.

Rose Hill often used this hall to welcome in potential residents and their families. The projector allowed the hard sell. Bernard remembered watching the heavily produced, almost fictionalised, account of euphoric residents living out their final days in nirvana.

Today, the projector displayed the queen who Bernard had fought, and almost died for, back in 1982. She was delivering her annual Christmas speech. She was spouting on about the unique British spirit that brought everyone together in times of crisis.

But no one in this room was British. They were Argentinian.

When Roy, the temp carer who was skilful with a carving knife but not so great with people skills, wandered towards him, Bernard decided that this was the perfect opportunity to unmask the first charlatan.

'If you could take a—'

Bernard shot him in the forehead. His head snapped back, his paper crown slipped off and he crumpled to the floor.

Bernard stared at the twitching carer, waiting for his disguise to melt away and reveal an Argentinian soldier hidden beneath. It didn't. He hadn't expected it to happen with Louisa because her skin had blackened and melted, but he was disappointed not to expose Roy. It seemed that, even in death, these Argentinian soldiers were very adept at concealing their identities.

The fire alarm kicked in.

He looked up. No one was charging him down, but

neither were they watching Her Maj anymore either. Several screaming residents and carers were already up and running for the far side of the hall where the fire exit was. Bernard hadn't expected them to run from him. He'd expected a battle. Maybe it was a test? Maybe this was still part of the ruse, and they were leading him into a false sense of security?

He wouldn't follow them into a trap. He lifted his gun, and shot Patrick, a rather pleasant young nurse, in the back. His Santa hat flew off and he slammed into a seven-foot Christmas tree. Bernard was surprised the tree didn't come crashing down. Instead, Patrick was held upright with his arms open. He looked like he was embracing the tree, rather than dying in its branches.

Back in his fighting days, Bernard had been a good shot, and it was like riding a bike – it never really left you. He shot two residents who were younger and quicker than some of the others hobbling to keep up. They both folded, upending a trailing resident.

After flinging open the fire door, some of the Argentinian killers, disguised as the innocent, fled to fight another day. Bernard had known already that he wouldn't be able to stop them all but that didn't stop it being a crying shame.

He looked at remaining residents. The bed bound. The spoon fed. The immobile. About eight or nine of them spread out over four tables. He couldn't resist a smile. 'You'll regret your choice in disguise.' He said, despite knowing they wouldn't hear him over the wailing alarm.

He had four rounds left in the chamber, and another magazine in the pocket of his jeans. He'd need to be economical with his final victims. He considered, and then decided to start with those who were sleeping through the ordeal. It may strike fear into the heart of the conscious pretenders and draw from them a confession of who they really were. After four headshots, it was clear that the plan was failing. The remaining residents simply stared in horror at their dead companions who were now face down in their Christmas dinners.

Despite the recoil on the gun being more suitable for a gentleman of his age, Bernard's hand still ached when he reached the end of the first magazine. He winced his way through the reload. The 8-round stainless-steel magazine featured tabs on both sides for ease of loading, and he was grateful for the modern engineering.

The Queen was just finishing her speech and wishing everyone a Merry Christmas. He looked up at her, and scowled. *This is how you repay me? The people I fought for you hunting me in the home I was supposed to pass away peacefully in? How could you let this happen? We're just meat to you lot … rotten, useless meat …*

After executing Brian, Lawrence and Paul, three residents who he'd recently formed a Backgammon club with, he moved onto the final table. Ronnie and Deirdre. He could smell shit. There was no dignity in death really, was there? Ronnie and Deirdre had been married fifty years, neither could walk unassisted anymore. They held hands across the table.

'Please,' Ronnie said.

Bernard couldn't hear over the alarm, but he could read the word on his lips.

'Please what? It was your choice to come back for me.' While watching Ronnie, he shot Deirdre in the forehead. The old man's face melted into despair. 'Wow, you really are good. Academy Award winning good. Maybe I should just clap, you lying bastard.' He shot Ronnie in the neck. He slumped from the chair and rolled onto his back. He writhed on his back for a moment as blood pumped out between his fingers. It was the most energy he'd ever seen this man exert. Maybe this was the soldier revealing himself from beneath the disguise?

Then he saw someone running towards the fire exit at the back of the hall. Kate the carer. Heart of gold. Stickler for the rules. At least the Kate *they* wanted him to know. Who was the *real* Kate?

Let's find out.

She slipped over the pool of blood spreading around the two fleeing residents he'd shot before. She came down with an almighty thump.

As he approached her, Bernard realised he was slowing down. All this killing was now telling on him. He wasn't the soldier he once was. Still, he reached Kate, and lowered himself down behind her. He was unconcerned about the blood soaking into his trouser legs.

Kate was crying and trembling. This felt like his last chance to truly expose them. He leaned down and hissed in her ear, 'Admit it ... *just* admit who you are ...'

She started to speak, but then choked on the tears and snot running into her mouth.

'Admit it ... and I'll make it quick.'

'I ... I ... please don't. Bernard ... this isn't you.'

He whacked her with the gun. Not too hard. In all honesty, he didn't have the strength in his old bones to do it too hard. It split her head though, and blood bubbled from her forehead. *'Tell me! Why couldn't you leave me be? Were the bullets in my gut not enough for you, you Argentinian prick?'*

'Please—'

'*Enough! No more bullshit.*' He stood up, pointed the gun down and shot her in the centre of the chest.

He watched Kate's eyes as they glazed over. Desperate for one sign that she wasn't who she'd claimed to be. But then she was gone, and he'd got nothing.

Up on the projector, a solitary boy in St George's Chapel was delivering a hymn. It was impossible for Bernard to hear it over the alarm pounding in his ears. He turned to view the carnage around him.

He shouted over at the many dead residents hunched over in their chairs. '*YOU MADE THIS HAPPEN!*'

He paused. Nothing. Just the wail of the alarm.

'*WHY COULDN'T YOU JUST LEAVE IT ALONE?*'

He turned and started to walk for the fire exit on the other side of the hall.

The phone in his top pocket vibrated. He pulled it out and saw that it was his friend. He read the message.

It is over, and you are healed. You can forget now, Bernard. Go in peace, and forget forever 1982.

WHEN AUDREY HOUGHTON had heard the first gunshot coming back from the toilet, she'd dived behind the Christmas tree. There she popped out her dentures and sucked hard on her hand to stifle the sounds of her terror.

After the Christmas tree shook, because someone had crashed into it, she couldn't believe it hadn't toppled and exposed her hiding place. *Was someone watching over her? Richard, perhaps?*

So, as the massacre evolved, she squeezed her eyes closed,

and thought of her deceased husband, Richard. Maybe if she was thinking of him when the gunman did find her, then it would be all the easier to find the big lug in death?

Once the gunfire had finished, she heard the gunman shouting, and was surprised to hear him over the fire alarm which was playing havoc with her tinnitus. '*YOU MADE THIS HAPPEN ... WHY COULDN'T YOU JUST LEAVE IT ALONE?*'

She opened her eyes. From where she was lying, she could see the end of the hall, and the fire exit many had fled through.

Bernard Driggs walked into her line of sight. Her hand was still in her mouth, so it smothered the gasp. He was holding a gun against his side, and was taking something from his shirt pocket.

Bernard! But he's the loveliest man ...? I don't understand ... Louisa and him make a wonderful pair ... unless ... unless ... did he disarm the real gun man?

Bernard took a mobile phone from his pocket. He read the message, said something which she couldn't hear, and then dropped it on the floor. His empty hand moved to his forehead. He looked unsteady on his feet.

He turned around to stare in the direction he'd just come from. The area that Audrey couldn't see. An area, Audrey assumed, that was littered with death. Bernard's hand slipped down over his face and covered his mouth. She watched his body fold in on itself. He slipped down to his knees, and went on to all fours, staring at the floor.

When he lifted his head to look ahead again, he shouted. '*PLEASE ... GOD ... NO!*' He manoeuvred himself upright, still staring. '*WHAT HAVE I DONE?*'

He took a deep breath, turned and looked at Audrey as

if he'd suddenly heard her, but she hadn't made a sound. She gulped and squeezed her eyes closed.

Trembling, sucking her hand for all it was worth, she knew this was the end. She tried to reassure herself, in these last terrifying moments, that her life had been full, and fair. She was ready. She had a picture of her and Richard on their wedding day back in her room. In her mind, she looked on this picture, as she did every day.

Some time later, when it became clear that the end wasn't *actually* coming, she opened her eyes and saw Bernard standing over her. Despite what he'd done, and the gun at his side, he didn't look like a monster. His face was blotchy, and his eyes were flicking left and right. Every now and again, the fire alarm made him flinch, despite the fact that it was actually continuous. It was as if his brain was shutting off momentarily, before being brought back with a sudden jolt.

'Bernard ...'

He sat down beside her with his gun on his lap, staring ahead.

'Bernard, what's—'

'I'm not Bernard.' He spoke loudly so she could hear him over the alarm. 'I mean I feel like Bernard.' He rubbed his face. 'But how can I be? I'm not capable of doing this. Who is capable of doing these things?'

Still lying on her back, Audrey reached over and settled her hand on his leg. 'What happened?'

He turned to look at her. 'He promised to heal me.'

'Who did?'

'He did.'

'I don't understand—'

'He takes it all away, Audrey, the pain. That's what he promises. To heal the pain ... but he's lied.'

She was losing control of the conversation, but it was so abstract in nature, she'd no idea of how to get back hold of it. 'We can get you help ... it's not too late.'

'My God ... Louisa ... I love her so much ...'

'Where is she?' Audrey said, regretting the question as soon as she'd asked it.

'The smoke ... the burning ... my God ... I'm a monster.'

Audrey put her hand to her mouth.

'Every time he took me under, every single time, he always said the same thing. If you ever hear it, Audrey, just run, run the other way and don't look back ...'

Bernard lifted the gun from his knee. 'My name is the Conduit. I am a channel.' He placed the gun against his forehead and closed his eyes. 'I become the piece that is missing from inside people, and I allow the thoughts, feelings and behaviours to move fluidly through me and within them.'

When Bernard pulled the trigger, Audrey barely flinched. Her nerves were shot already.

2

CHEWING ON A parsnip, DCI Michael Yorke eyed up the new puppy. He didn't really know what to make of it. All he saw was a bundle of black fur bouncing from wall to wall like a puck in a game of air hockey. He certainly didn't feel like the other residents of the house, who saw fit to drop everything at all opportunities, to fall to their knees and croon over it.

His lack of affection towards it was a major problem because the new puppy was his.

As a favour to Patricia, her friend and dog breeder, Sally, had delivered the Cockapoo first thing in the morning while Beatrice, his two-year-old daughter, had decided that the sole purpose of Christmas Day was to tear wrapping paper off a present in some kind of frenzy rather than actually appreciate the thoughtful gift inside. As Yorke watched Beatrice, he wondered how much better off his wallet would be right now if he'd just wrapped up blocks of wood. When the fur ball wandered in and nuzzled his feet, he almost jumped out of his skin.

'Merry Christmas, Mike.' Patricia leaned over and kissed his forehead. 'Her name is Rosie.'

Ewan, his adopted son, and Lexi, his girlfriend, melted to their knees, and went so gooey eyed that they were practically unrecognisable.

He looked over at his other Christmas present propped up by the fireplace. A second-hand Taylor acoustic guitar. Then, he looked down at the canine. The first present had been a masterstroke. The second ... well ...

'Thanks Pat, word please?'

When they were in the kitchen, he said, 'A dog?'

'I thought you'd like it.'

'Yes ... thanks ... but a dog is not just for Christmas.'

'The warning refers to children, Mike, not adults.'

'Are you sure about that? Anyway, did you not think it'd be better to talk first? Especially before introducing a whole new level of chaos into the Yorke household ...'

Behind him, he could hear Ewan and Lexi in hysterics as the puppy crawled all over them. He reached behind himself and closed the kitchen door.

'I'm detecting disappointment,' Patricia said.

'Not disappointment ... just concern. What do I know about bloody dogs?'

'You learn quick Mike. I grew up with them. This breed is great with kids too. Clever and affectionate.'

'Clever and affectionate, Pat? It's a dog ...'

'You'll see.' Patricia placed a hand on his upper arm. 'I thought it would be good for you. The distraction. She'll always be there for you when you've had a tough day. Think of the walks ... those long *cleansing* walks.' She smiled.

'I run for distraction. And I now have a lovely guitar too.'

'They're social animals, and you need more of the social in your life. You're too consumed, and this might bring you out of yourself a little bit more. Sorry if I messed up. As you know, me and Sally are close, she'd take Rosie back if necessary, we'd already anticipated this possibility.'

There was more raucous laughter from the living room. 'Look!' Ewan cried. 'They're cuddling! Rosie and Beatrice are cuddling!'

Yorke sighed. 'Not sure taking her back now will make me the most popular person in the house ...'

Patricia leaned over and kissed him.

'... not that I ever was anyway.'

So, as Yorke chewed on that parsnip, he wondered if he would even grow to like, never mind love, this dog. One positive from its presence, he realised, was that it had distracted him, momentarily, from his constant preoccupation with Jack Newton, the boy missing in Old Sarum.

Ewan was currently emptying the gravy boat over his turkey. 'This gravy is obscene, Auntie Pat.'

'Sorry,' Yorke said, 'But isn't "obscene" a negative word. Ever thought about just using the word "delicious"?'

Lexi and Ewan looked at him with confused looks on their faces.

'Never mind, don't answer that, but go easy, and save everyone else some of that delicious *obscenity*.'

Patricia was too preoccupied with Beatrice's attempts to drop food on the floor for Rosie to laugh at his joke. Or maybe, it just wasn't funny.

'Thanks again for letting me stay,' Lexi said. It wasn't the first time she'd said thank you. She must have been well into double figures by now.

Lexi had been having a lot of problems at home

recently. Her mother had died several years ago, and her father, a devout catholic, had become even more god-fearing in recent times. He'd become incredibly controlling, and was outraged that she was in a relationship with Ewan. She'd walked out of the house two weeks ago. At the time, her father had not made any effort to stop her. His last words to her were "good riddance, sinner". Because she was over sixteen, the law had not gotten involved, but he'd been around to the house on several occasions. Lexi had opted not to go back with him.

'You're very welcome,' Patricia said as an alarm sounded on her phone. 'Queen's speech!' Using a remote, she switched on BBC Radio 4.

They all listened to the speech. 'It is true that the world has had to confront moments of darkness this year, but the Gospel of John contains a verse of great hope often read at Christmas Carol Services – "The light shines in the darkness and the darkness has not overcome it."'

Yorke looked around the table. He agreed with her message. Despite having to move this year, after a brutal attack on his old home by a criminal he was chasing, he still had so much to be thankful for.

As the speech wound on, he felt his mind drift back to his childhood. The Queen's speech had never been a focus in his house. They'd have been lucky to get through the Christmas meal without a drunk mother and a tempestuous argument; a reflection on the previous year had certainly never been on the cards.

Despite this, he did have some fond memories of Christmas day. There were a couple of plastic-covered salt piles on his estate used to grit during winter. Himself, his sister, and all the other children on the estate used to gather there to run up and down them. If it had been snowing, it would make for a fantastic snowball fight.

It didn't matter who you were, or where you came from, everyone has good moments to retreat to.

And then he realised where the boy, Jack Newton, was.

He stood up. 'Excuse me.'

Patricia looked up at him with a creased forehead.

'Sorry … it's important.'

In the kitchen, he phoned Superintendent Joan Madden's mobile and braced himself for a frosty reception.

'Merry Christmas, Mike. It's a shame your name showed up on my mobile, or I wouldn't have answered. Glad to know you're enjoying a much-needed break. I'm certainly not now.'

'I know where Jack Newton is, ma'am.'

'How have you possibly worked that out on Christmas Day?'

'Nostalgia.'

'Come again?'

'Myself and DS Willows went through all the Nicholas Johnson interview transcripts with a fine toothcomb *again* last week. Johnson spends more time speaking about the past than anything else. What his parents did to him, how he was treated at school, that experience by the lake. You recall?'

'Of course. I was there for many of those interviews. It's not unusual. The monster was simply providing us with his origin story.'

'What does his narrative lack?'

'The location of the boy?' Madden said. 'Which neglected to give us before he strung himself up?'

'No, ma'am, that's just it. *I think he gave us the location.*

His story is a bleak one. His narrative lacks any happy memories, except one.'

'Okay, you're starting to get my attention.'

'Do you recall the treehouse?'

'No ... should I?'

'He mentioned it several times. These were the only happy moments in his whole narrative. The time when he used to hide away from his parents in that treehouse in the woods near his house. He said that this was the only time he really laughed – reading the Beano in that treehouse.'

'You're going to tell me that Jack Newton is in that treehouse, aren't you?'

'No, ma'am, because you already realise he is. Nostalgia draws people back. He was drawn back to a safe place. *His* safe place.'

'But is it Jack Newton's safe place?'

'I don't know that, ma'am. I hope to God, it is, but I really don't know.'

'I'll handle it, Mike, you go and be with your family.'

'But what about you, ma'am? I don't want to ruin your Christmas.'

Madden laughed. 'Come on now, Mike, you know me better than that. As if I celebrate Christmas Day. I'll be back in touch.'

The phone went dead. Yorke thought about himself on top of that salt pile hurling snowballs at his sister, and then thought about a lonely, little boy, hiding in a treehouse, reading a comic, evolving into something very different.

YORKE TRIED to look like he was focused on the game of Charades. Patricia's narrowed eyes told him she wasn't buying it. Every now and again he went to the toilet to steal a quick look at his mobile phone screen to see if he'd missed a call from Madden.

'Do we need to get that prostate looked at?' Patricia said with a raised eyebrow after the third trip.

Beatrice and the new puppy, Rosie, were taking a nap together at the side of the room. Everyone had already gone camera crazy over that scene. It would surely become an iconic image in the Yorke household for years to come. There was certainly no chance of marking his gift 'return to sender' now.

When Ewan mimed a slow run, using his hand to mimic his hair flapping in the wind, Lexi and Patricia hollered 'Baywatch' simultaneously, and everyone broke down in laughter. Yorke pretended to be amused, but it was impossible to make it convincing.

He was just too preoccupied with the life and death situation playing out without him.

In fact, the anxiety was getting to Yorke so much that he started to consider the cigarettes hidden in the kitchen. If it wasn't for his wife's razor-sharp stare, he'd already be out smoking next to the large snowball Beatrice had rolled earlier.

After the charades, they watched the *Snowman* on television, so everyone could revisit their childhood for twenty minutes. At the end of that, Ewan stood up and said, 'We have an announcement.'

Rosie ran over to Yorke and stood up against his leg. He looked down at her.

No surprises please, Ewan, Yorke thought, *not sure my heart can take any more of them today.*

Ewan beckoned Lexi over. She had her hands in the pockets of her dungarees. Once Ewan had his arm around her, she pulled out her left hand to show her Christmas present glowing from the third finger of her left hand.

Yorke reached down and picked up Rosie. The puppy suddenly felt like the least of his problems now.

YORKE WAS on his fourth visit to the toilet in less than two hours. This time, it wasn't to check his phone, but because he was reeling in shock.

Engaged? Where the bloody hell had that come from?

He didn't even know they were having sex for God's sake!

He'd had the conversation with Ewan regarding that but he'd been informed, *reassured* rather, that that stage of their relationship was a long way off.

And now they were bloody engaged!

At least she wasn't pregnant, and he knew that because it was the first question he asked.

'No, Uncle Mike ...' Ewan had said. 'That's not the reason at all.'

At this point, Patricia's relentless frown had turned into a glare.

'It's just ... we know. In fact, ever since I met Lexi, I've known ... why wait?'

I can give a thousand bloody reasons to wait. He hadn't said it, but he didn't have to. The awkward silence that followed suggested they'd sensed it.

'Congratulations,' Yorke had said, but it was too late; eyes were down.

So, Yorke had made his sharp exit.

He splashed cold water on his face, and looked at his reflection. He traced the long scar where his cheek had been split in half by a box cutter earlier this year. *For someone who has built a career out of saying the right thing, you are certainly very good at saying the wrong things to people you love.*

Christmas Day. Bloody hell. He'd managed to piss off everyone in that room today. Apart from his daughter, but she was asleep.

Time to re-emerge with a different attitude, Mike. A supportive one. The one you seem to give to everyone but those who are closest to you.

He opened the bathroom door and took a deep breath.

Besides, it doesn't mean that they are getting married next week, does it?

Not that this would be the first thing he said. First, he would hug his son, and his girlfriend ...

His phone rang.

'Hello, Ma'am.'

'He's alive,' Madden said. 'Jack's alive and we've got him.'

3

YORKE COULDN'T BELIEVE what he was hearing. He turned his car radio up.

There'd been a mass shooting in a care home in Leeds. Details were sketchy, but there were at least fifteen confirmed deaths; a mix of residents and carers. More were suspected. Part of the problem in identifying the true number of lives lost was the fact that *Rose Hill* was still on fire.

He listened to a nurse who'd managed to flee the scene. Repeatedly, she choked up, making it hard for Yorke to understand what she was saying. 'I don't understand it all ... he was never anything but a gentleman ... he just shot Roy in the head ... no warning, nothing ... and then we were running, those that could run, and I know it sounds bad, leaving them, but what could we do? It was terrifying ... I kept hearing the gunshots, and people were falling around me.'

Yorke sighed and pulled up alongside Jack Newton's home.

The reporter was now describing how an elderly female

resident had been cornered by the shooter but had eventually walked free after the gunman turned the gun on himself.

A brutal massacre *on* Christmas Day *in* a care home.

Yorke thought back to the verse from the Gospel of John included in the Queen's speech: "The light shines in the darkness and the darkness has not overcome it."

That may be true, Yorke thought, *but that darkness is making a bloody good go of it.*

He looked up at the house. It was the only house on the row without any Christmas decorations. He was here to deliver the news that Jack Newton was safe and being taken to hospital. Yorke had asked Madden for that honour, simply because he'd placed a hand on Malcolm Newton's shoulder last week and promised to find his missing son.

Something you should never do, but something Yorke always did.

He exited the car into the swirling snow. Malcolm Newton, and his wife, Sandra, opened the door. It was as if they sensed his presence. Why wouldn't they? They'd been living their lives on tenterhooks for the last ten days, and their senses would be in overdrive.

As he walked down the path, he brushed snow from his eyes, and gave them a smile, so as to calm them, and let them know he was here offering only good news.

This is the light you talk about, your Majesty, Yorke thought, *and when it shines, there is nothing quite like it.*

'WHEN I WAS A NIPPER,' the Conduit said, running his finger down the window, 'my mother told me a lie.'

He stopped his finger, but left it pressed against the

glass, so he was pointing outside at his snow-covered garden. 'She told me that every single snowflake was unique. What a thing to believe, eh? That every single one of those little white crystals has its own separate identity.'

Behind him, his dog grunted.

The Conduit smiled. 'I knew you'd appreciate that myth. But, you know, my mum didn't lie. Not really. You see it wasn't until 1988, that a scientist discovered two identical snowflakes. And by then, I was fully grown, and she was long dead.'

He paused to listen to his dog lapping water from a bowl.

'But still ... what a thing to believe ... infinitely more snowflakes than human beings, and every single one of them unique.'

He heard the rattle of his dog's chains.

'I believed so strongly in the force that was identity.' The Conduit turned. 'Yes, it was fragile. Yes, it melts away like a snowflake in the sun ... but it was there. Do you understand, my loyal dog?'

His dog yapped.

The Conduit sat back down at his dining table. He scooped a spoonful of cranberry sauce from a jar, and carefully positioned it beside a slice of turkey.

'But, alas, it was false. Uniqueness, identity ... simple myths. On first look, we may seem different, but we are no different.'

With a separate spoon, to avoid any cross-contamination of food, he scooped some stuffing, and placed that carefully on the other side of the turkey.

His dog whined.

'Don't beg, dog.'

Another whine.

'Are you not listening?'

The Conduit rose from his chair and picked up the pruning saw he kept propped up against the wall. The pole was already extended, and locked to two metres. He'd been using it on the garden tree several days before, cutting back some unruly branches.

The dog whined for a third time.

The Conduit moved towards his animal. Along the way, he noticed that the star was lopsided at the top of his Christmas tree. He was a tall man so he was able to right this particular wrong.

'You are what I allow you to be. Nothing more, *everything less.*' The Conduit reached down and stroked his pet's head. He liked to feel the indents that covered his shaven scalp. He ran his fingers over his thin and misshapen nose, broken on so many occasions, causing him to whistle as he breathed. He allowed the animal to lick his hand; he was asking for forgiveness. 'Good dog. We never beg for food.'

The Conduit turned, placed the pruning saw on the dining table, and picked up the dog bowl. Earlier, he'd stuffed it full of the raw giblets from the turkey.

When he turned back, his dog sat up, panting, desperate for its food, but not begging. Trying to be as obedient as he possibly could.

The Conduit knelt beside his animal, and starting at his iron collar, which was chained to a D-ring on the wall, he ran his hand all the way down his naked back, tracing the scars and welts, most of which were done by his pruning saw.

His dog enjoyed the attention.

'Identity ... such a fickle thing,' the conduit said, putting the bowl onto the floor.

His dog, who once carried the identity of Mark Topham, buried his head into the giblets.

THE SNOW beside the cathedral had been trodden down by walkers over the course of the day, so Yorke opted to circle it a few times in an effort to clock up a three-mile run. He was wearing running tights and, despite the very low temperature, had already built up quite a sweat.

He looked at his running watch, and saw he was moving into the third and final mile. If he'd had a running app on his phone, this run would be called the "post-case blowout." As it was, he didn't have an app; running was a private affair, and he was determined to keep it that way.

Although the run felt good, and felt, as always, *necessary*, he was plagued with worries. Ewan's engagement shocker was obviously high on the list of concerns, but he was also worried about his marriage. Patricia had displayed an extreme amount of patience on several occasions today. Occasions which, if the roles had been reversed, would have had Yorke reeling. Firstly, he'd left Christmas dinner to go to work. She'd understood why, and offered no objection, but he'd noticed an unfamiliar tone in her voice. And after his work duties, he'd returned home to excuse himself for a twenty-five-minute run. Again, she'd understood – it was his cleansing ritual following a difficult case – but just like before, there'd been *that* tone.

He bypassed the large Christmas tree in the gardens which, according to a recent press release, was "the size of two giraffes." He saw no reason to dispute this.

When Yorke and Patricia had first met, Yorke had been consumed by his profession. She'd been accepting of this, and continued to be so as their relationship had progressed. There had been promises never to question it. Promises which, on the whole, she'd kept.

But was this now the end of the road? Was bitterness finally creeping in? Resentment?

Was Rosie the dog her last attempt to try and break him out of the world he sometimes got lost inside?

He burst from the cathedral gardens onto Exeter Street. Over the road, the White Hart was dressed to the nines in flickering Christmas lights. He turned sharp right, and only just avoided skidding over a build-up of slush.

A well-wrapped elderly couple, supporting each other over the snow, approached. Despite the bitter weather, they looked happy. There was a lamppost taking a chunk of the pavement up, so Yorke stopped beside it to allow them past. It would be easy to consider the smile Yorke received merely gratitude over his display of good manners, but it was far more than that.

Yorke saw contentment in those smiles, and he liked it.

He hoped he too could look into the eyes of the young when he was old, and not feel loss, or even envy over what they had. And this is why he feared being alone.

Every day, he woke up, he couldn't believe the life he'd built with Patricia, Ewan and Beatrice. He never wanted to be without them.

He, too, wanted to look on the younger person at a ripe old age, and feel only contentment.

He vowed to make a change. Starting now. He had two weeks off with his family, and he intended to revel in every second of it.

ONCE THE CONDUIT had finished his Christmas meal, he picked up a napkin and dabbed at his top lip. A force of habit. For many years, he'd had a white moustache. It'd been part of the identity he'd sacrificed for this new life.

He smiled. *There it was again. Identity. That fickle thing.*

He listened to his pet's whistling breaths. It had finished gorging on the turkey's raw innards. These days the beast ate without complaint. There was far less need for the trusty pruning saw. Which, in a way, was a shame. There were many elements of the 'training phase' that the Conduit had enjoyed, but that had been the pinnacle. There was something truly exquisite about owning your animal with sadism.

He drained a glass of Vintage Bordeaux. 'There are times, dog, when I miss the early days of our relationship. The conversations especially.'

Earlier in this animal's evolution, while some semblance of Mark Topham remained, they'd embarked on a few conversations. Of course, the Conduit's IQ surpassed Topham's by some way - and many others for that matter - so the former police officer had been more of a sounding board.

Quite an unwilling one, the Conduit thought, *if memory serves me correctly.*

'There was one conversation, in particular, which often keeps me awake at night. It was about love, do you recall it?'

His dog didn't respond.

'Well, it was a long time ago, now, and there have been many *changes* since then. *Many.* Mainly in you, I might add, rather than myself...'

The Conduit felt sluggish as he rose to his feet. He was a burly man, and he felt heavy at the best of times, but he'd just eaten enough turkey to feed a small family. And why not? He wasn't about to waste it, or share it with the feral creature in the corner.

'Plato once said, "At the touch of love, everyone becomes a poet." How true that was for you, dog! I think your opening line to me was rather eloquent. Along the lines of, "You fucking monster, you took away the only thing I ever fucking loved."' The Conduit smiled. 'Yes, you were a true poet.'

He touched one of the teeth on the pruning saw lying on the dining table. 'I think my response was equally as poetic. Didn't I saw off a toe? Or was it two? Three glasses of wine has made everything rather foggy.'

The Conduit approached his beast again, and knelt. 'And speaking of foggy, dog, your nightcap should be kicking in around now. I bet you barely notice anymore.' He stroked the shaved, pitted scalp. 'Ever since I took you in, my dear little stray, I've fed you lysergic acid diethylamide.' The Conduit laughed. 'These days, the fog for you must be like a clear summer's afternoon!'

The beast's tongue hung out. It panted, but its breath was no longer steady, and it came in ragged gasps.

The Conduit pulled a handkerchief from the top pocket of his shirt, and dabbed at the drool on his pet's mouth. 'Good boy.'

The Conduit's phone vibrated in his pocket. It was an alarm.

He stood up, left his dog in the dining room, and headed into the living room. There, he sat on the couch and switched on the television.

He was in time for the headlines.

Rose Hill care home massacre. 16 confirmed deaths including the gunman.

The Conduit clapped his hands together and whooped. 'Bernard!' He then looked up at the heavens and showed the palms of his hands. 'Merry Christmas!'

4

MINUTES AFTER VOWING to ignore work for two weeks, Yorke faced his first challenge. A phone call from Madden.

The snow was absorbing light from the lamps, making it look heavier than it was, but it was still bad enough to force Yorke to seek out shelter. He found a large tree at the end of the road to take the call under. Fortunately, he was still warm from the run to stand still, but that wouldn't last long. Temperatures had been dropping as low as 3° these past few nights.

'Everything okay, ma'am?'

'Not really, Mike ... but I guess you wouldn't be hearing from me again if it was.'

Indeed. She was not phoning to see if he'd gotten his Christmas Day festivities back on track. 'Is it Jack? He should be back with his parents by now ...'

'Yes, he is. It's nothing to do with that.' She sighed. 'Are you sitting down?'

'No, ma'am, I'm standing under a tree in my running gear.'

'On Christmas Day? You are starting to sound more and more like me every time we speak ... well, anyway, don't sprint in front of a lorry in shock then.'

'I hate slow build-ups—'

'*The Conduit is back, Mike.*'

Yorke opened his mouth to speak, but nothing came out, instead everything suddenly became clear in Yorke's head ...

A survivor. The nurse on the radio. "I don't understand it all ... he was never anything but a gentleman." Someone else indoctrinated by the Conduit.

'You're not in front of a lorry, are you?'

'No.'

'We knew this day would come.'

'Yes ... but Christmas Day is some day to choose.'

'Inspired choice, Mike. I think you'll agree Dr Louis Mayers was always the showman.'

'It's the care home shooting in Leeds, isn't it?'

'Yep. We need you there tomorrow, Mike.'

'Hang on, ma'am. It's my holiday.' Yorke thought of Patricia's tone of voice earlier and imagined telling her that the two-week holiday was off. It meant he didn't have to worry about the cold just yet, because his heart had just started to beat like a drum again.

'Mike, I just got off the phone with former Detective Chief Superintendent Benjamin Rosset. He now heads up the HMET for West Yorkshire. He wants you, the SIO on the Christian Severance case, to assist tomorrow.'

The Homicide and Major Enquiry Team. It stood to reason. It didn't get any more serious than a care home massacre. It also stood to reason that they'd want the Senior Investigating Officer on the last case involving Dr Louis Mayers.

Knowing it was useless, Yorke tried to plead his case

anyway. 'There are other people who were involved in the Christian Severance case. I don't have to be your go-to on this one.'

'Sorry, Mike. It's the way it's going to be.'

'Will phone contact not suffice?'

'How do you think Rosset will feel about that?'

Yorke sighed. 'Unsupported.'

'So, I don't need to answer your question.'

'Please explain to me, ma'am, how they even know for certain that Mayers was involved?'

'One of the survivors ...' Madden paused. She was obviously looking through her notes, 'Audrey Houghton. She got trapped in there with the gunman, Bernard Driggs. According to her account, he went from full-on homicidal to placid and broken in a matter of seconds after reading a text message on his phone. He then killed himself, but not before he gave her a warning—'

'To avoid the Conduit.'

'Lightning fast, Mike. That's why you're always first choice.'

'Great. What happened after the text message?'

'Bernard Driggs warned her about the Conduit, about a man who promises to heal you, but then does something entirely different.'

'So ... somehow Louis Mayers had been getting to this Bernard Driggs, and indoctrinating him, just like he did with Christian Severance, and just like he did with Susie Long.'

Yorke paused to take a deep breath. *Susie Long.* The innocent young woman had stabbed to death his friend DI Mark Topham's boyfriend, after the Conduit had taken control of her mind with hypnosis and drugs. He had made Susie Long believe that Dr Neil Solomon was a threat to her. The Conduit's methods were powerful, and destructive.

Yorke continued. 'Who's been visiting him in the care home? This is the only way it could've—'

'Afraid not, Mike. The only person visiting him was his daughter. He was allowed out for a solitary daily walk between 10am and 12pm every day – this is the only time Mayers could have gotten to him.'

'CCTV and witnesses? Someone must have seen them walking?'

'I'm sure they have thought of that one, Mike. You may be the sharpest officer I know, but you're not the only capable one!'

'The text message? I bet there was two. One that switched him on, and the other that shut him down.'

'We'd love to know, Mike, but it looks like the phone went in the fire. He wasn't on a contract, so we can only assume he was using a burner.'

'Ma'am. I need this break. Things aren't so good at home with the family.'

'They never are, Mike, that's why I opted not to have one.'

Well, I chose differently, and I'm glad I did.

'I'm sorry, ma'am...'

Madden laughed. 'As if, Mike. I just heard the excitement in your voice. Nothing would keep you from this. There'll be no need to put myself out here by pulling rank, and risking HR on my back. You'll be in Leeds tomorrow.'

Yorke didn't respond.

'I'll give you two hours to play nicely. Bye Mike.'

Yorke decided there and then that next time someone called her a bitch in the office, he would not be coming to her defence.

ONCE THE NEWS HAD FINISHED, the Conduit switched the television off and lay back on the sofa. He always enjoyed this short period in between patients to reflect on his successes and failures. He had a growth mindset, and you couldn't grow without being critical as well as proud.

Bernard Driggs had been his hardest task to date. He was elderly, and so the PTSD had been gestating within him for a long time, winding itself around his unconscious mind like an anaconda. Its grip was tight, and Bernard had been suffocating to death in a care home.

Under his new identity, the Conduit had done some freelance counselling at a private psychiatrist's practice. Here, he'd been able to access old records on patients. It was through these old records, he was able to learn about Bernard's experiences in the Falklands war, his PTSD, the care home he resided in, and more importantly, his luxurious two-hour walks around the area. The only thing, Bernard claimed, that kept him sane.

The doctor had orchestrated a chance meeting with Bernard by a lake on his walking route. He allowed the handle on his plastic shopping bag to break at exactly the right time, so Bernard was drawn over to help save the tinned food from rolling into the water. After they started talking, it didn't take long for the Conduit to spin the lie that his uncle had also served in the Falklands. The friendship was formed. *Rose Hill* was out in the sticks, so there were plenty of quiet, secluded spots in the surrounding woodlands and parks for the Conduit to set up meetings in which he could develop his doctor-patient relationship further.

Bernard had first told his story on a bench, overlooking a rolling valley. 'Me and the others were hanging back on Mount Kent. It was dark and we were readying ourselves to seize the Two Sisters Mountain. Mount Kent was a ring of hills around Stanley, so it was chock full of no-man's land. Yankee Company, a fighting patrol, went before us, but that didn't end well at all. Our platoon was up next. We were yet to experience a full-scale attack ... and there is really nothing that can prepare you for it ... there is no order to the chaos that descends. Just a shit load of noise, and blinding flashes. It was all go, go, go ... mortars, artillery, arms fire ... lots of people falling around you. I'm sure it sounds scary, buddy, but unless you are there, it's really hard to explain how truly terrifying it really is. We were down on the ground and pinned back. Direct fire, but still coming from some distance ... Then comes the order to move in. Fucking unbelievable really. None of us thought that we could survive that. But you go. You *always* go. You look at each other, and no one suggests otherwise, and then you all charge forward together not wanting to let anybody down. We defied the odds and we got to the top of Two Sisters with few casualties, but shit happens. Shit *always* happens. I failed to pick up a loose Argentinian soldier. My two friends, Gavin and Bradley, paid the price. They were only boys. I was the old man of the crew – well into my thirties. I should have had their backs. Bradley took a bullet in his heart. Fortunate for him, his death was quick. Not so for Gavin. He was hit in the neck and drowned in his own blood. The soldier's third bullet went into my stomach, ruining my insides. You wondered why I'm in a care home at only seventy-four? Constant dialysis, buddy. And I'm not about to put that pressure on my daughter. As for that soldier, someone else did what I couldn't do for Bradley and Gavin that day and finished him before he finished me. For many years, I wished he hadn't. That mistake ruined my marriage, my friendships, my relationships with others ... my life really. It's a bloody miracle I'm sitting here today. But, you know, someone somewhere saw fit to give me another chance. It's a weird world. I found Louisa, and I found *some* peace.'

The Conduit nodded, put a hand on the old man's shoulder, and offered a solemn look. What he wanted to do was rub his hands together in anticipation. There was so much to work with here!

In the past, with patients such as Susie Long, his treatments, although efficient, had been quick. He often licked his lips over the memory of Susie stabbing Dr Neil Solomon countless times because she saw her murdering uncle rather than an innocent doctor. But, with Bernard, and another more recent patient, he vowed to go slower, and really fine-tune the process. He wanted to lift the cloud of PTSD from his patients and replace it with the ultimate displacement of these maladaptive emotions - an explosion of unrivalled violence.

So, he'd trodden carefully and meticulously with Bernard.

In fact, he hadn't introduced his chemical cocktail to him until they were at least three weeks into their meetings, or, if you will, treatment. And when he had administered the cocktail, he'd done so in smaller doses at first, slipping it into the cakes he often brought along with him for Bernard to enjoy.

The Conduit took a deep breath, recalling the first time Bernard had noticed he was under the influence. 'Sounds ridiculous, buddy, but do the colours looks different to you today? Somehow, they do to me.'

'Sorry?'

'The Valley. It seems to be brighter. Glowing almost. But the sun is not exactly shining, is it?'

'I hadn't noticed. How do you feel today, Bernard?'

'Good. Content. I always feel good after your cakes, though.'

'Euphoric?'

'Now, there's a word. Yes, I guess so. I didn't dream much last night. That must be it! More rest than usual. I often have horrendous nightmares.'

'Do you trust me, Bernard?'

'Of course, you know I do. Our chats. You make me feel so much better ... Of course, there is Louisa too ... she also knows how to listen.'

'You've still not told Louisa about me, have you?'

'No, but you know I don't understand why it's such a big deal. She won't say anything.'

'Still ... I'd rather maintain the status quo. I'm a professional doctor, and some people may not agree with what's going on here. Treatment outside of an official environment. I cannot afford to jeopardise my career.'

'I understand. So, I've simply told her that I meet an old friend for walks.'

'Ah ... good. Listen, Bernard, I'm going to ask you something now, and I need only one answer. For my treatment, I need willingness. If you answer in the negative, I'll walk away. Our friendship will remain, but the patient-doctor relationship will be no more. If you answer in the affirmative, I promise you a mindset change that cannot be rivalled. Do you understand?'

'Of course, and you know my answer already ...'

'Still ... humour me.'

'Of course.'

'My name is the Conduit. I am a channel. I become the piece that is missing from inside people, and I allow the thoughts, feelings and behaviours to move fluidly through me and within them. Nod if you understand.'

At first, Bernard had looked confused, but then he'd nodded.

YORKE OPENED the door to Emma Gardner. She was his beloved ex-colleague and loyal friend. Usually, it was impossible not to feel joy in her presence; right now, he was feeling anything but.

It was Christmas Day. There could only be one reason she was here. The Conduit.

Madden had been wrong about one thing on the phone conversation before. Yorke wasn't the sharpest there was.

After all this time, Yorke was still surprised to behold her thin profile. She'd lost so much weight since her days as a DI, which spoke volumes about how unhealthy this job could make you.

'Merry Christmas, Emma. Do you come bearing gifts?'

'Of course.' She held up a plastic bag.

Yorke's heart sank. She wasn't smiling. She *definitely* did have another agenda.

She was dressed casually in jeans and a Christmas jumper, again surprising him, because back when they spent nearly every waking hour together, she wore suits.

'You know something, don't you?' Gardner said.

Sharp, indeed. Yorke couldn't resist a smile. 'You're not going to wish me Merry Christmas?'

Gardner didn't smile.

Yorke sighed. 'You best come in. Pat and everyone will be pleased to see you.'

Gardner shook her head. 'No. In the car, Mike. I'm too shook up to put on a show.'

'Okay.'

Gardner had kept her car running, so Yorke welcomed the blast of warm air. She dropped the plastic bag on his lap.

'There's some guitar sheets in there for Ewan for *The 1975*, a band he likes. Patricia filled me in as you never answer your phone these days. For Beatrice, there's a colouring book on unicorns, stickers on unicorns, and a stuffed toy too.'

'Let me guess ... a unicorn?'

Gardner stared at him. '*Rose Hill* Care Home. Mayers is back, isn't he?'

Yorke sighed. 'Looks that way. What made you think of him?'

'The obvious. This wasn't some kind of extremist, this was a nice old gentleman winding down in a care home.'

'Yes, but anyone can crack, you know that.'

'That's some highly organised, efficient crack-up for someone in his twilight years.'

'He's a war veteran.'

'He was seventy-five, and madly in love with one of the victims according to some of the witnesses on the radio. Besides, why are you arguing against it, Mike? You already gave me the nod that Mayers is involved.'

'Just hasn't sunk in, yet. Not sure I want to believe it.'

'Why not? This is our chance to finally catch the bastard.'

Yorke stared at her, and couldn't resist a sardonic laugh. 'Our chance? You're joking, aren't you?'

'I'm not joking when the man who destroyed one of my best friend's lives is the topic of conversation.'

'I don't mean this to sound offensive, Emma, but you're a Marks and Spencer security guard. How were you planning on resourcing this investigation?'

'I don't need to. You are.'

'Am I?'

'Don't bother, Mike,' Gardner said, gripping the steering wheel, 'You knew Mayers was involved when I got here. They've made the link in Leeds and been in touch. You were the SIO on the last case involving him. That's your ticket in.'

'Spot on, except I've turned the ticket down.'

'What?' She tightened her grip on the wheel, and the whiteness of her knuckles burned through.

'I have two weeks off. I just can't keep doing this. Not to Pat. Not to Ewan and Beatrice.'

'Hello? But this is the Conduit. The man who killed Neil? Mark's partner ... have you been hit over the head?'

'There's always something. I've got to start putting my family first. Imagine if I marched in that house and told Pat that our next two weeks together were down the toilet.'

'She'd understand.'

'Yes, she would. But does that make it okay? It causes cracks, Emma. You know that more than anyone. That's why you got the hell out!'

'Anyway,' Gardner said. 'This is irrelevant. Madden won't let you off the hook.'

'She threatened as much.'

'Precisely.'

'But, I'm going to dig my heels in. Play a game of Chicken with her. She won't want the shit storm with HR. Besides, what's us finding him going to achieve? It's not going to bring Topham back. He's long gone, and God knows where. And if we did bring him back, then what? He's off to jail for killing a sex-worker. Is he not just best in the wind?'

Gardner took her hands off the wheel. Sighed, and wiped a tear away. 'I've not been totally honest with you, Mike.'

Yorke stared at her. 'Listen, Emma, please don't tell me anything that will get—'

'I know where Mark is, Mike.'

5

I T HAD TAKEN the Conduit a record number of sessions to build compliance in Bernard Driggs. He didn't possess the vulnerability of some of his previous patients, and the shell around his PTSD had hardened like dead skin on an athlete's foot.

However, after several weeks of "special" cakes and many attempts at hypnosis, the doctor finally broke through.

Treatment required the Conduit to be present in Bernard's darkest memory. So, the Conduit stood alongside him in that fateful moment when the Argentinian soldier had opened fire on him and killed his two friends.

The first time that Bernard had spoken to him in the visualisation had been particularly enjoyable. It had come in the aftermath, when the Argentinian soldier was already dead, and Bernard was lying on the ground holding his own guts in with bloody hands. 'It took me so long to accept it. For years, I blamed myself for the chaos of war. But that's the irony, isn't it? Chaos cannot be controlled. I could live through this event a thousand times, and it could happen over, or it may not do. Chance, *chaos itself*, could take those events either way.'

For the Conduit, this was always the most exciting part of the treatment. When the drugged patient found the bridge between clarity and disarray. The *sweet spot*. The point in which the patient was most malleable, and the doctor could do his best work.

It was at this point that the Conduit wanted Bernard to *reject* the original version of events. To do this, he had to alter the narrative. He took away the chaos. He gave Bernard the chance to stop the shooting. He created a scenario in which the Argentinian soldier was out in the open, with his rifle hanging by his side, begging for his life. At that point, Bernard could have shot him, but he was too scared to end someone's life up close and personal. This hesitation allowed the Argentinian a way back in. He took it with open arms. His rifle came back up and two innocent men lost their lives.

The first time the Conduit 'planted' the changed narrative, it didn't take. Bernard emerged from the hypnosis, shrugging off the new memories as a nightmare, and not the real version of events. Three visualisations later, and the Conduit was still stuck at square one. *This was one stubborn old fox!* But, eventually, like all the Conduit's previous patients, he started to crumble. On the fourth visualisation, Bernard emerged from the hypnosis in an anxious state. Sweating and trembling. The Conduit asked him to recall the events, and Bernard talked through them as if they were reality.

The fiction had taken root. Bernard Driggs was broken!

And now the Conduit could fix him.

YORKE WAS SHAKING HIS HEAD. 'Sorry, Emma, rewind. *You paid a Private Investigator?*'

Gardner took a long, deep breath. Spilling her guts to the person she respected most in the world had left her shaken. She followed the breath with a nod.

It was now Yorke's turn to take a long, deep breath, because hitting the roof with one of his closest friends was sure to rule him out as her confidante. 'Okay, okay ... from the beginning please.'

'Well, you know the beginning, Mike. You were part of the investigation to find him.'

Over eighteen months ago, battered and bruised DI Mark Topham had been in the midst of an alcohol-fuelled breakdown as a result of his boyfriend's murder. While he'd been finding solace in sex workers, Topham had become involved in a violent altercation with a young prostitute called Dan Tillotson, who'd then died.

After Topham fled Salisbury, the investigation had lasted months. Looking back now, it seemed to Yorke that they'd tracked down every person Topham had ever been in contact with. Yorke had seen more of the UK in those months than he'd ever seen before, or ever expected to see again in his lifetime.

Yet, it'd all come to nothing. In fact, it'd been so fruitless, that many at HQ had already written Mark Topham off as dead, and the search had quickly become considered a waste of resources.

'I wasn't having it,' Gardner said. 'He was my friend. *Our* friend. We owed him more than that. Knowing that I had a family to support, and that I couldn't just swan off and look for him myself, I found a PI called Robert Brislane.'

'How could you afford a bloody PI?' Yorke said.

'Barry is quite high up at his pharmaceutical company. He had a significant bonus that year. Also, I had some savings.'

'*Jesus*. How did Barry feel about this?'

'Pissed off. At first. But he knew I didn't have a choice. He'd almost lost me the previous year to that knife injury, and knew that I'd given up my job to keep myself safe for him and our children. When I told him it was Robert Brislane, or I was going back to the job, he agreed.'

'But still ... have you been paying this Brislane since then? That's almost eighteen months!'

'No, I paid him for seven months.'

'I don't understand ... why did you stop? Did you run out of money?'

'No. I stopped because he *found him.*'

Yorke's eyes widened. 'Found Mark?'

Gardner nodded.

'Where?'

Gardner wiped another tear from her eye. 'That's just it, Mike. I don't know. Because the day Robert told me he'd found Mark, he disappeared too.'

———

ONCE THE REAL version of events had been *rejected*, and a new narrative *adopted*, the Conduit set out to build a whole new event. This was a new challenge for the Conduit. Until this point, he'd only ever *adapted* and *tweaked* existing events – he'd never created a completely new one! And certainly nothing as audacious as this ... But, the doctor was confident that, with a generous helping of time and copious amounts of drugs and hypnosis, it was possible.

Right now, on the sofa, the Conduit clapped his hands together. *Oh, how right he had been!*

In this new event, the Argentinian soldier had not died instantly from the bullet delivered by one of Bernard's colleagues. From the ground, the Argentinian had threatened to return, in the future, with several of his comrades to finish off Bernard Driggs in a cold and cruel manner. They would wait until his guard was lowered in old age and they would pay him a visit in *Rose Hill* care home. There they would take on the form of the carers and other residents.

Now, to any rational mind, this was obviously complete nonsense. *How on earth did this Argentinian plan to transcend death and return in another form? How could the soldier possibly know where Bernard Driggs would be residing in later life?*

But the level of believability was irrelevant because, as the Conduit would be pointing out in his notes for the science journals, "anything can, and will, be believed when the mind is under severe pressure".

And Bernard's tweaked narrative, in which he had frozen when he could have saved his comrades' lives, caused severe pressure.

So, Bernard Driggs bought it, hook, line and sinker. Maybe not back in his waking life – the Conduit never put this to the test – but certainly under hypnosis. And from that point onwards, the plot accelerated at breakneck speed and the Conduit realised that Christmas Day would be an optimum time to test out his treatment.

The Conduit trained Bernard's mind to respond to certain messages. Upon receiving these messages, he would fall under hypnosis again, and believe, whole-heartedly, in the threat issued to him all those years ago on an Argentinian battlefield. On one of their walks, he presented Bernard with a new phone and a Christmas present. He instructed him not to open the gift until the big day, and not until he received a text message. 'I want to know, immediately, your response when you see my gifts! So, only open them when I text you, so I'll be at hand to receive the reply.' Of course, there would be no text back. There didn't need to be. The Conduit knew what his response would be already.

The Conduit was very confident that no one would be searching Bernard's belongings (and the contents of his present) when he returned from his walk. Who would suspect Bernard Driggs of anything? This was a good thing, because within the wrapping slept the lighter fluid and a box of matches, for Bernard to burn *Rose Hill* down, and a Smith and Wesson Shield EZ.

So, early today, he'd driven himself, and his burner phone, to the other side of Leeds. Here, he'd sent the first text message to *activate.* Ten minutes later, he'd sent the second to *deactivate.*

Then, he'd dropped the phone into the River Aire, returned home, and waited for news of his success.

The Conduit took a deep breath.

Emil Kraepelin, Sigmund Freud, Eugen Bleuler, Nathan S. Kline, Aaron Beck ...

And now, Dr Louis Mayers.

He would change the face of modern psychiatry and take his place beside his illustrious forefathers.

GARDNER GAVE Yorke a potted history of Robert Brislane's seven-month hunt for Mark Topham. 'The last time I heard from him was on that day you came to see me, back in February, during that atrocious ash cloud - not long after that shit show with Borya Turgenev.'

Yorke flinched. The mere mention of his name caused the scar on his cheek to burn.

'Robert phoned because he'd found Mark in Leeds. Obviously, I had a lot of questions. I was desperate to know exactly where he was, and whether he was safe, but Robert just kept telling me it wasn't that simple. He said I had to come to Leeds. So, the next day, I phoned in sick, and headed up there to his hotel.' Gardner ran a hand through her hair.

'And?'

'When I got there, he'd gone.'

'Checked out?'

'No. They phoned up to his room and he wasn't there. It was a fairly cheap hotel with low standards. I only had to pretend to be his wife and they let me into the room. I waited for him. Spent the whole night there, and he didn't return. The next day, I called his wife to see if he'd headed home. No luck. So, I contacted the police ... after I'd searched his bags.'

'*What?*' Yorke said. 'You left DNA over all of his belongings. What if he turns up dead?'

'I used gloves, Mike. Besides, I told the police I spent the night in his room, and they would expect some DNA transfer from that anyway. Look, I was completely open and honest about my contact with Robert.'

'How did they feel about you two working outside the law to track down a wanted murderer?'

'How you'd expect. But I just stressed that Robert hadn't done anything illegal.'

'You were only aware of what he saw fit to tell you. You know how some of these investigators work.'

'True, and I was paranoid for a time, but if they ever suspected me, or think I crossed some kind of line, they must have moved on because I haven't heard from them in a good while. To begin with, it was me pressing them for information on the investigation, rather than the other way around! I didn't need my experience as a detective to know that they were going nowhere.' Gardner reached into her inside pocket, and pulled out a large box of tic tacs. 'There was a time when I considered hiring another investigator to find the missing one, and I even brought it up in conversation with Barry. Yes, ridiculous, I know. I'm already responsible for one person's disappearance.'

'You don't know that.'

'Oh, I do.' Gardner shook a tic tac out. She held the box out to Yorke. He shook his head.

'Mark may not even have been in Leeds,' Yorke said. 'You only have that one brief phone call from Robert. You saw no actual evidence.'

Gardner threw a tic tac into her mouth, leaned over and opened the glove compartment opposite Yorke. 'The brown envelope.'

'What is it?'

'I searched Robert's belongings, remember?'

'You didn't say you found anything.'

Gardner smiled. 'I didn't say I hadn't.'

'Are you about to show me evidence that should be with the police up in Leeds?'

'Close the glove compartment then, Mike.'

Yorke narrowed his eyes. 'I can't believe this. Are there any jobs going at Marks and Spencer because I might be applying there next month?'

'Stop exaggerating. No one will ever know you looked in that envelope.'

Yorke sighed, took the envelope and slipped out an A4 photograph. He recognised the person and the location. Both sent his heart racing.

The Parkinson Building. A prominent landmark in Leeds and one of its largest buildings. Yorke recalled being able to see the clock tower at its highest point miles away on the motorway every time he drove towards Leeds to begin a new semester.

This building sat at the entrance to Leeds University; a central part of Yorke's life for three years back in the early nineties.

Sitting on the third step up to the door into the Parkinson Building was their ex-colleague, and friend, Mark Topham. He had shaved his head, grown stubble, and traded in his tailored designer clothing for shapeless, loose-fitting attire. He was dishevelled, and so unlike the Topham they'd worked closely with.

'So Robert did find Mark ...' Yorke said.

Gardner nodded. 'Then lost him again.'

'And himself in the process. Bloody hell, Emma. This photograph should be with the police. Withholding this has not been your finest decision. You should have at least come to me sooner.'

Gardner snorted. 'Come to you! You want to lock him up!'

'Yes ... you do remember what he's done, don't you, Emma?'

'Yes, but I don't believe it's as it seemed. I want to hear his story before he's dragged in like some kind of animal.'

Yorke sighed. 'So, why are you here then if you don't trust me?'

'Desperation.'

'Thanks!'

'Now that I know Mayers is in Leeds too, I'm worried that he may have both of them. Robert and Mark.'

'That's a leap—'

'Come on, Mike! Why else would Mark be in Leeds unless he'd found Mayers? And if he found Mayers, no one is safe. Robert and Mark are in danger, I know they are.'

'Or were in danger, Emma. This picture is ten months old.'

'I'm not giving up.'

'Okay, say you're right, what then?'

'We go up to Leeds. You have a way in with the force up there—'

'Emma, that's not happening.'

Gardner stared at him. Her eyes were wide. He was used to seeing her look *driven* from their time working together, but this wasn't *drive*. This was obsession. Bordering on the fanatical.

'I'll go on my own then.'

'That's not happening, either.'

'You going to cuff me?'

'You're being ridiculous.'

'I was wrong.'

'Wrong ... about what?'

'About the fact that you'd do anything for your team.'

'You're not making any sense.'

'Iain is dead, Jake has gone, and Mark needs us. If we're not going to help him, who is?'

The dig hurt. Yorke broke eye contact with Gardner. 'But this isn't the right way. Ditching authority like a couple of rogue agents. Would we even get anywhere anyway?'

'You will be working with the police up there – hardly rogue.'

'While dragging a civilian along as part of the investigation?'

'I'm not a civilian, and you know it. And no one knows Mark like I do. Together, we can find him. And Robert too.'

Yorke rubbed his temples. Then, he picked up the envelope and threw it back into the glove compartment. 'I'm sorry, Emma.' He closed it, and then opened the car door.

He looked over at her. Her eyes were still wide. She trembled slightly. He had to force back his own tears. 'I'm going to go and be with my family. You should do the same.'

He left the car and closed the door behind him.

6

THERE WAS NO point trying to rekindle the Christmas Spirit in the Yorke household. That ship had well and truly sailed.

Ewan and Lexi had disappeared upstairs to celebrate their ridiculous engagement in privacy. Whether they were having sex or not was the least of Yorke's concerns now that they were preparing to commit their entire lives to each other. Patricia was watching EastEnders, which was always a positivity-sapper.

He watched Beatrice push a doll from the roof of her new doll's house. 'Susie's dead.' She then prepared another doll for a simulated suicide.

He walked around the side of the sofa, and saw the bundle of black fur. Even Rosie had given up bouncing off the walls and gone to sleep.

He sat down on the sofa and said. 'Sorry.'

Patricia muted the television. 'You don't have to apologise.'

'Yes, I do. It's ridiculous, I know.'

'We knew what we were getting into when we hooked

up. This is the way our jobs are. I've got the part-time excuse now ... you don't.'

'But it's Christmas Day.'

'And you've returned a child to their parents. Could your commitments be any nobler?'

'Roles reversed, I'd hate it.'

'Roles reversed, you'd *accept* it, for what it is. Important.'

'How long though? How long really before it comes between us. Before it does to us what it did to Jake and Sheila, to countless other people I know? I brought a Russian hitman into our house earlier this year for Christ's sake!'

She stood up and walked over to him. She smiled. 'Him? He was no match for the Yorke family.'

Well ... technically, it was Jake that helped us out on that one, Yorke thought, feeling a pang of loss.

She sat beside him, and put her hand on his knee. 'We're stronger than that. We met in blood remember?'

She was right. She was a forensic pathologist, and they'd met while she was examining a murder victim. 'I prefer to say we met on the job.'

'Same same ...'

'... but different?' Yorke said with a raised eyebrow. 'I get all that. But, we've decided to have a family together. *Us.* Not just *you*, who is happy to suffer because her husband is addicted to his job. *Us.*'

'You're tired. Emotional. You're thinking too hard. Any problems that exist between us are just in your head, Mike—'

'No. I can see the discontent even if you won't acknowledge it. Sometimes I hear it in your tone of voice, sometimes I see it in your eyes. It's there. We can't just ignore it.'

She rubbed his knee. 'Don't get wound up. Listen, we've got two weeks together—'

'Yes!' Yorke said, sitting upright. 'We have now. We almost didn't. They were at me again, trying to pull me away from my family for the umpteenth time. Don't worry, I—'

'Slow down. Who was at you?'

Inside, Yorke cursed his foolishness for mentioning it. Even bringing it up brought gloom into their lives. *Why couldn't he keep his big mouth shut?*

'Who?' Patricia asked again.

So, Yorke told her about the phone call from Madden telling him that Mayers was back. Before he'd even finished the story, Patricia's hand was over her mouth and she was deathly pale.

See, there it is, more angst sweeping through the Yorke household like a bloody tsunami.

She took her hand away. 'Jesus, I'm sorry, Mike. I really am.'

Yorke creased his brow. 'What're you sorry about?'

Patricia looked confused. 'That man ... that *monster* ... what he did to your friend.'

Yorke gulped. He recalled standing in an interviewing room with his hands on Topham's shoulders, desperate to achieve the impossible and hold him together. He'd watched his friend's world break in two.

'Madden wants you to help, doesn't she?' Patricia said.

He nodded. 'So, I obviously told her what she could do with the request.'

'What? I don't understand?'

'I told her I was spending the two weeks with my family.'

'And she let that one lie ... *Madden?*'

'No ... not exactly, but I'm unshakeable on this one.'

'What're you doing, Mike?'

'What do you mean?'

'This isn't you. There is no one else, *and I mean no one else,* better equipped to find this beast than you.'

Yorke stood up. 'So, now you're going to try and talk me into it too?'

'It's not something you can refuse to do.'

Yorke took a step away from where she was sitting. 'I turned it down for us ... for our family ... for you.'

'Do not,' Patricia held up a finger, 'use any of us as an excuse, Mike. That is not fair.'

'This is ridiculous.' Yorke said, turning and walking to the lounge door. He stopped with his hand on the handle, and turned back. 'I want to be here with all of you.'

'You want to find this bastard. To say otherwise is just a lie.'

He turned back from the door. 'I *never* lie to you.'

'No, you don't,' Patricia said. 'You're just lying to yourself.'

'So that's it then? I go, and what, Christmas is over? Why can't someone else stop him?'

'What happens if they can't? You'd blame yourself. And have you forgotten Emma? What happened to Mark tore her to pieces. How would she feel if she ever finds out that you had the opportunity to stop him?'

Yorke flinched and looked away.

'What?' Patricia said. 'There's something you're not telling me.'

Yorke told her about Gardner and the conversation

before in the car. He also told her about the photograph of Topham on the steps in Leeds.

Patricia rubbed her temples.

'Could you imagine me and Emma heading up north on some kind of crusade?' Yorke said with a shrug.

Patricia looked at him. She didn't say anything. She raised her eyebrows.

'You can't be serious.'

'What's the alternative then Mike?'

'What do you mean, what's the alternative? Emma goes home and spends time with her family, and I stay home and spend time with mine.'

'Jesus, Mike, for the most intelligent man I know, you can be thick as pig shit sometimes.'

'What do you mean?'

'Phone Emma now.'

'Why?'

'Just do it, Mike.'

Yorke phoned Gardner. 'Voicemail? Now what?'

'Phone her home.'

Yorke obliged.

'Hello, Barry?'

'Mike?'

'Yes ... Merry Christmas.'

'Merry Christmas to you too!'

'Sorry to disturb you today but is Emma there?'

'Yes, she just got back from seeing you. She's upstairs, packing.'

'Packing? Why?'

'For her trip to Leeds tomorrow with you, you plonker! You need to ease off the mulled wine.'

Yorke felt the blood drain from his head. 'Yes ... that's right ... sorry, I was just going to pack first thing.'

'Shall I grab her then?'

'No ... just tell her, I'll collect her at 8.'

'Fantastic. Will do.'

After ringing off, Patricia stood up, walked over and kissed him. They touched foreheads for a moment. 'I'm proud of you.'

Yorke sighed.

'While you phone Madden, I'll go upstairs and pack your things.'

———

WHEN THE CONDUIT wrote letters to his friend, he opted for a fountain pen over the keyboard, and *always* plumped for a cursive style. If he made a single mistake, he rewrote the letter again. He had one friend, and as such, could take the time to offer perfection to them.

He was on the final paragraph of a rather long-winded affair. He sat back on his dining room chair, took a refreshing deep breath, and looked over at his dog convulsing on the floor.

His eyes were rolled back, his teeth were clenched, and he was frothing from the corners of his mouth.

'Sorry, dog, I got a bit carried away with your cocktail this evening. I can only imagine what you are seeing in that storm. Flashes of a bygone era with Neil, I guess, before his insides were sliced like salami. But pay little attention, dog, don't let it upset you. That time, your old identity, doesn't exist anymore. Glowing embers on a long-dead fire. Nothing more.'

He smiled at his pet. Granted, he looked as if he were suffering, but he would be fine. He'd already rolled him onto his side. No need to put anything in his mouth. It was a common myth that you could swallow your tongue during a seizure – it was virtually impossible.

The Conduit turned his attention back to his letter, trying to shut out the groaning and clattering.

He was writing a letter about minimalism. Living a life with fewer possessions. He found the idea intriguing, and knew that his friend, the recipient, was currently experiencing this minimalistic lifestyle.

It was a shame that his friend never replied. The Conduit closed his letter by remarking on the possibility of extending minimalism to cover relationships. The fewer entanglements the better, in a life that carried too much emotional baggage for many.

The Conduit looked at his pet. The seizure was coming to an end. He was whining rather than groaning.

'Yes, dog, but don't you worry, our relationship is in no danger. You certainly don't bring emotional baggage. Not since I hollowed you out.'

7

BOXING DAY

YORKE SLIPPED OUT quietly.

Since his conversation with Patricia the previous evening, he'd accepted that his family wouldn't hold this departure against him. They'd concede that there was something grossly wrong in the world right now, and that he was off to try and put it right.

However, despite their blessing, Yorke knew that they'd be disappointed. He'd be leaving a gaping hole in the Yorke household for the rest of the Christmas season.

So, he quickly kissed Patricia and Beatrice, said 'congratulations' to Ewan and Lexi for the thousandth time – which was now coming across as more of an apology for his initial reaction – ruffled Rosie's fur, and then made his exit smooth and swift, in the hope that they could revive their celebrations.

He drove to Gardner's house. She was already at the door waiting for him. After she'd installed herself in the passenger seat of his police-issue Lexus, he turned to her. 'Did you know I'd cave? Seriously?'

'Never a doubt.'

'Shit.' Yorke indicated to pull out. 'That's exactly what Madden said. Am I really that much of an open book?'

'Yes.'

'It was a rhetorical question.'

'I know. Still thought it best to answer it.'

'Well, if you're coming with me, you better stay on your best behaviour.'

'So, I'm coming with you now then?'

They exchanged a smile. He passed her a wad of paper, stapled together.

'What's this?'

'I have an old academy buddy in the West Yorkshire Police. I contacted him last night, and he pulled the necessary strings to get that fast-tracked to me. It's all the records from the investigation into Robert Brislane's disappearance. It came through on e-mail about an hour ago.'

'Jesus, that's a different level from fast-track.'

'Good thing about being this long in the tooth, Emma, is that you're owed a lot of favours, and a copper always repays his favours. We've got a long journey ahead of us. Before I meet Benjamin Rosset of HMET, I really want to be completely informed. If you start to feel travel sick going through the notes, there are some tablets in the glove compartment.'

She scowled. 'You're all heart.'

Over the next hour, Gardner fed him the details of the case. Yorke could feel himself growing more and more frustrated. The investigation was half-hearted at best.

'Bloody hell,' Gardner said after reaching the end of the notes. 'Was your buddy involved in *this?*'

'If he was, he wouldn't be my buddy anymore.'

'Well, now I know why I didn't get much when I pestered them.'

Yorke stopped at the Service Station for a coffee and left Gardner in the car. While they prepared his order, he sat down and scrambled around the many holes in the West Yorkshire investigation looking for something.

'Mike?' The waitress called, holding up his tray of coffees.

'Thanks.' He winced. He was all for good service, but knowing his name just felt creepy.

When he got back to the car, wielding a skinny Latte for Gardner, and an Americano for himself, he felt more inspired. 'Whenever we investigate the murder of a married woman, we always throw so much at the husband.'

'That's because uxoricide is so common, Mike. Remember that training course we went on? 35% of female victims are killed by their husbands.'

'Yes, that's right. But because mariticide is rarer we give it limited airtime.'

'You thinking Robert's wife?'

'I'm thinking that our colleagues barely looked into Robert Brislane's wife.'

Gardner nodded.

'The ratio of mariticide to uxoricide is 3:4. Not as rare as some may think, eh?'

'But I'm hoping Robert is missing and not dead.'

'Do we really need to go through the statistics of how many missing people are dead too?'

Gardner gave him a cutting smile. 'I did say I was hoping.'

'Take a look at a map, Emma. Do you know that Coventry is approximately half-way between Salisbury and Leeds?'

'I do.'

'Fancy popping in to see Mrs Brislane? See how she's adapting to life without her husband?'

Gardner smiled. 'Shit! I've missed *this*!'

ALAN SANTS, wets his pants.
Alan Sants, wets his pants.
Alan Sants, Alan Sants.
Alan Sants wets his pants.

Using a ruler, Alan Sants adjusted his four Chinese Mud Men figurines, so they were exactly four centimetres apart. These four mud men on his shelf, dated from the early 20th century, were a gift from his mother. She, too, had received them as a gift. Not from *her* mother, but an exporter from Beijing, who sent his cloths and silks over to be sold in her sewing shop.

Alan loved the figurines, and not just because they were an antique artefact from South China, and so worth some money, but because they were rugged and real. Untarnished by gloss and commerce.

His four Mud Men were all fishermen. They wore hats to protect them from the sun, and dark brown sandals. There was some glaze on the clothing. Some yellow, some blue and some green. But the face, hands and feet were left unglazed, and the natural colour of the mud was exposed.

But what Alan loved most about these rustic figurines was the fingerprints of the sculptor. Forever burned into the fired clay.

Once, when he was younger, he took these wonderful figurines to school to show his friend. He was thirteen years old. A group of children of different ages, sizes, and gender, clubbed together to tease him over his interests. One young girl even took one off him and threatened to smash it. When a large damp cloud spread over his trousers, she gave it back, but not before a new song came into being.

Alan Sants, wets his pants.
Alan Sants, wets his pants.
Alan Sants, Alan Sants.
Alan Sants wets his pants.

That song had been sung to him countless times. All the way through school. All the way through college. Branding him, like the fingerprints of a sculptor on a little Chinese Mud Man. Only stopping after his escape to University.

He heard Eddie McLarney farting behind him.

When he turned to look at the naked rugby player sprawled on his bedsheets, he chewed his fingernails. Not from nerves. He never really felt nervous. Neither was it from revulsion, although he did feel this often. It was disorder which made him chew his nails.

'Why do you always wear that *fucking* bowtie?' Eddie said.

Alan chewed harder. This disorder was extreme. The only reason he was in this situation right now was because the desire for sex had been particularly strong last night.

But there was no desire right now. 'It's time for you to go. I have to leave ... soon.'

'Answer me. Why the bowtie? You look like a *fucking* ponce. Didn't *Doctor Who* wear one?'

Alan touched the material with his fingers. He turned to look in the mirror above the mantelpiece. He loved the symmetry of a bowtie. 'I just prefer it to a tie.'

Eddie snorted. 'So? You don't have to wear a fucking tie either. You're not working for a corporate company, you're at Uni!'

'My mother always said, "Clothes make the man. Naked people have little or no influence on society."'

'Is that a jab at the boy with his bollocks out on your bed?' Eddie gave a snort of laughter.

Alan tried to ignore the disorder and focus instead on the order in the room and his reflection. His brown bow-tie. His Mud Men. The black curtains of hair that framed his long gaunt face. 'I have to leave.'

He farted again. 'I can see myself out *after* you leave.'

Alan's left eyelid twitched. He turned from the mirror. 'I'd prefer it if you left *before*.'

Alan could only imagine the havoc Eddie would wreak with the order of his room. The Mud Men, for example. What if he picked one up? It was inconceivable.

Eddie slumped out of bed and dressed with a sneer on his face. 'I knew this was a bad idea.'

We both knew it was a bad idea, Alan thought, *but that didn't stop it happening, and it won't stop it happening again.*

After dressing, Eddie stood opposite him. They were both tall, but where Alan was very thin, some would say emaciated, Eddie was wide and muscular. He'd already admitted to using steroids in oral form. It was a slippery slope, Alan had thought, but never said anything. He didn't really care less if Eddie started injecting himself or not.

Eddie poked him in the chest with a fleshy finger. 'You know the drill.'

'Yes ... I say *fuck all* about us.'

'Shit.' Eddie smiled. 'Word perfect. You do listen.' He showed him the palm of his hand, and swung it to strike him, stopping at the last moment. 'Not even a flinch. You like it that much?'

Alan didn't like it. He'd just got used to it.

'Remember, I call you, you don't call me, Mr Bowtie.'

Eddie left the room.

Alan sat on the edge of the bed, running his hand over his arm, feeling the sting of the bruises Eddie had left there. Then, he leaned over and slipped the backpack out from under the bed. He checked it was completely zipped up. He had a gift in there, and he would hate for it to get wet in the snow.

———

THE SAT NAV said that they were ten minutes from Helen Brislane's house. Yorke was glad they were close, the general mood had taken a turn for the worse over the last hour, and the distraction of an interrogation would be welcome, and should hopefully get the two investigators' juices flowing again.

Gardner was just relaying her experiences with CBT. 'It did help, at first, it really did. It helped with the guilt I felt after shooting Lock. It also helped after I was stabbed. I could really get at that paranoia, those thoughts of dying, and leaving Anabelle alone. But it just didn't help with Mark. I just couldn't get over what I saw. Do you remember seeing Dan Tillotson?'

Yorke nodded. Seeing a young lad in his twenties beaten to a pulp wasn't something you shifted with ease.

'And I see that boy all of the time. How could Mark do that to someone? Mark? *Our Mark?*'

'You know, better than anyone, he wasn't himself. The grief over Neil changed him ... as it would anyone.'

'But grief, or no grief. Yourself, or not yourself, how could the gentlest man start behaving like a wild ape?'

'Well, Darwin might offer you some rationale for that.'

'And you're right. We all have those moments. Those moments we're *overwhelmed*, but with most of us there is a failsafe switch, isn't there? I know I've pressed it a few times.'

'My finger is hovering over it nearly every day,' Yorke said with a smile. 'Look ... mental illness is a force. We've seen it time and time again in our job. The people who do these things are often not the people they once were. People change, and sometimes what they change into, is not something that is easily understood. I know I struggle to.'

'But I don't believe he's changed, Mike. I can't believe it. He was a good man. *Is a good man.* He cannot have lost that. It only seems like yesterday, I was sitting across from him in the kitchen. Yes, he was drinking too much. Yes, he was plagued with nightmares of Neil being stabbed. But there was no aggression in him then, and I don't believe there is now. I mean are we even 100% sure it was him that killed Tillotson?'

'Apart from the DNA?'

'He could have been defending himself?'

'From what? There was no weapon. You'd expect more of Topham's blood and DNA on the victim if they were actually fighting.'

'Well, when we find him, I guess we'll finally get the truth.'

'You are speaking about him as if he's still alive?'

'He is.'

'It's good to be positive, Emma, but I think you should start preparing yourself.'

'No. I won't accept it. Have you accepted that Jake is gone for good?'

'That's not the same, Emma.'

'Why? He's gone. Missing too.'

'Yes, but Jake's not dead.'

'So where's he gone then?'

'Just to cool off. He'll be back.'

'Cool off from what?'

Cooling himself off for getting in too deep. For getting involved with the wrong people. For doing some immoral things. And it was the right move. It means he is safe. For now.

But Gardner could not know these things.

'His broken marriage for a start. Anyway, now is not about Jake, it's about Mark, and I'm just asking you to prepare yourself, that's all.'

Yorke drove past Helen Brislane's house and to the end of a cul-de-sac. The dead end opened up onto a small park, scattered with a few benches, and a children's weathered playground. Yorke pointed it out. 'Handy if you've got kids.'

'They don't.'

'It may be best if you wait here—'

'Not a fucking chance. And I've met her already.'

'So, she knows you're not an officer?'

Gardner looked away. 'Not really, no. She never asked for a badge.'

'Bloody hell, Emma, you know the trouble you can get into?'

Gardner shrugged. 'I'm coming in, Mike, so you can lay some ground rules now, or we can have the argument on her doorstep?'

'There is only one ground rule, don't speak. If you wind her up, and she lodges a complaint, both me and you are going to get strung up.'

Gardner mimed zipping up her mouth.

As they walked towards the house, Gardner said, 'What if *you* piss her off?'

Yorke touched his chest. 'Me?'

'You are pretty good at that if I remember, Mike.'

'Memory is fallible, Emma, and if you're going to play cop, you best start calling me sir again.'

'Did you miss my subservience, *sir*?'

'Well, it's not the respect,' Yorke said, 'Because I never bloody got that.' He knocked on the door. 'What a way to bloody well spend Boxing Day.'

THE GIFT WAS WEIGHING on him, so Alan tightened the straps on the backpack. It seemed to help. Then, he crossed over the road to avoid the long walk past a row of shops in Headingley. He didn't like the windows, or parked cars. He didn't mind his face, but he avoided reflections that showed his upper body.

To be reminded of his scoliosis was to be reminded of the lack of order and symmetry in his body. His curved spine caused him to lean to one side. One of his shoulders, and one of his hips stuck out. His ribcage was also an uneven mess.

As he walked the street, he became aware, as he always did, of the stares. He didn't need to make eye-contact with any of these people to know where they were directing their attention. That was one of the advantages of being a freak of nature. There were predators out there who preyed on the disadvantaged, so your senses became acute.

Eddie McLarney was one such predator.

He looked up at the *Original Oak* public house. It was dolled out in festive decorations with fake snow stuck on the inside of the windows. The proprietors had even gone so far as to stick an inflatable Santa on the roof.

Opposite the *Oak* was the road on which everything had changed for Alan many months before ...

It was late, and dark. After a trip to the cinema, Alan jumped off the bus in Headingley. It was the nearest stop to his flat in his apartment block. He hated walking through a drunken crowd, so he always opted for a weekday night to visit the cinema. But students were students, and even though the crowd wasn't heavy, it was big enough to cause him discomfort.

He kept his eyes down, felt the stares roll over his misshapen body, and made a beeline for home.

Eddie McLarney intercepted his path.

They knew each other from university. He studied psychology too. They'd even shared a discussion group for one module. Of course, there'd been little discussion between them, and when there had, Eddie had been solely focused on fulfilling a stereotype. Alan had found it confusing. Everyone knew Eddie was a drunken rugby player - was it totally necessary to perform all the time?

'Where are you going?' Eddie slurred his words. He bounced from one foot to the next to keep himself standing. The smell of marijuana was pungent.

'Home ...'

'Not before you have some of this, Mr Bowtie.' Eddie held out a joint.

'No, thank you.'

'Why are you so *fucking* stiff?'

Alan tried to step around him.

Eddie stopped Alan dead in his tracks with the palm of his hand. 'Answer the question.'

'It's not really a question though, is it?' Alan said. 'It's more of a conclusion. That's what you think of me. Could I change your mind even if I wanted to?'

A ghost of a smile flickered over Eddie's face. 'I knew there was more to you.'

'*Oi bender!*'

Eddie pulled his hand back and addressed the person shouting towards them. 'Fuck off.'

'*Where're you fucking going?*' The person said.

'I was getting some air, then into the *Sky Rack*.'

'Who's your boyfriend?' The friend was closer to them now, so there was no need to shout, but he did so anyway.

Alan didn't turn to look. He started to walk ahead again.

'*Oi! Where the fuck do you think you're going?*' The friend said.

Alan stopped.

'Leave it out, Mickey, you prick,' Eddie said.

'Why? Do you fancy him? *Everyone, over here*, Eddie is just coming out of the fucking closet!'

'You bell end,' Eddie said. 'He's on my course.'

Alan chanced a step forward.

'Oi, you bent-backed faggot.' Mickey said. 'You do as you're told, and fucking stop, or I'll twist you into shape.'

Alan sighed, and stopped again. He didn't turn, but he could hear that there was now a crowd of them behind him, bantering over Eddie's sexuality. He decided to give it a minute and when they were suitably wound up by each other rather than him, he would slip away. He looked down at the second hand on his watch, and watched it sweep.

'I saw you kissing Quasimodo,' Mickey said.

'There's an alley back there, Eddie,' another grunt said, and laughed. 'You can go and ring each other's bells down there.'

'The bells ... the bells ...' said one of the knuckle-draggers, adding an exaggerated slur to his voice to mimic the disabled Quasimodo.

'I know,' Eddie said. 'I've been down that alley with a bird. Not quite the behaviour of a queer now, is it?'

'I feel I don't know you anymore,' Mickey said. The group all burst out laughing. He was their leader, and they hung off his every word.

'Fuck off,' Eddie said.

'You're going to have to prove yourself to us,' Mickey said.

Alan saw it had been one minute and started to walk away from the cavemen—

He was pushed sharply. If there hadn't been a lamppost for him to grab, he would have gone face down on the pavement.

'What did I say, cripple?' Mickey said.

Alan didn't move.

'Turn around so I can look at what my friend likes so much.'

His sheep laughed again.

A young couple were walking in their direction. If he broke into a sprint now, he could maybe reach them and get some back-up.

They crossed the road. The safest move on their part. They didn't want to cross paths with this lot—

Another shove. Not quite as hard, but enough for him to lose his one-handed grip on lamp post. He stumbled forward.

'*Turn ... the ... fuck ... round.*'

Assaulted from the back, or the front, Alan guessed it was all the same. Anyway, they were out in the open here – would they really risk their university places by assaulting him with potential witnesses around?

He turned.

There were five of them in total, including Mickey and

Eddie. The three chuckling followers had their arms draped around each other, and were stumbling back and forth, with eyes half-closed. It was a pathetic sight.

Having his masculinity questioned was sobering Eddie up. He was no longer swaying and was just scowling. Alan noticed that Mickey was notably smaller, and slimmer than his rugby chums. The littlest man definitely shouted the loudest in this group.

'I'd just like to go home,' Alan said.

'You would? On your own, or with my friend here?'

More guffaws from the sheep.

'For fuck's sake,' Eddie said.

Mickey narrowed his eyes and turned to glare at Eddie. 'Go with him. Get it out of your system, brother. We won't ever mention it.' A wry grin spread across his face. '*Honestly.*'

Eddie shoved him. 'You're being a fucking bell end.'

Mickey shrugged. 'Prove it then. Prove you don't want to fuck him.'

'How?'

'Lamp the puff.'

'I'm leaving,' Eddie said.

'That's proof of something alright.' Another grin spread across his face.

'Why don't I lamp you instead?'

'Guess you could. Then you can go home and celebrate with your princess.'

'Do you want to get me kicked out of Uni? Have you forgotten what happened to Tom?'

'No one gets booted out on one punch. You just say he provoked it. You have four witnesses.'

Alan took a deep breath through his nose. He wasn't particularly anxious by what was unfolding in front of him and just really wanted to go home. He'd spent a fair chunk of his childhood being bullied. There was very little out of the ordinary in this whole scenario.

The drunken sheep chanted. '*Lamp the poof! Lamp the poof!*'

'For fuck's sake!' Eddie said. 'But not the face.'

'Because he's pretty?' Mickey said.

'No, because I don't want to be pulled in on GBH.'

'*Lamp the poof! Lamp the poof!*'

Eddie turned and slammed his fist into Alan's stomach. The wind was forced out of him, and he slid down the lamp post to his knees. He took a deep breath and looked up.

Mickey threw an arm around Eddie's shoulders. 'Welcome back! *Skyrack?*'

Eddie pulled away. 'Yes.' He looked back at Alan and their eyes met.

Alan smiled.

Eddie creased his brow.

'Come on,' Mickey said, pulling at Eddie's arm.

'Yes, coming,' Eddie said, but he was unable to pull his eyes from Alan's.

Mickey started to move away.

'I understand,' whispered Alan, loud enough for Eddie to hear.

'For fuck's sake, Eddie, he's not your boyfriend anymore,' Mickey said.

'*Coming!*' Eddie turned.

As they were walking off, Eddie looked back, reigniting the eye contact for a moment longer—

Someone stepped up behind Alan and said, 'Long before we were born, a British prime minister said something that stuck with me ever since I heard it as a child.'

One of his university lecturers walked around to the front of Alan and offered a hand to help him up from his knees. 'He said, "Courage is fire, and bullying is smoke".'

Alan took Dr Alexander Harris' large hand and was back on his feet in a moment.

'Tell me, did you anticipate the outcome of that encounter?' Harris said.

'Yes.'

'And did you fear it?'

'No.'

'Precisely.' Harris smiled. '*Fire*. There's *real* strength ... and *sharp* focus in you. What's your name?'

'Alan Sants. I'm a Psychology Major. You may have seen me in your lectures?'

The burly man pushed his hand through his tangled white hair. 'I'm sorry, Alan, there are many students in my lectures ... so ... did you see the *smoke?*'

'Sorry, Dr ... the smoke?'

'Courage is fire, and bullying is smoke, remember?'

'Yes ... I guess so. They're afraid of what's different. I'm different I guess. They're pretending to be courageous and powerful, but they're masking their anxieties.'

'Almost ... but there is something else. I saw the whole thing.' He pointed over to the alley that Mickey had suggested to Eddie before. 'You may wonder why I didn't intervene. I'm well into my fifties, Alan, and I've been around the block, but you'd nothing to fear in that encounter. Smoke is dangerous, but the burning house is ultimately doomed, and those boys have no wish to hasten their demise. They were never going to really harm you. Too much to lose. But, I digress. There was something interesting about one boy's behaviour there. Did you spot it?'

'I'm not sure ...'

'The way he looked at you, Alan. His hesitance over delivering the blow. The lingering stare. He bullied you for an entirely different reason. He bullied you because of what he fears about himself.'

Alan was startled by the direction of the conversation. What was Dr Harris doing out here anyway? This was a student area. Yes, there were restaurants dotted about, but you rarely saw the teachers and lecturers out here, probably because they wanted to avoid awkward encounters ... such as this one.

'But, you're tired. I'm tired. I have just met a group of church friends for Italian, and whenever there is a wine menu, there is only one outcome. Would you like me to walk you home, Alan, you have nothing to fear from me?'

Alan thought about it. His professor was a very interesting man. 'Honestly ... I'm fine. Thank you though.'

Dr Harris nodded, and then reached up to his top lip. He opened his thumb and forefinger there as if he was stroking a moustache. 'Fire, Alan. That's what I see. *Fire* ...'

Now, all these months later, as Alan walked to the bus stop in Headingley, avoiding car windows and shop fronts, he considered these first encounters with Dr Harris and Eddie.

He considered them very deeply.

8

THE COFFEE WAS disgusting, but Yorke drank it anyway. Not to be polite, but because he was desperate for a caffeine hit.

Gardner looked across at him from the other sofa. She, too, was probably wondering what dead animal Helen Brislane had dropped into the cafétiere.

During his many years on the force, Yorke had been into many expensively furnished houses, but this really took the biscuit. The sofa he was sitting on was probably worth more than his car – at least it felt like it; and there was nothing fake about the crystal in the massive chandelier that hung from the heart of the room. Yorke wondered if he was in the wrong job, and briefly speculated over how much he would get paid for following cheating spouses and taking photographs like her missing husband had done.

At first, Helen had expressed surprise that, after all this time, the police were still interested in finding her husband. She'd assumed they'd given up. Yorke explained that this wasn't the case, while wondering why she'd not taken it on herself to badger the police more. This was his first red flag.

Helen had quickly turned on the tears and delivered a sermon on their fairytale marriage.

Rehearsed. Two red flags and they'd only been in the house ten minutes. Why the hell had the officers investigating this case not taken a good look at her?

Helen was the type of person that really wanted to look good. To the extent she stopped looking so because she tried too hard. She was caked in make-up, and the outfit she wore to potter around the house was more suited to a cocktail party. She was drinking mulled wine. She either knew how bad her own coffee was, or she was doing it to settle her nerves. *Something to hide, Helen?*

'That job,' Helen said, 'I *just* knew it'd be the end of him.'

'The end of him?' Yorke said.

'Well, he's dead, isn't he?'

'Do you know something we don't?' Gardner said.

Yorke stared at Gardner. The gagging order he placed on her outside had lasted less than fifteen minutes.

'He's been missing since February. Do you really think he's still alive?'

'We try not to draw conclusions, Mrs Brislane, we just try to find the truth.'

'What do your past experiences tell you? Everyone knows the statistics.'

'Statistics and past experiences aren't always the answer,' Yorke said. 'We prepare ourselves for that outcome, but we don't give up hope, and you shouldn't either.'

Helen nodded.

'You said in one of your interviews that you spoke to him the evening before he disappeared.'

'Yes, he called me. He always phoned me in the evening when he was away.'

'How did he seem?'

'Fine. We spoke for a while. He is good at that. Talking.' She smiled. 'He loves the sound of his own voice ... but, I don't mind. I love it too.'

'Did he talk to you about the investigation he was working on?'

'No. He didn't like to talk shop. He also took a professional attitude and wanted to keep the confidence of his clients. Besides, we had more than work in our lives. I mean, he'd tell me if he was having a hard time, or if one of the cases wasn't coming together, but the details weren't there.'

'So, he didn't say anything about how he was doing on this investigation?'

Helen sighed. 'I seem to remember him saying it was looking good. He said the case would be wrapped up soon, and he'd be home by the weekend but, no, nothing more. You know, I'm sure I said all of this in the interviews ...'

'Yes, you did,' Yorke said. 'But memory is a funny thing. A bit of time, and things sometimes come back to you.'

'Or things alter and become a work of fiction,' she said.

'True as well ... however, do you remember anything else?'

'No, sorry, nothing has come back to me.'

'Have you ever been to Harewood House?' Gardner asked.

'Harewood house? No, can't say I have. Where's that?'

'Near Leeds. West Yorkshire.'

Helen shook her head. 'Doesn't ring a bell, sorry.'

'That was where he was last sighted.' Gardner looked down at some notes which she'd made on the journey. 'Automatic Number Plate Recognition tracked his car on the day he disappeared. He left his hotel and was last picked up by cameras at 2.10pm on the A61, Harrogate road, heading in the direction of Harewood House. ANPR *never* picked him up again.'

'I never knew about this before.'

Yorke and Gardner exchanged a glance.

'Despite the fact they searched the area?' Yorke said.

'News to me,' Helen said. 'So, what did they find?'

'Nothing really, but it's a big area. They didn't have the time or manpower to search all the areas that ANPR won't reach. That's a lot of woodland and forest, and some quite substantial reservoirs too.'

'I can't believe I didn't know about this.'

Despite the excess blusher, Yorke could see her grow pale. This newsflash had disturbed her. She took a mouthful of her mulled wine. 'Do you *really* think he's alive, Detective?'

'I never said I thought he was alive,' Yorke said. 'I just always hold out hope.'

'Well, if he drove into a rural area, and never drove out of it, what conclusions can we draw from that?'

'Like anything, Mrs Brislane, ANPR is not infallible. He could have been missed coming out of the area.'

'Yes, but wouldn't he have been picked up sooner or later somewhere else?'

Yorke nodded. 'Probably.'

'And yet you still remain positive?'

Yorke looked down and pretended to make notes. He wasn't at all positive about Brislane; in fact, he felt fairly certain he'd come a cropper. But he wasn't about to share this.

'Stranger things have happened, Mrs Brislane. Now, please, think again. Have you ever been to Harewood House? Or, do you know if your husband has ever been there? It's an Eighteenth-Century stately home.' He glanced around at her impressive décor again. 'With incredible interior design, priceless art, landscaped gardens, that kind of thing.' *Should be right up your street, shouldn't it?*

'Never been. Never heard of it. Sorry Detective.'

'Can I just ask you about Dr Moss?' Gardner said.

Helen snapped her head left to look at Gardner. 'Yes.'

'You told the interviewing officer that you were with him from 3.00pm the day that your husband disappeared.'

'I was.'

'For marriage counselling?'

'Yes.'

'Is it standard practice for someone to see a marriage counsellor without their other half?'

'I don't know ... I'd never done it before, and I may never have to do it again. Dr Moss liked to have individual sessions with us – that's all I know.'

She was getting snappy. Yorke tried to ease Gardner down with a stare. He didn't remember her being this aggressive in interrogation when they worked together; however, cases like these, which were extremely personal, could have this kind of impact.

'You said before that you were very much in love,' Gardner continued. 'Why did you have to see a marriage counsellor?'

Yorke inwardly groaned. His stare clearly hadn't worked.

'We were happy. *Very*. We just thought we could be even happier.'

Strange answer. But, fair enough.

Yorke continued the interview for quite some time. He remained persistent, but polite; his trademark style.

Composure had taken him to the truth more times that he could remember. He took detailed notes. In the past, whenever his investigation had come to a dead end, he read back through his notes. It was the perfect safety net. 99% of the time the answer was buried in there somewhere.

There was one question he still wanted to ask. He'd saved it until last, so as to glean as much information as he could before potentially sending her flying off the handle. It was an important question and often spoke volumes in a case such as this. 'Did you or your husband ever have an affair, Mrs Brislane?'

Yorke noticed her turning pale again.

'No ... *he* would never do that.'

'Thanks, I just wanted to clear that up.'

'*We loved each other.*'

'No one is questioning that.'

'It seems like you are.' She pointed at Gardner without actually looking at her. 'She certainly did when asking me about marriage counselling.'

She clearly hadn't been subjected to difficult questioning last time.

'Have you met anyone else?' Gardner said. 'You know ... since?'

Helen turned and glared at Gardner. 'Since what? You've just told me he might still be alive. So, are you asking me if I'm currently being unfaithful?'

Yorke didn't like Helen's tone with Gardner. 'Could you answer the question please, Mrs Brislane?'

'There's no one else' Helen swept back her fringe. 'I miss my husband very much.'

'I'm sorry for the situation you're in,' Yorke said.

'Thank you, Detective.'

Yorke brought the interview to a close.

Yorke was already convinced that Helen knew a lot more than she was letting on, but what he saw sitting by the front door as he put his shoes back on, sent his suspicion into overdrive.

As they were walking to the car, Gardner said, 'Well, maybe she didn't have anything to do with it.'

'Jesus, you are rusty.'

'What do you mean?'

He beeped his car. 'Emma, there were more red flags than a communist parade in that house.'

'Enlighten me.'

'In the car.'

Once they were in the car, and Yorke had raised his concerns with Gardner, she asked, 'So now where?'

Yorke started the car. 'To see a doctor.'

A WALK through the quiet Leeds University Campus on Boxing Day was a pleasant experience for Alan. There was no one to trap him with a horrified stare.

The buildings were all closed, so he sat on a wall opposite the School of Psychology. He slipped off the backpack with his friend's present inside it. He placed it on the wall beside him. He rolled his rounded shoulders and listened to his curved spine crack and reflected on that first night Eddie McLarney had come to his apartment ...

'Just wanted to say, I'm sorry. That's it,' Eddie said.

'Okay,' Alan said at the door, playing with the top buttons of his shirt. He'd already removed his bowtie, and so felt *uneven* without it.

'Don't make this fucking harder than it has to be, Mr Bowtie.'

Back to his default mode. Aggression, confrontational.

'I wasn't ... it's late so ...'

'You invite trouble, you know that. It's mainly your fucking fault.' Eddie paused and chewed his bottom lip. 'Can I come in?'

'Yes.' Alan stepped to one side.

Alan knew he shouldn't be inviting disorder into his house. He'd spent his life avoiding it. He'd end up chewing his nails. Except ... tonight, for some reason, it was exciting him.

He thought about Dr Harris' words that night in Headingley. *'The way he looked at you, Alan. His hesitance over delivering the blow. The lingering stare. He bullied you for an entirely different reason. He bullied you because of what he fears about himself.'*

Eddie passed Alan in the doorway, and they both turned to face each other. Alan closed the apartment door behind him with one hand.

'I faced my fear by letting you inside,' Alan said.

Eddie creased his brow. 'What the fuck are you talking about?'

'You can face your fear too.' Alan leaned in and kissed him.

Eddie pulled back. 'Jesus! You *are* a faggot!'

He pushed Alan hard against the door. It winded him. It reminded him of the attack the other night. He felt the beginnings of an erection. 'You can leave then.'

'Yes. Get out of my fucking way.'

Alan leaned against the wall, still trying to get his breath back. Eddie stepped forward and his left hand closed on the door handle. With the back of his right hand, he slapped Alan across the face.

Alan's closed his eyes. He felt his erection pressing against his trousers, smiled, and opened his eyes.

'You really are a fucking freak, do you know that?' Eddie said, opening the door. He left.

Now, these many months later outside the School of Psychology at Leeds University, Alan opened his eyes. He was smiling that same smile the night that he'd given Eddie a chance to face down his own fear. He'd opted out that time, but the second time, the very next evening in fact, well, that had been a whole different story ...

'Are you ready to face me?' Alan said.

'No,' Eddie said.

They were lying on their sides, backs to one another.

Alan could feel his big lover's trembles through the mattress. He reached up and stroked his cheek, sore from the slap he received after tonight's lingering kiss. He was also sore below. Eddie had been forceful and aggressive. Feeling him release his fear had been worth it. In this instance, pain and pleasure had come together harmoniously.

Alan turned over to face Eddie's back. 'No one is who they appear to be, you do know that, don't you?'

No reply.

'I've met someone. I've learned so much from him. He's taught me that we are not legible texts to be read and deciphered.'

Still no reply.

'Would you like to meet him?'

Eddie flipped over and grabbed Alan by the throat. 'I should fucking kill you.'

Alan smiled.

Months later, and Eddie had still not accepted his invitation to meet Dr Harris. This didn't bother him too much; after all, Alan cared very little about whether Eddie received any help for his fear. He was welcome to continue coming to terms with his sexuality in the only way he managed to do anything in his life, by bullying and aggression; and, in return, Alan was able to tease himself with these small bursts of arousal and pleasure.

Whenever he sat for more than ten minutes, he became stiff as a plank. He stood up and stretched, groaning. He picked up the backpack, looked at his watch. It was almost time for the doctor.

And to give a present to a dog.

9

'GOING TO SEE a doctor without waiting two weeks for an appointment,' Gardner said, walking alongside Yorke towards the house, 'been a long time since I did that.'

'Perks of the job,' Yorke said, 'But don't be asking him about your in-growing toenail.'

Gardner smiled. 'He specialises in marriage ... so, it might be wise for you to ask him for advice?'

She was kidding, of course, but the joke struck a nerve. He kept this hidden though and simply returned her grin.

Yorke knocked on Dr Moss' door. A tall, dark man, wearing a Christmas jumper, opened the door.

The first thing Yorke did was look down at his shoes.

Before, on their way out of Helen's house, Yorke had noticed three large items of footwear. A pair of Birkenstocks; a pair of Moccasin slippers; and a pair of brown Caterpillar boots. They must have been size 12s, if not bigger. Yorke had explored this with Gardner in the car. Robert Brislane had been quite a short man, and she didn't remember him having particularly large feet. So, if these shoes didn't belong to Brislane, who did they belong to?

Dr Moss had big feet.

Yorke could feel his heart rate rising.

After spending the morning with the well-presented Helen Brislane in her glamourous house, Yorke wasn't surprised to find himself now being led into a pristine office, with sophisticated décor, by a doctor with groomed eyebrows, an expensive haircut and suit, and chiselled features.

Yorke would be asking Gardner later if they'd taken the wrong turn somewhere and ended up in Beverly Hills rather than Coventry.

As Yorke and Gardner took seats opposite Moss, the doctor opened up a tin of breath mints, popped one in his mouth, and then slid it across the table. 'Would you like one?'

He expected Gardner to descend on them like a wild animal.

'No thanks.' It seemed like it was tic tacs or nothing.

Moss lifted a pile of unopened presents from his desk and placed them on the floor, so they could all see each other clearly. 'Patients,' he said. 'They are always generous.'

'You going to open them?' Yorke said.

'Later, with a brandy.'

Yorke nodded. 'So, are we okay to ask a few questions about Robert now.'

Moss sighed. 'For a moment out there on the doorstep, Detective, I thought you were going to tell me that you'd found him. It's a shame ... he's a nice man. How can I help?'

'I know you've already disclosed confidential patient information in interviews.'

'Yes. It was uncomfortable and, fortunately, it's rare that

I must do this. But when someone has been missing for several days, and their life could be in danger, disclosure is in the patient's immediate best interests. I'm just sad that you couldn't use any of the information to locate him.'

'Well, hopefully, we can dig up something today. Could you sum up what marital problems Helen and Robert were having?'

'Typical ones to be honest. They were still very much in love, but there were communication issues that were having a negative effect on their relationship. They kept trapping themselves into something I call the "history jail cell". Everyone's perceptions of past events are different. For example, if you tell your spouse that they were impolite to your in-laws, and your spouse believes that they weren't impolite, no amount of arguing is going to solve the problem. It will reach a stalemate because you both perceive the event in a different way. In that "history jail cell", the argument rages until someone gives up. It's exasperating and it saps relationships.'

Gardner and Yorke exchanged looks. Yorke wondered if she, like him, was considering herself guilty of the "history jail cell" too.

'So, what jail cell were Helen and Robert trapped in?' Gardner said.

'One of the most common. Having children. He vehemently denies saying he would ever consider children; she seems to think he did. The situation couldn't be resolved. She wanted children, he didn't. There was no point in revisiting the promises that may, or may not, have been made. They just had to learn to live with that disagreement.'

'So, in your professional opinion, do you think they'd have separated?'

'I like to remain upbeat. I want to help solve the issues. This was a large dilemma. It always is. One partner desperate for children, and the other desperate not to have them. But I've come out the other side with this issue successfully on many occasions.'

'How?' Gardner said. 'Surely those feelings don't go away?'

'No, of course not, but if they learn to live with their different desires and need, and find some common ground, then it will succeed.'

'But, I still don't see how,' Gardner said. 'How do you sacrifice having children if you are desperate?'

'People have done far more in the name of love before now.' He smiled. 'So, in answer to your question, this was the main reason they came to me, and I was confident that I could help.'

'Thank you,' Yorke said. 'Do you often see patients alone?'

'Yes, of course. It's a safe space. You can often get to the root of problems when you take away the physical trigger of conflict which, I'm sorry to say, is often the spouse.'

'Okay,' Yorke said. 'You provided an alibi to Helen Brislane on the day Robert disappeared, is that correct?'

'Sorry,' Moss raised an eyebrow. 'An alibi? Has a criminal act taken place?'

'It's standard procedure, doctor, to establish the whereabouts of anyone connected to the missing person.'

'Helen was with me. I told the officer back in February.'

Yorke looked down into his notepad. He pretended to be reading from it, and even tapped some unconnected notes to firm up the pretence. 'Yes, we have that on record. But I did notice that the investigating officer never asked for paperwork.'

'Paperwork?'

'Your diary ... your appointment sheet ... I guess that would be with your receptionist?'

For the first time, the unflappable Moss looked uncomfortable. It was similar to how Helen Brislane had looked when she was asked about new relationships.

'Yes ... but I've changed receptionist since then. Surely my word is enough?'

'Sorry, sir, not really,' Gardner said. 'We always ask for evidence.'

'Well, the last officer didn't.'

Yes, but they were incompetent, Yorke thought. 'There shouldn't be a problem, doctor. I assume you keep your appointments on a database. Could you not just ask your receptionist to send them over?' *Preferably, without you altering them.*

'*It's Boxing Day.*'

'Yes, I understand it's inconvenient timing, but I'm sure you appreciate the importance of our request.'

Moss nodded.

For another fifteen minutes, Yorke continued to probe the "confidential" details surrounding the Brislanes' marriage counselling. After deciding he was going to learn nothing new, Yorke thanked the doctor for his time, and both him and Gardner were back outside for a heavy burst of snowfall.

'Anabelle will be pleased,' Gardner said. 'It'll revive her snowman. It was looking rather emaciated earlier when I left.'

Yorke didn't respond.

'Let me guess ... more red flags than a communist parade?'

He nodded. 'Both of them are guilty of something. I'll

bet anything that those were his shoes sitting snugly in Helen's rack.'

'Sitting snugly in Helen's rack? Did you really just say that?' Gardner said. 'So what now?'

'I'm going to contact Madden to ruffle someone's feathers about the level of incompetence in this investigation...' Yorke looked at his watch. '... and I predict it will take less than an hour for one of Leeds' finest to get back to me, cap in hand, willing to pick up the reins in this missing person investigation.'

'Shit,' Gardner said, 'I was really starting to enjoy this.'

'Ah, don't worry, we'll still be pulling the strings. They can just do the legwork.'

THE SNOWFALL WAS THICKER, but Alan did not worry about the present in his backpack. He'd covered it in plastic before wrapping it, and even if the paper did get wet, the gift inside was in no danger.

He pulled up his hoodie and turned onto the doctor's road. He always worried that someone may recognise him as a student going into his lecturer's house. He wouldn't want to get the doctor into trouble.

Even now, damp from the snow, and chilled by an icy breeze, Alan felt warmer merely being in the vicinity of the psychiatrist. That's what this doctor offered. And he'd offered it ever since the moment he'd helped Alan to his feet that night in Headingley.

Dr Harris was an enigma. A warm cradle that softened and soothed. That offered safety and security.

That healed ...

... The day after Dr Harris had reached out a hand,

Alan had waited behind in the lecture hall. He'd approached the doctor while he was logging out from his laptop.

'Dr Harris?'

'Yes?' Harris didn't look up from his screen.

'I just wanted to say thank you for last night.'

The doctor finished what he was doing first, and then looked up. 'Ah, the boy with the fire. Alan, isn't it?'

'Yes.'

'What're you thanking me for?'

'For helping me up. For making me feel better about the whole situation.'

'Well, you're welcome, but I cannot say I did very much. Bullies are bullies, and heroes are heroes. I just simply pointed out which side you were on. Well, I'm glad to see you're back up and at it, Alan, and don't think me rude, but I'm going to have to dash I'm afraid. Got an appointment with a coffee, and a colleague too. Yes, the colleague is secondary to the coffee.' He chuckled. 'I think I told you about the extensive wine menu I was subjected to last night?'

Alan nodded.

Harris smiled again. 'See you later, young man.'

As he walked away with his laptop under his arm, Alan danced from foot to foot, desperate to say something, but not knowing exactly what. When Harris reached the lecture room door, Alan called out. 'Dr Harris?'

Harris turned, but he didn't say anything.

'Do I look like a freak?' Alan said loudly.

Harris started to walk back towards him. 'A freak? What's that exactly, Alan?'

'Someone different, odd...'

Harris stopped in front of him. 'Well, we can't all be the same. It really doesn't work like that.'

'Maybe, but I'm so peculiar that I can never fit in.'

'Why? Because you dress differently and have scoliosis of the spine? The colleague I'm meeting, Chris, has halitosis so bad it curls your toes; yet, he's the most popular man I know. I struggle with the notion of a freak. If people define you as a freak, it is nothing but an opinion, and we all know the weight of opinions, don't we? However, if you define yourself as a freak, that is a whole different scenario. Then, I guess, it can become a fact. Do you think you're a freak, Alan?'

Alan opened his mouth but couldn't find an answer.

Harris held up the palm of your hand. 'Don't ... think about it. But it is a question *you* have to answer. No one else can, and especially not me. I, myself, had to make a very similar decision a very long time ago.'

'And what did you decide?'

Harris smiled and looked at his watch. 'I really have to go.'

'Dr Harris, I really want to see you again.'

'Why?'

'I know you practise in a medical centre near Roundhay Park. Can I come?'

'I'm afraid not, Alan. I'm not permitted to treat my own students.'

'Please,' Alan said. 'There's something about the way you talk to me, you *help* me. No one else has ever made me feel so calm.'

'My ex-wife would be surprised to hear that. Look, Alan, we've barely spoken for more than ten minutes.'

'I spend most of *every* day dazed and lost. I cannot

remember the last time that I didn't feel like that. Until last night. And now too...'

Harris sighed. 'Well ... I guess with you being so complimentary. Pad?' He nodded down at the notepad in Alan's hand.

'Sure.' Alan handed it over.

Harris wrote his address down. 'This Saturday, 5pm. That's my home address. Come around the back of the house though. You really can't tell anyone, you do know that don't you?'

'I don't talk to anyone, Dr Harris.'

'Yes, you do,' Harris said. 'You talk to me ...'

Now, these many months later, Alan was walking down the path at the side of Dr Harris' house to his back garden, as he'd done on so many occasions.

The path had not been used since Alan's last visit on Christmas Eve, so the deep snow broke in at the top of his boots and dampened his socks. He turned into the small garden. It was hard to tell now, in the dead of winter, but Dr Harris kept his garden in good condition. He looked up and noticed that he'd been trimming back the branches on both old oaks in the far corners of the garden.

The first time Alan had been to this garden, he'd been impressed. Not so much by the vast array of flowers, but rather the symmetry. Both sides of the garden took on the same pattern, and colours. Dr Harris had been meticulous in the planting.

On that particular day, Harris had stepped up alongside him and said, 'Do you like my garden?'

'I like the balance and the order.'

'Yes, me too.'

'I have no balance and order.'

'In what way?' Dr Harris said.

'Look at my body.'

'Physically? Well, yes, you aren't the most evenly shaped person, but you know, not many people are evenly shaped.'

'Most are more evenly shaped than me.'

Dr Harris pointed at Alan's head. 'But how is the balance and order *in there?*'

'I don't know. Not good, I guess.'

'Let's go inside and begin. Let's find out. But first, try one of these. I've been baking.' He held up a tray of cookies.

Inside, Alan sat on the couch in the doctor's office. They talked for a while, until Alan started to feel light-headed. 'Sorry, doctor, I feel dizzy.'

'It's been a hot day, lie back on the couch and I'll get you some cold water.'

Alan lay back. He looked up at the walls. It was covered in colourful artwork. It seemed to be swirling and moving. He closed his eyes.

'Are you okay?'

Alan opened his eyes and saw that the doctor was now kneeling on the floor. His face, which now took on an unusual reddish tint, was closer to his.

'I feel funny,' Alan said.

'Drink some of this.' Harris cupped Alan's head and lifted it slightly, so he could press a glass to his lips.

'Thanks.'

'Can I be honest with you, Alan?'

'Yes, of course.'

'I gave you something. It was in the cookie.'

'What?'

'Nothing dangerous. Just something to help you relax. I noticed you were on edge. It makes it easier for me to help you. I give it to all of my patients.'

'Is that really allowed?'

'Of course. It's a legal drug. But don't worry about that now. You could just go with it?'

'It is starting to pass. I'm less dizzy, now, and I do feel more relaxed. Quite happy, actually.'

'Euphoria is always a welcome side-effect,' Harris said and smiled.

Harris lowered Alan's head back down and put the glass on the floor. 'I'm sorry for not asking your permission regarding the medicine, Alan. I can be quite impatient when it comes to healing. The sooner I can help, the better. If you are feeling betrayed, or disappointed in any way, I'll not be able to help you.'

'No ... it's okay,' Alan said. 'I trust you.'

'Good, Alan, because that will make what I'm about to tell you that little bit easier. I have another name, another persona if you will, one that I use to really help people. Do you mind me becoming that person now?'

Alan shook his head. He noticed that the reddish tint had spread from the doctor' face and bled into the surroundings.

'Good. My name is the Conduit. I am a channel. I become the piece that is missing from inside people, and I allow the thoughts, feelings and behaviours to move fluidly through me and within them. Do you understand?'

'Yes.'

Despite the peculiarity of the situation, Alan felt comfortable. More so than ever before. Maybe it was the drug, maybe it was just the gentle rhythm of Dr Harris' voice, or maybe it was just the hope of a better tomorrow. Whatever the reason, he welcomed the doctor into his mind.

And he led him down a dark path that he wouldn't normally travel down.

He was thirteen years old on a Friday night. The only night of the week Alan was forbidden to leave his room. And when his parents checked on him, on the hour, every hour, until one in the morning, they would knock quietly on his door, and he would unlock it. They'd ruffle his hair, kiss him on the forehead, and tell him how much they loved him. They'd ask him to lock the door again, and when in bed, think about all the wonderful things they could do that weekend as a family.

Alan stumbled from the dark path, sat upright on the sofa and, gulping for air, looked into the doctor's eyes.

Harris placed one hand on Alan's shoulder to steady him. 'Breathe, Alan.'

After Alan had caught his breath, he said, 'I'm sorry.'

'For what?'

'For losing it.'

'On the contrary, you didn't lose anything.'

'I don't understand.'

'*Finding* the darkness is the first step.'

'I don't understand.'

'Tell me, Alan, are you repulsed when you look in the mirror?'

'It depends. Not by my face, but the rest of my body, yes ... yes, I am. The lack of order ... the uneven—'

Harris held up the palm of his hand to silence him. 'I want you to consider the possibility that it isn't your appearance that repulses you, but something else – something inside you, inside that darkness. What happened back then when you were thirteen?'

'I can't recall much. I remember this one time being crouched on the balcony looking over. I recognised a younger lad from my school being dropped off by his father. He looked terrified, while his father looked unstable. Drink, or possibly, drugs? I don't know. I remember, a few days later, following that boy home by hopping on the same bus. He was from a rundown council estate in Chapel Town.'

Harris took a deep breath. 'Were your parents exploiting families in poverty?'

'Yes,' Alan said.

'Did you realise that at the time?'

'In my own immature way, I must have done. But there was obviously a lot of denial. At first, I tried to convince myself that they may have been helping. We were wealthy, they weren't. My mother ran a successful company importing from China that she inherited from her mother ... at least, that's what she always told me. I hoped, *I really hoped*, they were just giving back.'

'When did you find out the truth?'

'When they were arrested and ... and ... something else happened.' Alan felt tears in his eyes.

Harris still had his hand on his shoulder and gave it a gentle squeeze. 'What else happened?'

He stared at Harris. Tears were running down his face now. 'I don't want to go there.'

Harris brushed his tears away. 'But that is exactly where you must go. That is the source of everything. It is only through going back into the darkness, and *accepting* it, can you start to heal from it. The revulsion you feel is not from your crooked posture, it's from what lies deep into those shadows. It's where you must go ... next.'

'I don't know. I really don't know if I can face it.'

'Do you want me to go with you?'

'Yes. Would you?'

'Of course, but first ...' He pulled a small contraption

from his pocket and switched it on. It produced a slow flashing light. 'I must hypnotise you. Let me be your conduit, Alan, let me help you embrace the darkness.'

Alan nodded.

The Conduit held the flashing light in front of his eyes ...

Alan was distracted from this memory and pulled back to the present day by a tapping at the patio door behind him. He turned from the snow-caked garden and the skeletal trees.

Dr Harris was standing there. He was smiling at him through the glass.

10

I T WAS LATE afternoon when Yorke and Gardener reached the hotel carpark in central Leeds.

Moments before, he'd finished a conversation over the speakerphone with DS Paul Breaker from the West Yorkshire Constabulary. Breaker hadn't been involved in the shambolic Alan Brislane investigation; he was just the unlucky boy that was now picking up the pieces. He was polite and sounded competent. Yorke wasn't surprised. Madden would have raised merry hell on her phone call, and knowing they were now under scrutiny, this northern constabulary would be putting the best on this old investigation.

Yorke relayed, in detail, his interviews with Helen Brislane, and Dr Eli Moss. He discussed his suspicions regarding the relationship between them, and the possibility that this may have started prior to Brislane's disappearance. Yorke advised Breaker to contact Moss' former secretary to query Helen's appointment with Moss on the day her husband vanished. As far as Yorke was concerned, the appointment sheet that Moss himself would send over would be null and void.

'And if you find out that there never was an appointment, try and find out where Helen Brislane got to when she was supposed to be with him.'

'Don't worry, sir, I will be doing.' He sounded assured.

'And phone me night or day with anything.'

Outside Welcome Break, in the carpark, Yorke turned to Gardner. 'I'm going to go and meet DCS Benjamin Rosset about the massacre. You check us in, please.'

THE INCIDENT ROOM that Rosset led Yorke into was far more impressive than the ones he was used to back in Wiltshire. It was stocked so full of technology that the room hummed. He couldn't remember seeing so many officers together in one space; some were at standing desks on the phone, others were hunched over computers. There was even a line forming at the photocopiers. Did austerity take a wrong turn somewhere when it arrived in Yorkshire? Yorke wondered what the point of him being here was; if they couldn't solve a crime with this kind of resourcing, then God help them all.

Rosset smiled. 'I can see from your expression, Mike, that you think we're throwing a lot at it.'

'The thought had crossed my mind, sir, but I guess the response fits the crime. Besides, if you've got it, use it.'

'Yes ... it does look impressive, I admit, but then, it has left some investigations operating on a shoestring. I hope it doesn't turn out to be a robbing Peter to pay Paul situation. But I made this call for the following reason.' He took Yorke to the incident board and pointed at a sickening collage. 'We didn't get the fire out in time.'

Yorke's eyes flicked between the images. He counted sixteen bodies burned beyond recognition, each with a name tattooed beneath the photograph. Yorke wondered as to Rosset's motivations for displaying them so boldly at the front of the room. Motivation for his team, perhaps? He didn't query it.

'You have to go back to the Cumbria Shootings in 2010 to find something this bad. Twelve died that day. Let's hope this monster, Mayers, opts for the same way out as Derrick Bird ... but until then, he's loose, and so,' he turned back to look at an incident room which probably looked more like a *Virgin Media* Call centre, 'no expense spared.'

He turned back and tapped a photograph of an elderly lady. 'Thank God for Audrey Houghton, or we'd have no idea what went on in that place. Not much evidence survived that inferno. We found the charred tin which contained the lighter fluid that started the fire in Drigg's room. We also have his gun of course. A Smith and Wesson Shield EZ. A good choice for the elderly. Easier to handle for those with arthritis. I don't want to be ageist, and I know he was ex-military, but do you really think Driggs negotiated the dark web to acquire himself one of these?'

'No, I don't,' Yorke said. 'Mayers gave it to him. On one of their little walks – along with the lighter fluid I expect.'

Rosset raised an eyebrow. 'While he was controlling his mind?'

There was a tone. Yorke looked away. There was no point in being angry. Why would you believe it? Unless you'd lived through it. He looked back. 'Have you read the files on the Severance investigation, sir?'

'Twice. Look, Mike, you shouldn't blame me for being

sceptical. You know I've watched my fair share of Paul McKenna shows, and I'm sure there is truth to hypnosis, but this ... the slaughter of sixteen innocent people ... you cannot tell me he wasn't aware of what he was doing?'

'Oh, he was aware alright,' Yorke said. 'But that's hardly the point is it? The point is not what you're aware of, it's what you *believe*. Let's go to your office and talk. You invited me here because of my personal experience with the Severance case. The files are thorough, but they're not everything. By the time we've finished talking, you will know that Bernard Driggs was just another victim in this whole sorry affair, and your priority then will be to stop there being anymore.'

YORKE DIDN'T NEED to provide chapter and verse. Rosset had spent the last twenty-four hours poring over the Christian Severance files. What Rosset needed was an understanding of what made the crazy doctor tick. Then, he would truly understand what a devastating adversary he faced.

'Louis Mayers chooses patients based on their background. He looks for those considered damaged. And not just damaged, but rather, *devastated*. Christian Severance had been abused by a teacher, Susie Long had witnessed her uncle euthanising her grandmother—'

'Bernard Driggs had witnessed his friends being killed during the Falklands war. He also sustained a catastrophic injury that almost killed him.'

'Yes. So he would fit the profile.'

'But why is he turning them into monsters? What's the point?'

'The point to Mayers is bigger than any of us could ever imagine. He, too, experienced trauma. Before he became the Conduit, he was a successful psychiatrist in the treatment of insomnia. Renowned, rich ... he had it all. Two of his insomniacs, high-flying bankers addicted to cocaine, entered a state of psychosis due to sleep deprivation. Because they knew each other, they came together, and shared their beliefs. They believed that they were victims of a malicious doctor experimenting on them—'

'Sounds like they were about right!'

'I don't think so. I think what happened next created the Conduit. The two patients purchased guns. The day they went for Mayers, they killed three other patients and his receptionist. Unbelievably, Mayers survived his wounds. As you can imagine, he suffered devastating PTSD. That's when Dr Martin Adams came into the picture. He was working on a new therapy for PTSD at the time. *HASD. Healing. Acceptance. Sharing. Displacement.* He offered Mayers treatment under this new programme.' Yorke then went on to explain the principles in more detail.

'And this is where all of this started. With this *HASD?*' Rosset said.

Yorke nodded.

'So is it worth contacting Dr Martin Adams, the pioneer of this shitstorm?' Rosset said.

'Yes, if he's willing,' Yorke said, reaching for the coffee on the table between them. 'His project fell by the wayside, for obvious reasons, and I heard he was struggling to get his career back on track.'

Rosset made a note.

'But I cannot say for sure how much use he will actually be. The way that Mayers twisted and adapted this treatment, first with Christian Severance and several others, and then, even more catastrophically, with Susie Long, have made this therapy a rather different animal.'

'Well, considering the purpose of the treatment was to *heal* someone of their PTSD, it seems to me he is just making it worse. He's just antagonising his patients.'

'He would disagree with you. The philosophy remains intact. He wants to *heal*, and believes he is doing so. The healing takes place when the patient *accepts* the trauma within them, *shares* it with the therapist under hypnosis, before *displacing* it.'

'Displacing, or murdering?'

'In this instance, Mayers sees it as the same thing. Whatever it takes to free the patient from the shackles of their anxieties.'

'They're hardly healed though if they then go and blow their brains out?'

Yorke nodded. 'I've thought about this a lot. I guess the patient is irrelevant to Mayers when the process is over. Keeping a healed patient alive is just too much high risk for him. Look, I'm not saying that Mayers actually healed Bernard Driggs, obviously I do not believe in the effectiveness of his barbaric treatment, but it's not what I believe that is important. Mayers will have *believed* Bernard was healed. He'd achieved all he was going to achieve, and now Bernard would simply be a liability. So, he would have programmed him to commit suicide.'

'Or Bernard could have just woken up, seen what he'd done, and then shot himself from guilt?'

'Possibly. But again, this is irrelevant, as we do not care less about the success in Mayers' approach. All we care about is what Mayers *believed*. He thinks he is on the road to greatness. Somewhere he is recording everything he does in great detail. One day, when he is dead or alive, I don't suppose that matters too much to him, he will unleash his discoveries.'

'So he believes he's changing the face of psychology? Wow. That really is a new level of grandeur!'

'I've come across it before,' Yorke said. 'When obsessives like this *believe* something this much, and when they are *driven* to this extent, the combination is not only powerful, but deadly.'

'You're telling me.'

They continued talking until they were interrupted by a Management Support Assistant bringing in another tray of coffees.

Rosset stirred four sugar cubes into his. While watching this in disgust, Yorke weighed up whether to tell him about the other reason he was in Leeds. Some of the resources back there in the interview room could be put to excellent use in the hunt for both Robert Brislane and Mark Topham. And if their disappearances were connected to the Conduit, could he be impeding this investigation by holding back on this information?

Yes, he could.

It meant betraying Gardner, but what choice did they have in all of this anyway? If Topham was still alive, which was unlikely, he was going to prison for a very long time. Gardner didn't seem to want to accept this, but it was completely non-negotiable. It would break all of their hearts, but if Topham was still alive, he was going back to Salisbury to face justice.

So, when all was said and done, full disclosure was surely the only option.

He took a mouthful of coffee and was just opening his mouth to say something when there was a knock at the door. A wiry male officer, wearing a suit so tight that Yorke wondered how on earth he could walk, poked his head in. 'Sir, they've recovered the phone Bernard Driggs used.'

'Destroyed though, surely?'

'No. Audrey Houghton just pulled it out of her bag. She doesn't know how it got in there. The doctor at the hospital that contacted us suggested that she probably put it in her bag while she was in shock before she fled the building, and then forgot.'

'Where is it now?'

'It's on its way here.'

Rosset turned to Yorke. 'Listen, it'll be a good half hour until it gets here, and then another chunk of time for the relevant parties to have a good look at it. Would you like to go and get settled in your hotel, and then I'll contact you when we have something? You can even come back in then after you've refreshed?'

Normally, the answer would be a resounding *no*. Walking away from a moment like this in an investigation was like walking into a clearly marked electric fence. Instinct wouldn't allow it. But, he had Gardner back at the hotel. Hopefully, she would just be twiddling her thumbs, waiting for him, but knowing Gardner, he doubted that very much. He had to be really careful that she didn't cause any serious problems while they were up here.

Yorke nodded. *When I come back*, he thought, shaking Rosset's hand on the way out, *I'll tell you everything about Topham and Brislane, and Gardner will just have to accept that this is the right thing to do.*

ALAN SANTS STROKED the dog's head. It leaned back and nuzzled his hand.

'It's strange,' Alan said. 'But the more I see him, the more I pet him, the more I really do see him as an animal.'

'We're all animals, Alan,' Harris said.

'Yes, but there is an order, I guess.'

'Yes, an order *we* imposed. Anyway, let's not get into that. I'm just pleased to see that you two have become so close. Mark relishes your visits you know. He's far happier when you're around than when he's stuck here alone with little old me.'

Alan's eyes settled on the pruning saw leaning against the wall. He knew that Harris had been cutting back trees, but he also knew the saw had *other* uses.

'I have a present in the bag.'

'Not for me though, I hope. I told you presents are wholly inappropriate when I'm treating you.'

'No, the present is for Mark. I think he'll like it. I think you will too.'

Harris stepped alongside Mark and settled his hand on his shaved and pitted head. 'The wonderful thing about a diet of deprivation is the gratitude you can then feel. Mark will be grateful. Of that you can be sure.'

Alan had been a month into his therapy when he'd first met Dr Harris' dog Mark. It was a significant day in Alan's development because it was also the day that he'd finally reached the darkness inside himself ...

In the visualisation, Alan stood by the Conduit and watched his younger self from the side of the room. Despite knowing that the doctor couldn't get involved with what was about to happen, he was grateful for his presence.

His restless thirteen-year-old self was rocking back and forth in bed. The room always felt warmer on a Friday night, probably because there were always so many people downstairs, and hot air rises. He'd already undone the top buttons on his pyjamas, but it wasn't cutting it, so he sat up and peeled the entire thing off.

The knock at his door made both Alans, young and old, flinch.

His younger self looked at his bedside clock. It had been less than an hour since his parents' last check.

'Don't open the door,' Alan said.

He felt the Conduit's hand settle on his shoulder.

'I don't want to stay. I don't want to see.'

The Conduit didn't reply. Alan looked at him. The doctor offered a sympathetic expression, but then gestured for him to look back. They'd worked long and hard to tunnel into this dark memory, and it was now essential, that they observed it.

When Alan turned back, his younger self was already padding across the room, eager to see his parents.

'*Please,*' Alan called out. '*It's not mum and dad. It's not them ...*'

The younger Alan couldn't hear the man from his future.

Alan took a step forward. The Conduit gripped his shoulder. The strength of the large man prevented him moving any further. He shouted instead. '*THEY BROKE THE RULES ... THEY CAME UPSTAIRS!*'

His younger self opened the door and stepped backwards in surprise. A Chinese businessman, late forties, with silver hair stood there. He came into the room, knelt, and offered a gift.

'A Mud Man,' Alan said. 'He was the exporter who'd given my mother them before. And now he's giving me one too.'

With wide excited eyes, his younger self took hold of the Mud Man.

The businessman turned and closed the door.

Alan turned back to the Conduit. 'I still don't know if he thought I was just one of the children my parents brought to the house. Another one of those poor children from that Chapel Town estate, who were earning ridiculous amounts of money for their parents. For years, I thought who would do that? Sell their own children? Sell *other people's* children? But as time has gone on, I've realised that innocence is often a fairytale, and so many more people hide away poison than you first might think.'

The Conduit spoke for the first time in this visualisation. 'You must watch.'

Alan didn't want to watch, but he also didn't want to let the Conduit down. The man beside him was his last chance. Justice had failed him. So, too, had the health service. This could be his final opportunity to *heal*.

To no longer be a *freak*.

He turned and watched.

At first the businessman was gentle. He petted the boy, and attempted to soothe away the anxiety, but eventually, his true intentions were revealed. Before long, they were lying down on the bed together.

Alan didn't need to see the terror on the face of his younger self. He remembered it all too well. He still felt it most days, and he most certainly felt it right now, watching.

When the man became aggressive, Alan was glad to see the fight in the boy. Yes, he'd lost – his damaged self in the present was living proof of that – but, still, the fight made him proud. He scratched at the man's face, kicked at him, spat at him, and it was only when he was turned over, and the bigger man flattened him down with his weight that the battle was lost.

Alan cried as he watched the next few minutes of his memory.

When his parents arrived too late to prevent anything, Alan felt no sympathy for their despair. Their faces melted.

'Alright for other children, but not their own?' Alan said to the Conduit. 'In a way, at least some good is about to come from my experience.'

'What?' The Conduit asked.

'Watch. Watch their whole sordid little enterprise come crashing down.'

His father was a small, slim man, but he was agile, and prone to displays of sudden aggression. He grabbed the businessman by his hair and dragged him off his son and the bed.

The man landed with a thump on the wooden floor. He scurried backwards and was a pathetic sight. Naked from the waist down.

'That's my son,' his father said, approaching.

'I didn't know, I didn't know.' His Chinese accent was strong.

His father started to kick him.

The boy was crying, and his mother was already over there consoling him. She had her arms around him. 'I'm sorry ... I'm sorry.'

Over the sounds of the businessman being pummelled, Alan could barely hear his younger self explain to his mother what had happened, but two words came through loud and clear. 'Mud Man.'

Her eyes widened and she took the Mud Man from her son's hands.

Alan traced the palm of his hand. He remembered the pain he'd felt there all those years ago. He'd clutched it in a fist so tightly during the ordeal that it had drawn blood.

'It was a good Mud Man,' Alan said. 'He carried a long fishing spear. It was sharp to the touch.'

Seeing that her husband was in the process of beating a man to death, his mother darted over to him and placed her hands on his shoulders.

It seemed to work. His father backed away, gasping for air. The businessman groaned and rolled onto his front. In the background, the boy curled himself up into a ball and continued to sob.

As his mother embraced his father, desperately trying to calm him, the man made it up onto his knees.

His father came away from his mother. 'A fucking Mud Man?' He grabbed it from her hand and swung back towards his son's abuser. 'You gave my son a fucking Mud Man and then raped him?'

The businessman was on his feet now. He was unsteady. There was blood running from his nose, and his lip. He stood at the open door with his back to the balcony just outside.

'I didn't know,' the rapist continued.

'Are you fucking blind? This is the first floor. You were told to stay on the ground floor.'

His father stepped forward and the bastard held up the palms of his hands. 'Please ... I was looking for the toilet.'

'The toilet is on the ground floor. Would you like this back now you blind prick?' He held the Mud Man upside down in his right fist, so the fishing spear was pointing down. He drew his fist back and stabbed the businessman in his left eye.

He screamed. Blood and fluids spewed down his face. He reached up and covered his punctured eye with his hands, while the father slammed the spear into the other eye.

'Now I accept your excuse,' his father said. 'You're blind. You made a mistake.'

The man stumbled backwards, clawing at his damaged face. He hit the balcony backwards, flipped and was gone.

His mother and father approached the balcony and looked over.

'Hitting the ground floor put him out of his misery,' Alan said to the Conduit. He gestured at his younger crying self. 'Mine was set to continue.'

'And what happened then?'

'The sick bastards and the children below who'd not already fled the house when the noise had started upstairs, didn't think twice about leaving when the body landed in front of them. I think my mother and father tried to do something about the dead man, but it was all too late. Chaos had come, and chaos breeds weakness. The children saw the weakness in the enterprise that held them, and summoned the courage to come together, and get help.'

'And your parents are still in jail?'

'My father, yes. My mother, no. Cancer. She tried to get out on compassionate grounds. She was refused, but she died in hospital, and I was allowed to hold her hand.'

'And how did that make you feel?'

'Relief.'

'Why?'

'Because the guilt was too much for her too bear.'

'Some would say *deserved?*'

'She deserved it, but I didn't want to see her suffer.'

'That's very noble. And your father?'

'I speak to him on the phone.'

'Do you ask him why they did what they did?'

'No.'

'Why not?'

'Because I know already.'

'How?'

'Because the darkness that exists in him, and existed in my mother, exists in me too.'

Alan looked around Harris' office. Without even realising it, he'd been eased out of the visualisation. He sat up on the sofa. Harris was busy making notes behind the desk.

'How do you feel?' Harris said.

'I understand it more now.'

'*Acceptance.* Now, come with me. You shared with me and now I want to *share* something with you.'

To date, Alan had only seen the back room and the office of Harris' house, so he was surprised to be led into the interior.

He was further surprised by the naked man lying asleep on his side in Harris' dining room.

'What the—?'

'Sit for a moment, Alan, do not let shock overwhelm you. There is much to be learned here.'

'*Who is this?*' Instead of sitting, Alan moved closer, so he was standing directly over the man.

'It's not who it is, it's *what* it is.'

'I don't understand ...' Alan knelt and looked at the man's scarred body. He ran his fingers over a metal collar that fixed him to D-ring on the wall.

'He *was* Mark Topham. A police officer in fact,' Harris said.

Alan stared up at Harris with wide eyes. 'This is torture.'

'On the contrary, Alan, he is happier than he has ever been. Do you know what a lobotomy is?'

'Of course.'

'Well, they used to give them to people *consumed* by madness. Some considered it barbaric, but then, these critics weren't the sorry souls trapped in hell. Just imagine the release of pressure that came with the cracking of the frontal lobe, Alan. One minute, they were clawing at their faces, the next minute, they were as calm and obedient as a trained dog.

'Mark came to me in this condition. He was rabid, beyond help. He wanted to kill me. It was too late for me to help him in the way I'm helping you, and how I've helped many before you, but there was something I could offer him.

'I could release the pressure. Not with a lobotomy, you understand. That is too crude a method. It also takes too much of the person away. Mark still exists in the animal you see before you. He still understands the world around him. But he is completely under control, and is obedient.'

Alan ran his eyes down the sleeping man's body and they settled on the mass of scar tissue around his groin. He looked back up at Harris. 'You've castrated him.'

'He is a dog, Alan. If I'd left him with desire and instinct of that nature, how would I have truly tamed him?'

Alan stroked its head. It stirred, opened its eyes and nuzzled his hand.

'Mark likes you, Alan.'

Mark licked the back of his hand. Alan pulled it away in disgust.

'Don't think of Mark as human anymore, Alan. He's not. Now, come back to the office with me. I wanted to show Mark to you as a warning. This is the only option if you do not *displace* the darkness within yourself and you become consumed by it ...'

Now, these many months later, having grown attached

to Mark, Alan was eager to give him his present. He opened his backpack and presented the gift to Harris.

'You best open it for him, doctor,' Alan said. 'He'll chew through the plastic inside and make himself ill.'

Harris unwrapped the present. He smiled. 'He'll love it, Alan. He really will! Where on earth did you get it?'

11

AFTER SPEAKING TO Rosset again, Yorke lay back on his hotel bed. He sighed. Although the news regarding Bernard Driggs' phone had been predictable, it didn't make it any less disappointing.

Mayers had used a burner to send the messages that activated Bernard. That phone would be lying at the bottom of a river somewhere no doubt.

The messages had verified Yorke's theory that Mayers would have used Bernard's experience in the Falklands war to indoctrinate him. Both messages referred to 1982, the year of the conflict, and the second message made reference to the fact that he'd now been *'healed.'*

Yorke was also fairly confident in the second theory he'd presented to Rosset. That once you were 'healed', you became expendable. He suspected there was something in the second text message that made suicide seem preferable than heading straight to the police station to identify Mayers as a psychological puppeteer.

He would have shared the disappearances of both

Topham and Brislane with Rosset at this point, if not for the phone call he'd received earlier from Breaker.

In contrast to Rosset's update, Breaker's update was unpredictable and anything but disappointing.

Dr Moss' retired secretary had pulled out an old diary, which she'd 'always used as a back-up' to the computerised diaries she didn't trust. eli had a full schedule that day, but there had been no mention of an appointment with Helen Brislane. Both Helen and Moss were being picked up for further interrogation. Yorke told Breaker he'd be waiting by the phone on 'tenterhooks.' Breaker, probably under pain of death from his superiors following the Madden grilling, promised not to let him down.

The investigation was moving rapidly under Breaker, and Yorke didn't want to crush it under the weight of Rosset's army unless it hit a dead end.

He phoned Patricia. It was great to hear her voice. He still felt painfully guilty, and when she asked him how he was feeling after his long drive, he welcomed her thoughtfulness like a soothing balm.

'Never mind me,' Yorke said. 'Has the sofa survived the first twenty-four hours with Rosie the dog?'

'She treats it better than you do, Mike. She's not spilt any tea on it yet.'

Yorke laughed. 'How are the engaged couple?'

'Getting in some practice and behaving like a married couple already. Bickering one minute, cuddling on the couch the next.'

'Well, tell them to take after us, and weight it more towards the cuddling.'

'So, you've come around to the idea?'

'It was hardly an idea was it! We were just told it was happening!'

'True. But they need our support and, with our support, we can ensure it goes properly. Well, as properly as it can do when you're still a teenager!'

'By *properly* do you mean an *extremely* long engagement, with church lessons, and a vow of celibacy before the wedding night?'

Patricia laughed. 'Beatrice would make a nice bridesmaid though ...'

They talked for a while. It was only near the end of the conversation that Patricia asked for an update on the search for Topham. He didn't say much, simply because there wasn't much to say at this time.

After the conversation, Yorke closed his eyes for a moment. He realised how exhausted he was from the journey up here, so he sat up straight before he fell asleep.

He texted Gardner. 'Burger and a pint?'

She texted back. 'Already eating a processed burger, and swilling some Northern swamp juice.'

Yorke texted back. 'Sold. See you downstairs in five.'

Eddie McLarney was a pretender.

He'd spent most of his life faking it, but right now at University, he was having to dig deeper than ever before. Keeping up appearances with the rugby boys required a whole new level of focus.

At first, he hadn't minded the theatre. The drinking, the misogyny, the fighting. He could manage this part of the act, and actually took some pleasure at being so adept at performing.

But recent months had taken their toll. This wasn't who he really was. Behaving in such an aggressive and obnoxious manner for so long had made this persona his default. He struggled to behave in any other way.

He feared his life after University. Did the role he currently occupy exist outside of this University bubble? And if it didn't, would he be able to break free of the default?

He doubted it. Simply because he'd failed to be himself with Alan, and he'd *really* started to like the strange boy.

The problem was that when you'd pretended for as long as Eddie had, switching off that vile tap was near impossible; it had rusted open, and aggression and hatred gushed out.

He indicated to turn off into the row of garages adjacent to his shared house. It was only when he was parallel to his own, and had climbed out to open it, did he see that the garage door was ajar.

There was no chance he'd left it open when he'd taken the car out last night. He just didn't do that. He checked and double-checked every door he ever closed and locked. He was the only one who owned a vehicle, so he didn't suppose anyone else from the house had been in there; unless they were seeking out one of the tins of dried-up paint. Someone must have broken in.

Well, if it was a joyrider they'd been bang out of luck, because Eddie had the car. However, it could be a squatter …

Eddie went back to the boot of his car and rustled around in his junk for a tyre iron.

Then, he went back to the garage, knelt, grabbed the edge of the open door, took a deep breath and pulled it up.

He felt scared but wasn't about to show any fear.

He was the great pretender, after all.

ALAN NODDED down at the gift in Harris' hands. 'I got it last night.'

'Where from?'

Alan smiled. 'Earlier in the evening, I watched Eddie type his security number into his phone. I put one of my sleeping pills in his beer so after he was asleep, I knew he wouldn't wake. Then, I texted his best friend, Mickey.'

Harris grinned. 'Didn't I say the fire was with you? Always with you, never with them ... what next? Come on, be quick, Mark has noticed his gift and is looking eager. What happened with that bully, Mickey?'

Alan took a deep breath through his nostrils and knelt beside Mark. He stroked his pitted head and allowed the dog to lick his hand. Months before, it had repulsed him; now, he welcomed it. 'I pretended to be Eddie and told him to meet me in his garage in twenty minutes. I told him I'd scored some weed. That we should smoke it in the garage, before the rest of them got stuck into it.'

'That easy, eh?' Harris had placed the gift for Mark down on the table and was rubbing his upper lip. Alan had noticed him doing this before; it often happened when the doctor's adrenaline was up. It was as if he was playing with a moustache.

'Yes. He even opened the garage for me when I got there.' Alan rubbed the back of Mark's neck. The dog closed his eyes.

'Did he recognise you?'

'I turned the headlights onto full beam. He couldn't see anything.'

Harris clapped. 'Bravo! And then?'

EDDIE PUT his hand to his nose. It didn't help. There was shit and blood, and the rich combination seeped into his pores. Someone was dead. You didn't need to be a fucking Crime Scene Investigator to work that one out.

He didn't bother reaching for a switch. There was no lightbulb. He'd left his car running outside. Although the headlights weren't pointing directly into the garage, they offered something.

His eyes fell to the pile of flattened cardboard boxes at the end of the garage beneath the empty shelves that had once held pots of paint. These pots had been lifted down and used to weight down the corners of the boxes.

Readying the tyre iron, he edged towards the boxes. The smell of shit intensified, but he didn't cover his mouth again. He wanted both hands on the tyre iron.

For all his bravado, Eddie felt like crying. He wanted to run from the garage and call the police. But this moment, this *horrendous* moment, was kind of like a test. Could he maintain the veneer that he'd spent so many years building around himself?

To run now would bring that all crumbling down. It would expose the queer within.

It was much darker at the back of the garage, but he could see well enough to know that a body lay beneath the cardboard boxes. They were sodden with blood.

An argument between two squatters that went wrong?

He would have liked to believe that, but when he moved his eyes along to the end of the boxes, he recognised the trainers that poked out from the bottom.

Mickey's.

HARRIS REACHED for the empty salad bowl on the dining room table. 'So Mickey never saw you at all?'

'Oh he did, but not until the very end.'

Harris used a cheese knife to slit through the layers of cling film that Alan had wrapped Mark's gift in. The smell was pungent. It brought Mark up on all fours, straining against his chain.

'Tell me about it.'

'He waved and shouted at me to turn the full beam off, but he still backed into the garage to allow me in. I checked both ways to ensure that no one was coming. There wasn't, so I edged the car slowly forwards. Only when I had the entrance completely blocked, did I switch to normal headlights. At first, he was still squinting, but when his eyes had recovered enough to see who'd paid him a visit, his face dropped.'

'I bet it did.' Harris held the gift over the salad bowl and pressing on the back of the plastic. The slimy, jellied matter started to slip loose.

'Once I'd given him long enough to realise that I was the fire, and he was the smoke, I drove forward. I didn't drive fast, because I wanted to return it to Eddie without too much damage, so I pressed him against the back wall, and kept my foot on the pedal until I crushed the life out of him.'

'Are you sure no one came past?' Harris hacked at the contents of the salad bowl with the cheese knife. Mark started to whine.

'No begging, dog!'

Mark stopped.

'Are you sure you weren't seen?' Harris said.

'Yes. I reversed slightly, and let him slide to the floor. I left the headlights on, but turned the engine off. I did my research, and was as careful as I could be. I put on a protective suit, overshoes, a shower cap, a facemask, you name it. I felt like I was in a sealed container. Only then, did I get out of the car and close the garage door.'

'What made you decide to do what you did next?'

'For so many years, Dr Harris, I've watched these people parade around with a sense of grandeur, desperately trying to reduce anybody who is different, who isn't playing their game, to nothing. Like you always say, they're the cowards. They're the hollow people. We, freaks, although I know you hate the word, are filled with so much substance. They fear us because of our variety, our ability to offer something different to their mundane existences.'

'And so?' Harris said, laying down the offal for Mark.

'And so, Dr Harris, I hollowed him out.'

THE GREAT PRETENDER, Eddie McLarney, felt his veneer splinter.

He backed away with one hand to his mouth, and with the other, he threw the cardboard back towards the body, hoping to re-cover it. Unfortunately, it missed its mark, and Eddie was forced to look on Mickey's mutilated abdomen a moment longer.

His belly had been slit open. One side of his gut had been tugged and torn enough so it hung over his side. The other flap lay loose, but uneven.

Eddie could not tell what Mickey's killer had done to his insides. It wasn't good that was for sure. Insides looked messy at the best of times, but Mickey's looked far too soupy.

He stumbled against the wall, desperate to keep himself upright. He closed his eyes, but it was useless, because Mickey's broken insides were frozen in his mind.

It was only when he tried to take a desperate, deep breath and gagged that he realised he was currently puking down his front.

After he'd finished throwing up. He reached into his pocket for his mobile phone. He needed to call the police.

'GOOD DOG,' Harris said, stroking the back of Mark's head as he feasted on the offal.

'I worried Mark would struggle with it,' Alan said. 'Some of his guts felt stringy and gristly. I tried my best to scrape away anything too inedible.'

'I may have taken his balls, but I didn't take his canine teeth, he'll be fine. You did a good job, Alan. I might save the stomach for later. He seems content with intestines for the moment. I do worry about repercussions now though. There must have been a lot of blood ...'

'I was careful, doctor. I covered the seats in Eddie's car with plastic and, when I was done, I undressed carefully inside the car and wrapped everything up in the same plastic. I drove everything to a quiet piece of woodland, burned what I could, and buried the gutting knife.'

'Impressive, Alan,' Harris said. 'But the car was the murder weapon, and even if the damage was minor, there will be traces. What happens when Eddie calls the police?'

Mark growled as he struggled to chew his latest mouthful.

Alan smiled. 'Eddie won't call the police.'

———

WHILE LOOKING DOWN at his phone, and punching in the first nine, Eddie noticed an envelope on the floor beside Mickey's body. He reached down and picked it up. He felt his spine freeze. Not because the envelope was smudged with blood, but rather because of the name written across the front.

Eddie.

With trembling hands, he slipped a small card out. The message was typed.

I have a video of you and Mr Bowtie fucking. Call the police, and it goes viral.

The breath caught in his throat.

Without really thinking, he screwed up the small card and the envelope and crammed it into his back pocket.

He then stared down at the solitary nine on the phone screen. Right now, he wanted to scream, '*Fuck you,*' to the world ... so what if it knew *who* he really was?

He pressed the second nine.

Today was the first day of the rest of his life. He pressed the third nine.

He felt tears running down his face. Nothing had ever felt as surreal as his best friend, mutilated on the floor beside him, while he considered releasing himself from the pressure of the never-ending theatre. His finger hovered over the call button.

Press it ... press it ... it's time to free yourself ...

He put the phone in his pocket.

Yes, the great pretender's veneer had splintered today, but it wasn't ready to break.

ALAN'S PHONE started ringing and Harris looked at him with a raised eyebrow.

Alan looked at the caller ID. 'I know you didn't want a Christmas present, Dr Harris, so I went and got myself one instead.'

Harris nodded. He felt overwhelmed right now. The boy's evolution this last few months really was something to behold.

Alan answered the phone. 'Hello.' He looked up at Harris. 'Eddie ... what's wrong? Slow down ...' he smiled. 'Really? Jesus ... call the police ...'

Harris looked down at Mark who, having wolfed down half of the offal in the salad bowl, had decided to take a nap. He then looked back up at Alan. He was lost for words. Despite what had happened all those years ago with Christian Severance, he'd been given another chance.

First, Mark Topham. Then, Bernard Driggs. And now, Alan Sants.

Although he didn't believe in a higher power, it was as if someone somewhere wanted him to succeed.

'I don't mind, Eddie, you still have to call the police ... so it ends up on the internet, so what? *Someone is dead ...*'

Harris carefully wrapped the stomach back in the plastic. He wanted that to be Mark's treat later.

'Okay ... we can discuss it first ... I'm at my doctor's house. I'll text you the address. Make sure you close the garage door. You don't want any children stumbling on that ...'

After Alan had rung off, he started to text the address.

'What are you doing, Alan?' Harris said. 'Is that safe?'

'There is nothing to worry about, Doctor. This is one

broken bunny.' He pressed send and looked back up at Harris, smiling. 'And I want you to teach me how to fix him.'

'I QUITE LIKED that Northern swamp juice,' Yorke said, putting down the empty pint. He nodded at Gardner's half-full pint of bitter. 'And it clearly grew on you too. What's that? Your third?'

'Fourth.'

'You're not on holiday you know!'

'Might as well be for how involved I am in this investigation.'

Yorke rolled his eyes. 'Number one: you quit. Number two: what part of the investigation are you actually missing out on? I'm sitting here with you, and I've filled you in on everything I know.'

'I'm talking about tomorrow morning when you piss off back to Rosset's military camp.'

'Well, what do you want me to do? Go home? You're the one who wanted me up here.'

Gardner sighed. 'Sorry, just frustrated. Too many years working alongside you. Just missing it, I guess. Feel like an observer. Nothing better than getting your hands dirty.'

'Sounds like you want back in.'

Gardner looked away, betraying the hidden truth that it'd been on her mind. 'No, Mike. Nearly dying took its toll.'

It took its toll on both of us, Yorke thought, *because it was my fault.*

'There're still moments, Mike, when I let my guard down and ...' she paused and took a mouthful of beer. 'I see Chloe Ward coming at me. Her eyes wide, looking possessed. I guess she was, in a way, by that twisted doctor. And when the vision comes, it's not the pain of the knife wound because everything is cold and numb in a flashback, it's more the sheer helplessness of knowing that you cannot stop what is going to happen. That loss of control. I don't ever want to feel that loss of control again. *Ever.'*

Yorke almost told her that these same feelings of impotence came from other areas of your life, not just police work. His adopted son telling him about his engagement, for example. But, to a certain extent, she was right, this job *did* serve up the most extreme of situations. He felt the scar on his face tingle. He only had to cast his mind back to Borya Turgenev to confirm that.

'Anyway,' Gardner said, 'Change the subject, or there's going to be a lot of tossing and turning tonight. So, Leeds, eh? You went to university here, didn't you? When was the last time you were back?'

It'll be me tossing and turning all night if we take the conversation down that road, Yorke thought.

'A long time ago. Graduation day.'

'Like it that much, eh? To be fair my university days disappeared into a haze of alcohol and marijuana too ...' She put her hand to her mouth.

'Don't worry! I'm not going to pull you in. I'm not that hypocritical!' Yorke smiled.

'Don't tell me the great, and pure, Michael Yorke, was no angel at university?'

'Is anyone? I had a friend who smoked constantly. He used to smoke through a porcelain gnome.'

'What?'

'It was a bong, in the style of a gnome. You burnt the marijuana in a small funnel in his pocket, and then smoked through the rolled-up newspaper he was carrying. He used to call him his Chuckle Brother.'

Gardner raised an eyebrow. 'Okay ...'

Yorke smiled. 'It was great fun. *He* was great fun. His name was Brandon.'

'And do you stay in touch with Brandon?'

Yorke's smile fell away. 'He passed, I'm afraid.'

'Oh, I'm sorry.'

Yorke looked down. 'It's okay ... it was a long time ago.'

'So, you haven't been back because of that?'

'That and other things ...'

'Go on.'

Yorke opened his mouth to reply, but then closed it again.

'Look, sorry, I shouldn't pry.'

Yorke smiled. 'As I said, it was a long time ago. Maybe, another time, okay? I'm feeling worn out after that journey. I'm getting another beer, and I'm getting you a lemonade?'

'*Pardon?*'

'Four is your limit, Emma. It could be a busy day tomorrow.'

'God, I hope so, Mike. If I end up in the hotel room all day, I'll go nuts.'

12

DECEMBER 27TH

W HEN YORKE RECEIVED the phone call from Breaker that morning, he acknowledged that Gardner would be very pleased. It was going to be a busy day.

As opposed to the original inept investigation into Robert Brislane's disappearance, this one was moving at breakneck speed, and was getting results.

Breaker's team had recovered CCTV footage of Helen Brislane buying a train ticket in Coventry and heading to Weeton station on the day that her husband disappeared. Weeton was six miles from Harewood House. The area in which ANPR had picked up Robert's car for the final time.

'Where did she go when she stepped into the station carpark?' Yorke said.

He heard Breaker sigh. He knew the answer already. Yorke had been in this situation on more than one occasion before. 'Let me guess, no bloody CCTV footage.'

'Vandalised and not replaced. Budget cuts. I laid into them, told them it wasn't an excuse.'

I'm sure they listened ...

'We also have footage of her returning to Coventry early evening,' Breaker said.

'Alone?'

'Yes. We've watched it several times, no sign of the husband. Sorry to disappoint.'

'I'm not disappointed. *We have her*. Helen *clearly* met with Robert on the day he disappeared rather than Eli Moss as she claimed. We also have that lying cretin too for obstruction. Make sure it's you that interviews her, Paul.'

He desperately wanted to go himself. Capable or not, Yorke did not like leaving a red-hot suspect to an officer he'd known less than twenty-four hours. But Rosset would think it strange if he didn't make an appearance this morning regarding the massacre investigation.

While dressing, Yorke made some suggestions to Breaker of how he would approach the interrogation. Really, his suggestions were instructions. They would be followed. The shadow of Madden and top brass would still be looming large. As he fastened his tie with his phone glued between his ear and his shoulder, Yorke delivered one last request. 'Helen arrived on the train. That means she either got a taxi to meet Robert somewhere, or he came to meet her. I can't remember how far the search of the area extended during the last investigation, but it didn't extend as far as Weeton. Have some officers start identifying taxi drivers who operate in and around that area. One of them could very easily have picked her up and taken her to Robert. Also, look for any police reports around that area in recent history. Where there's smoke, there's fire. Someone may have seen or heard something and reported it. You just never know.'

After wishing Breaker luck with the interview, he

ended the call, brushed his teeth, texted Patricia a photograph of him smiling, and set off to wake Gardner.

———

WHEN EDDIE MCLARNEY opened his eyes, he thought the world was on fire. So, he closed them, took a deep breath, and tried opening them again.

No, not on fire, but different. Brighter, sharper, more intense somehow ...

He was lying on a sofa in an office. There were framed photographs around the room, but he couldn't identify who was in them. They seemed to melt away when he tried to focus on them.

Someone familiar was walking towards him, someone pale, and wearing a bowtie—

Memory hit him like a cannonball. *Mickey! Dead. Split open in the garage...* He bolted upright, gasping for air. Alan towered above him. 'Eddie. It's me.'

Alan ... thank God ... but Mickey? 'HE'S DEAD!'

Alan knelt beside him. 'Try and relax, Eddie. We gave you something to help you sleep when you arrived here last night. It's left you groggy.'

Eddie started to cry. 'I can barely remember getting here after ... after ... Mickey ... you gave me a drink ... Jesus, Alan, what've you done to me?'

'Nothing dangerous, Eddie, you're perfectly safe.'

'None of this is making sense! I feel completely out of it.'

'Do you see the man behind me?' Alan said.

On a chair behind Eddie was an older, larger man. His head was wide, and his white hair was tangled and unkempt like a mound of hay. He stroked his upper lip as he observed.

'I see him,' Eddie said.

'That is the Conduit and, today, he is going to help me to help you.'

'What kind of fucking name is that? I don't need anyone's help! We need to go to the police!'

Alan shook his head. 'That is not an option.'

'Jesus ... I should have just fucking gone to the cops. I'm such a dick!'

Alan raised an eyebrow. 'Have you finished?'

'I should have fucking called them!'

'HAVE YOU FINISHED?'

Alan's voice sounded like a drum in Eddie's head. He reached up to clutch his ears and slumped back on the sofa, crying. He closed his eyes, wishing that the fiery world he'd just awoken to would just disappear.

'It's not working, Conduit,' Alan said.

'Patience,' the Conduit said. 'Just offer a little more persuasion. Exactly how we planned.'

'Open your eyes and look at what I'm holding, Eddie,' Alan said.

Eddie opened them and saw that Alan was holding a syringe.

'I was hoping that it wouldn't be necessary. I don't want to risk hurting you in order to heal you, but if necessary, that's what I will do.'

'I don't understand—'

Alan reached forward and seized Eddie's arm. He felt the pressure of the grip, but he lacked the motor control to pull it away.

'No more talking, Eddie, for now. Nod if you've had enough medicine and are ready to be helped. Shake your head if you need a top-up.'

Eddie nodded.

'Good, now sit back and listen.' Alan released Eddie and he slumped back into the sofa.

Alan leaned over to pick a notepad off the floor and read from it. 'There is darkness in all of our lives, Eddie. No one is exempt. That is what I have learned over the years, through my own experiences, and through everything that the Conduit has shared with me. Rather than always trying to smother the darkness, push it away, contain it – sometimes we need to embrace it. The sense of freedom that comes from that is indescribable. I am living proof of that, Eddie. I killed Mickey, and I've never felt better.'

'No ... I don't want to hear this—'

'I told you, *no more talking!* This is easier if you are willing, Eddie. I do not want to hurt you. Only heal you. Please nod if you want to be healed?'

The panic inside him was indescribable. He could feel it rising up, ripping through his body, desperate to escape, but when it reached his mouth, it emerged as little more than a whimper.

'NOD EDDIE!'

Eddie nodded.

'Good.' Alan said, leaning over and picking up something from the floor. 'I'm going to hypnotise you, Eddie. The medicine will make this easier, but your consent will make it even easier. Let me find the darkness inside you Eddie and let me help you embrace it. Do you consent?'

Eddie whimpered again.

'DO YOU CONSENT?'

Eddie nodded.

Alan, the boy who Eddie had developed strong feelings

for, held a flashing red light in front of his eyes, and he fell deeper under his spell.

YORKE HAD NEVER BEEN in a briefing with so many officers. It was impersonal and, as he watched Rosset deliver the agenda for the day, he realised it was easier. With so large an audience, officers were far less likely to argue, and voice controversial opinions. Something Yorke had been up against in the past.

Yorke had taken his seat with the HOLMES 2 operatives. They threw data into the vast computerised crime brain at a remarkable speed. Yorke had always assumed he'd had the fastest operative known to crime fighting in Jeremy Dawson. He looked around the table. It seems he'd been wrong. Jeremy wouldn't even make it into the top three.

At this moment, Rosset had projected a map onto an interactive whiteboard of the area around *Rose Hill* care home. Using an electronic pen, he drew a red line to show the route Bernard Drigg's walked every day. He used arrows to indicate the direction, and numbers to indicate where Bernard would usually stop to sit on a park bench. The recreation of this route had been pieced together through extensive interviews with Bernard's surviving carers. Bernard had spent exactly ninety minutes outside the care home every day. In terms of finding witnesses, it was difficult. The problem was that it was a very rural area. There were no shops on the route, and therefore no CCTV or witnesses that encountered Bernard on a regular basis. Most of the walk took place through a large park that had been donated to the council by the owner after his death.

Being an avid dog-lover, the benefactor of the park, had wanted the local residents to have a fantastic place to walk their own pets following his passing.

Rosset shone his laser pointer at the top of the map, at the northernmost area of the park.

'Number 6. The bench overlooking a valley,' Rosset said. 'As you know, yesterday, we got lucky with Malcolm Sinclair, a professional dogwalker, who came forward following our public request. He saw Bernard talking to a large man on more than three occasions. We've shown him *this* picture of Dr Louis Mayers.'

Rosset moved his pointer along the board to an A3 photograph of Mayers. Most people in this room, Yorke included, wouldn't see it clearly from this distance. It didn't matter to Yorke. He knew the photograph well. It had branded itself on his memory a long time ago.

'He said he had the same stocky build, and large features, and it *could* be the man, but he refused to commit. He said that if it was him, he now had much longer hair, and that long white moustache was gone. Today, we have a forensic artist with Sinclair. We're also modifying the photograph we have of Mayers. We're going to take away the moustache, lengthen his hair, and add a few years to him. Then we are going out hard with that image. There is little doubt in my mind that the person on the bench with Bernard was Dr Louis Mayers. He told Audrey Houghton he'd been manipulated by the Conduit before he committed suicide. You should all be completely up-to-date with the operation involving Christian Severance and the Conduit, from HOLMES 2 and, today, we are lucky enough to have the most senior officer involved in that investigation, DCI Michael Yorke, here with us. You know the details, but facts and figures are emotionless. What DCI Yorke told me yesterday made my understanding of Mayers, his motivations and behaviours, more organic. And it left me cold. It is important for you to have the same understanding as me. We're dealing with something out-of-the-ordinary here. DCI Yorke?'

Yorke stood up and turned to face his audience. 'There's no need for me to introduce Mayers, simply because he has made his introduction already, and the manner by which he has done so, is heinous and distressing. You also clearly do not need a warning to be on your guard. The injuries sustained to one of my officers on the last investigation, and the personal tragedy sustained by another, will all be in the documents you've read on HOLMES 2. I'm also not going to stand here and give you a psychological profile of Mayers because that has been done on more than one occasion, and are also available for you to read. All I can give you is my perspective on the man who believes himself to be a conduit of some kind, and I hope that this will be enough of a personal touch to direct you to the right outcome.'

Yorke went through everything he'd discussed with Rosset the previous day: that Mayers chooses incredibly damaged individuals and that Bernard fitted this profile because of his experiences in the Falklands; the shooting at Mayers' old medical practice; the way the doctor adapted Dr Martin Adams' pioneering HASD therapy into a newer, more vicious beast; that Mayers was programming his 'healed' victims for suicide to cover his tracks; and, most importantly, the doctor's delusions of grandeur.

Yorke didn't get any questions. Instead, a stunned silence settled over the room. Because the monologue had completely taken it out of him, he was glad to sit back down beside the HOLMES 2 operative who was typing so fast that Yorke wondered if the computer was actually able to keep up with her.

'Long story short then,' Rosset said, 'We stop this monster before he does any more damage. Assignments are pinned to the board, but I just want to go through a few priorities. Dr Martin Adams, pioneer of HASD, will be with us by mid-afternoon. Kim, you're rolling out the red carpet. Make him welcome, his help may prove invaluable. Brian, I want you to do the 'park duty' today, quiz as *many* of those dog-walkers as you can, take the new image of Mayers – we *need* more witnesses. All it takes is for one person to have seen our doctor catch a particular bus and the fuse is lit. Ronnie and Silvia, continue through your list of therapists that Bernard has seen over the years. Dr Louis Mayers is a therapist, or at least, believes himself to be one. Where is he most likely to be finding these patients with traumatic experiences? If he isn't still practising under a new identity himself, he is most certainly getting inside information to identify targets. There are, of course, countless other priorities; hence, the reason that I have made the word *budget* obsolete this week.'

After answering several questions, Rosset thanked his captive audience, and led Yorke back through to his office. On the way, Yorke decided it was time to share Robert Brislane's disappearance. He began with an excuse, which was partly true. 'For complete transparency, I want to share something else that I've been looking into over the last couple of days. I wanted to ensure it was relevant before complicating your already complicated investigation further. Someone went missing, someone who was searching for DI Mark Topham.'

Rosset stopped and turned to look at Yorke. 'Mark Topham. Murder suspect?'

'Yes,' Yorke said, sighing. 'Complicated, you see.'

Rosset raised an eyebrow. 'Complicated because Mayers killed his lover?'

'Yes,' Yorke said, feeling himself reddening.

'So, do you know where he is?'

'Of course not, sir. I'd be no use to anyone in jail.'

'Do you blame me for asking? After that revelation?'

'I'm not here looking for Mark Topham, sir, I'm here to help you. Obviously, if I find him, I'll do my duty. For what it's worth, I think he's dead. But I have become interested in the private investigator looking for Topham. He disappeared, and the investigation has been a disaster. I believe he might be dead, but I do not believe it was down to Mayers. I want to be transparent with you, sir, but I believe you're making good use of your resources at this time.'

Yorke's phone started to ring. He pulled it out of his pocket and looked at the screen. It was Breaker.

'Sorry, sir,' Yorke said to Rosset, and answered the phone.

Rosset, clearly irritated, shrugged.

'Sir ... unbelievable. You have the Midas touch!' Breaker said.

You wouldn't think it, looking at Rosset's body language. 'Go on.'

'Asking me to look for police reports around Weeton has struck gold. An elderly farmer, Andrew Campey, made a complaint regarding trespassers on his land. In a wooded area just south of his farm.'

'Who were the trespassers?'

'Don't know, sir, *because* it was never investigated! Campey regularly complained to the police about children trespassing. It was never followed up on.'

'Okay ... but I'm assuming Campey took a look himself?

If anything serious had gone on in that patch of woods, we'd surely know about it by now.'

'Not necessarily, sir. Campey died of a heart attack *that evening*. No wonder it was never investigated. Why bother?'

Yorke felt his heart rate increase. 'Who lives there now?'

'No one. The property has been left to his son, Dom Campey, but is standing there vacant.'

'Okay, Paul, I don't want you to abandon the plan. I want you to continue to Coventry. That interview with Helen Brislane must go ahead. Ask an officer to contact Campey's son and have him meet me, and your officer, at his father's farmhouse. Do you know how far away his son is?'

'Less than an hour out.'

'Fantastic. Tell him it's important, and that we want to take a look on his land regarding an old complaint. Don't give him any more than that.'

'I won't do.'

'Please text me the address. I'll head straight there.'

After the phone call, Rosset raised his eyebrow again. 'Still unconnected?'

'I think so, but I have a lead that I must check out.'

'Good. I'll tag along so you can fill me in on absolutely everything. I trust you Mike. I understand why you don't want to *clutter* my investigation, but you know, as well as I do, that no matter how valid an opinion is, one is *never enough*.'

EDDIE COULD FEEL Alan in his head. Not just the gentle music of his voice, which coaxed him further and further in the darkness, but *his whole being*, holding his hand, encouraging him down into the dark heart of the memory.

They were in Eddie's parents' bedroom. The curtains were drawn, and the room was dimly lit by bedside lamps.

Absent from school due to sickness, twelve-year-old Eddie stood at a full-length mirror, dressed in his mother's underwear.

Eddie turned to look at Alan beside him. 'News to you, isn't it? Obviously you knew my life was a lie, but you didn't know to what extent, did you?'

He turned back to look at his younger self, modelling his mother's black lingerie.

'Saskia,' the boy said, turning side on, narrowing his eyes, trying to look seductive. 'My name is Saskia.'

Eddie approached so he could stand behind his younger self. He wanted to feel again this happiness. This total freedom. Long before he'd built a solid wall around himself which could absorb the fiercest of blows. He wanted to touch himself but knew this wasn't possible.

'It's only a visualisation,' Alan had told him.

Eddie watched his younger self head to the dressing table, spray himself with perfume and then rustle around in the make-up drawer. After he found the red lipstick, he leaned into the mirror and started to apply it. 'Beautiful,' he said to his reflection.

'What the fucking hell are you doing?'

Both Eddies, young and old, turned.

It was his father. A man that Eddie had both feared and loved as a child. A self-proclaimed *traditional* man. A man who worked hard for his family but expected respect in return. A man with values so outmoded that he socialised only with people with the same values so he was never called out on his bigotry.

The mean man's eyes were wide as he stalked into the room. 'What're you wearing?'

Eddie was between the boy and his father. He should have been blocking his younger self's view of the twisted old prick, but as he wasn't actually there, that didn't happen.

'Mum's clothes,' the boy said.

'I can see that. Why?'

'I don't know.'

His father approached. Eddie tried to stop him. It was useless. His father passed through him as if he were an apparition and, when he turned, the old bastard already had his younger self by the shoulder.

'What's that on your face?'

'Lipstick.'

'Why?'

The boy was starting to cry now. 'I don't know.' His voice was cracking.

Eddie started forward. *'Take your fucking hands off him!'*

His father yanked the boy's head back by the hair and swept his feet out from under him with his foot. While down on his knees, his father kept tight hold of his hair, forcing him to continue staring up at him.

Eddie turned to Alan, who was watching from the back of the room. 'Okay ... I've had enough ... bring me out ... I've had enough!'

Alan nodded forwards, gesturing for Eddie to turn and watch the end.

'Wind the lipstick out, son. All of it.' His father said.

While crying, and begging to be released, the boy wound the red lipstick out. It was clearly a new stick and was still of reasonable length.

'Now put it on,' his father said.

'It's already—'

'*Put it on!*'

The boy painted his lips again.

'Carry on!' His father said, still pulling on his hair.

'I don't understand—'

'*Carry on, paint your whole fucking face!*'

'Dad—'

'*Your ... whole ... fucking ... face.*'

Eddie watched his younger self draw lines of red up and down his cheeks.

'Your head too.'

The boy scribbled on his forehead.

'Is that the best you can do? A little faggot like you can do better than that.'

The father snatched the lipstick from his son. With his grip still tight on the boy's hair, the bastard pressed the lipstick hard against his head. He continued where the boy had left off, and drew thick red lines across his forehead, up and down his cheeks, and over his chin.

Then he did it again. Harder this time. The lipstick started to buckle, causing thick splodges of red wax to break off on his face.

Eddie's younger self was squealing, and was trying to pull away, but his father's grip on his hair was too strong.

Once his father had worn the lipstick down to the holder, he threw it to one side, and placed the palm of his hand on his son's face. He started to rub aggressively. 'You want to wear make-up, gay lord, you wear it. All over your fucking face.'

When his father released his son, his entire face glowed red. He wept uncontrollably.

'Good, cry. Wash it the fuck off. And never let me see anything like that again.'

His father stormed out. Eddie stared at his younger self for a moment before turning and glaring at Alan.

'You think you're so clever, don't you?'

'This is your memory, Eddie.'

'So ... it means little. After this, I vowed never to talk to the old wanker again. Yes, it's hard when you live in the same house, but he died a year later in the streets fighting with a rival football fan. Not surprising really. He lived his life aggressively and died the same way. I made my peace with him at his gravestone a year or so back. Told him I forgave him his ignorance. I told him I understood what it was like to live in a world that value appearance over substance. I know now why he didn't want this for me. He wanted me to appear the right way, wanted to spare me labels and criticism.'

'So you've *accepted* this experience already?'

'Yes. So whatever this is, this visualisation, it's a waste of your fucking time.'

'On the contrary, it is anything but. We're now ready to move forward.'

———

FOR MANY YEARS, the Conduit had believed that the special bond he'd experienced with his former student, Christian Severance, was an enigma that could never be found again.

Alan Sants had just proven him wrong.

In fact, this relationship was far stronger. It had taken the Conduit much longer with Severance to lead him down the right pathway and when the fireworks finally did go off, *and go off they did,* he'd still had some doubts about him. Severance had been driven, and tenacious, but he was also torn. He wanted revenge on those that had wronged him, but he did not believe in collateral damage. He still held on to some broken belief in innocence.

Alan was different. He was just as driven, and as tenacious, but there was no sign of him being *torn*. Alan knew exactly what he wanted. For the first time in his life he had a purpose, and nothing would stand in his way.

His cool and methodical execution of Mickey was nothing short of genius.

He'd not asked for the Conduit's help, nor had he needed any help. His plan, so far, had moved with perfection. To know that Eddie McLarney would scurry here like a rat from a sinking ship ... *the confidence! The audacity!*

It'd taken time and effort to prep the fireworks with Severance. With Alan, he'd merely lit the fuse!

His new student ended the visualisation, and Eddie slumped backwards, twitching and dribbling.

Alan turned to look at him. 'He said he'd *accepted* it.'

'I know. I heard.'

'So, now what do I do?'

'Now you must make a choice.'

'Go on.'

'About how you wish to heal him.'

'I want to alleviate his suffering, make him healthy again.'

'Too obvious. To be healthy is merely the absence of disease, and to feel good. What do you think will make young Eddie feel good? What is his disease?'

'The mask he wears. The face he shows to the world. It's not really him.'

'So, now you know what you have to do. His acceptance is no good if it makes him persevere with his disguise ... his false veneer. Turn his *acceptance* to *rejection*. Make the darkness in that memory destructive again. You can do that, Alan. *Easily.* Because this is the point that he is poised delicately between clarity and disarray. *The sweet spot.*'

'Yes,' Alan said, widening his eyes. 'And when he reaches his lowest point, I'll make him take off the mask.'

'Bravo!'

13

OVER THE YEARS, Yorke's investigations had taken him to his fair share of farmyards, but he'd never been to one that dealt exclusively in pumpkins before. He was rather disappointed that there wasn't a single pumpkin to be seen. Not because of the sheet of snow that covered everything, but because the seeds had needed to be sown in April and Andrew Campey had been dead since February.

'Dad did well for himself.' Dom Campey zipped up his waterproof. After a groggy start, the snowfall was having a mid-morning burst of energy.

'Pumpkins sell well around Halloween, I imagine,' Rosset said.

'Understatement,' Campey said, 'but, I was in no fit state to sow. What happened to Dad hit me hard. Now, I'm just planning to sell the place and move on. My own business is doing well enough.'

'Glad to hear it. What do you do?' Yorke said.

'Carpet fitting.'

Yorke, Rosset, Campey and the two officers Breaker had

sent, trudged through the snow. Despite the heavy snowfall, the sun was bright, and the bare land around them glowed white. Yorke was reminded of the vastness of Antarctica on the nature documentaries he so often watched. The idyllic illusion was quickly eroded when they sighted the skeletal trees that blotted the landscape.

There was a short blast of wind. The travellers hugged themselves. When it had passed, Yorke said, 'So, Mr Campey, your father regularly complained about trespassers?'

'You can't see it,' Campey said, pointing west, 'But there's a small, winding dirt track alongside our property that's large enough for a small vehicle to get down. The entrance to the track is overgrown so not many passersby give it a second thought. If you follow that track, it leads into the woodland ahead, makes it about half-way in, and then is blocked off by a fallen tree. Local teenagers drive in there, and smoke dope. From the house, you can often see the headlights on the track and in the woodland. My father used to phone the police. Twice the little pillocks were collared, and twice they got off with a warning! Then, the kids got savvy, and stopped putting on their headlights.'

Yorke nodded, thought for a moment, and then said, 'So, on the day in question, when your father made the complaint, how did he spot the trespassers if there were no headlights?'

'There were in that instance. My father phoned me before ...' he paused and sighed, 'his heart attack. He said he'd seen headlights.'

'Yes, but it was daytime, why would any trespasser have headlights on?' Rosset said from the other side of Campey.

'On a gloomy day, it can get quite dim in those woods. Whoever the trespassers were, they put the headlights on when they got among the trees. So, I suspected these must have been a different set of kids, not the savvy ones.'

'Did you never think to go and have a look, see what had bothered your father?' Rosset said.

'Why would I have done that? My thoughts weren't with teenagers getting high in the wood. They were with my father, who I'd just lost. When it did cross my mind a few days later, I had no reason to assume they were still there, did I?'

'We understand,' Yorke said, 'And we are sorry for your loss.'

They entered the woodland. It was indeed gloomy. Lack of foliage ensured that most of the snow fall still penetrated. Yorke felt the cold sting on his face. He tightened the hood on his ski jacket.

Campey walked ahead of the four officers. He was heading in a diagonal direction, cutting deeper into the heart of the woodland. They clambered over several fallen branches. Rosset slipped at one point, but one of Breaker's officers was there to catch him before he fell.

'Around here,' Campey said, swooping around some icy brambles. 'You're now on the dirt road. When the trees were planted, they obviously wanted to leave this free for wagons and whatnot. Not uncommon.'

'Where's the fallen tree that blocks off the road?' Yorke said.

'Not far at all. A minute or two this way. Spent most of my childhood in this wood. Keep an eye out. You might see my name carved into some trees.'

There was a build-up of snow on the path, but nothing like what they'd trudged through earlier on the field. Yorke looked up at the twisted branches along the sides of that path. They weaved into each other forming a monstrous cobweb. But with cobwebs, you'd expect spiders, flies ... *life.*

This place was dead.

As a university student, Yorke had discovered Brandon, his best friend, murdered. In that moment, a cold sensation had started up in his neck, and spread, furiously, all over his body. He'd once described it to Patricia. 'It's as if something's freezing your soul.'

Whenever Yorke encountered death, the cold flared. He'd learned to both fear it and trust it as a signal as to what was to come.

It flared now. He already knew his neck was covered by his zipped-up ski jacket, but he checked anyway.

The dirt track curved sharply, and ahead was the fallen tree, and next to that, a white Audi TT. The registration plate was too dirty to read, but Yorke already knew it would be Robert Brislane's. This was the car that ANPR had picked up. It would also be the car in which Robert had met his end.

He didn't need the cold in his neck to tell him that.

'Looks like I should have come earlier,' Campey said.

They approached cautiously.

'Mike, do you think your man is inside?' Rosset said.

'I don't know,' Yorke said. 'If he was out in the open, the teenagers using this spot since February would have phoned it in anonymously.'

'Wouldn't they have phoned in an abandoned vehicle anyway?' One of Breaker's officers asked.

Yorke and Rosset were both surprised by the naivety of the question. It was Campey that answered it. 'If you think that, you don't know teenagers these days ...'

Rosset smiled. 'The teenagers who came in obviously

weren't law-abiding, but let's not tarnish them all with the same brush. I have one at home actually.'

Uninterested in the dialogue, Yorke moved ahead. He circled the abandoned Audi. All of the windows were smashed and the tyres were flat. 'It looks like the teenagers had some fun with it,' he called back.

Yorke went around to the boot, pulled some gloves from his pocket and put them on. He tried to open it. Locked.

Rosset came up alongside him.

Yorke pointed out some red staining on the white surface by the rear registration. He turned back to the officers. 'Get a team out here. He's in the boot of the car.'

THE START of the visualisation remained the same.

Eddie watched the confused boy admire himself in his mother's lingerie. 'Saskia ... my name is Saskia.'

After his father came into the room and smothered the face of his younger self with lipstick, Eddie turned back to Alan. 'It was for the best. My father was helping me. My tears now will have protected me for years to come.'

Alan nodded for him to turn back.

Eddie sighed, turned and watched the vile show again. Even though he knew exactly how it evolved, he still flinched throughout.

'You want to wear make-up, gay lord, you wear it. All over your fucking face,' his father said, covering boy's face in makeup and then releasing him.

This is different, Eddie thought. *Where're my tears?*

His younger self turned to the dresser table behind him, reached into a packet of make-up wipes and grabbed a handful. 'I will wear make-up, Dad, but I'll wear it how I want to,' the boy turned back, 'and not all over my *fucking* face.' He started to wipe it off.

Eddie smiled. *You tell him, fella!*

His father's eyes widened.

The boy continued to wipe. 'I don't want you to call me your son anymore. I'm your *daughter—*'

His father slapped him hard across the face. He stumbled backwards. The dressing table stopped him from going over.

Eddie's smile fell away. *Yes, precisely why I never provoked him. Such an obvious outcome.*

Still the boy refused to cry, continuing instead to scrub at his face, before rearing up again. 'Don't deny it, Dad. You've known for a long time. I dare you to go back to work and tell your friends that your child no longer identifies as male—'

Another slap.

This time, his backside went up onto the dressing table. He slid backwards, crashing into the mirror. It didn't smash, but he gasped as the wind was knocked out of him.

'You want to stay in this fucking house, you do as you are fucking well told.'

'I'll do whatever I'm told if you let me be who I want to be.'

He raised his hand. 'You're a fucking man, and you'll stay one in my house.'

'You think Mum will kick me out?'

'She does what I tell her to do.'

'Because you hit her too?'

'I don't hit women. Now, get yourself into the bathroom—'

'You hit me. I'm a woman.'

'One more time—'

'And you'll beat me. *Do it*. Take your belt off and whip me. I'll die before I change my mind again. This is it. This is who I am.'

His father's hand settled on the buckle of his belt. There it stayed while he bared his teeth and stared down at the son who he thought was betraying him.

'This is bullshit. I'm going back to work. You can explain yourself to your mother tonight.'

He turned and walked away.

Younger Eddie continued to rub at the lipstick. Obviously, it wasn't coming off. He'd need a shower to shift that amount of wax, but metaphorically, he was stripping away the lies.

Eddie turned back to look at Alan with tears in his eyes.

He felt proud.

THE CONDUIT ALSO FELT PROUD.

Very, very proud.

Alan's technique in leading Eddie through the process of *rejection* had been scintillating entertainment.

Before the Conduit had been impressed by his protégé's tenacity, now he was impressed by his sheer creativity.

The Conduit would be the first to admit he was regularly in awe of himself, but to be in awe of another was unheard of. Until today.

Until now.

The Conduit wanted so much to stop Alan and congratulate him on a tremendous session, but he stopped himself, and remained patient.

The reason?

Alan was about to start the visualisation all over again

and that was one show he simply could not, and would not, put on hold.

———

THE QUIET WOODLAND didn't stay quiet for long. Crime scenes had a tendency to turn the most isolated and forgotten areas into a hive of activity.

One of the officers who had accompanied Yorke, Rosset and Campey into the woodlands took on the role of first attender and began a logbook.

Technically, Breaker was leading the investigation into Brislane's disappearance, but right now, due to his absence, Rosset's rank ensured he was overseeing this crime scene. Yorke wasn't short of experience either, so both ensured the scene operated smoothly.

An officer had taken Campey back to the house. A crime scene was no place for civilians.

Both Yorke and Rosset had been there when they cranked open the boot, and *both* had backed away in disgust. Not only because of the stench, but because the corpse had made a significant journey towards decomposition. The body was partly liquified. Forensics would be needed to identify it.

As the forensic pathologist pored over the dead man, Yorke and Rosset retreated to the tree.

Yorke had already informed Rosset of everything he knew regarding the Robert Brislane investigation on the journey to the farmyard, but the senior officer was still struggling to look Yorke in the eye. Yorke didn't blame him. He should have told him everything much earlier.

'And you don't think this was Louis Mayers?' Rosset said.

'I don't,' Yorke said. 'I think it was his wife.'

'She must have had some help getting that body into the boot then,' Rosset said.

'Possibly. Let's see what the pathologist says.'

When the pathologist came over, he unhooked a facial mask, and let it dangle from his ear, so he could speak clearly. 'On first inspection, the likely cause of death looks like a gunshot wound to the abdomen. He wasn't shot in the boot though.'

Yorke nodded. Having seen the blood traces on the outside of the boot, he'd suspected this already.

The pathologist gestured back at the car with his thumb. Scenes of Crimes Officers were buzzing around the vehicle. 'We've found blood stains on the driver's seat, and *Luminol* picked up blood traces alongside the vehicle, leading to the boot.'

'Was he dragged or carried to the boot?' Rosset said.

'No evidence of dragging.'

Rosset flashed Yorke a scornful look which said: *how big is this female suspect?*

'However,' the pathologist said, 'he could have just walked there himself and climbed in. He was alive when he was in the boot. There are scratch marks and bloody handprints on the interior of the boot.'

A white-suited officer came running over, holding a see-through evidence bag. Yorke and Rosset sidestepped the pathologist and approached to meet the officer on his journey.

'Sir, I found a wallet. The driver's licence belongs to Robert Brislane,' the officer said.

Another SOCO threw his hand in the air. He was standing by the passenger door of the Audi. 'I found a gun under the seat.'

14

AFTER ENDING THE phone conversation with Yorke, DS Paul Breaker returned to Helen Brislane in the interview room. His entire interview strategy, which had been configured by Yorke earlier, was now out of the window. Yorke hadn't needed to provide another strategy because this interview had just become very straightforward.

Breaker sat beside his colleague and restarted the interview. 'I have some bad news, Mrs Brislane.'

She put a hand to her mouth.

'We've found a body.'

She started to cry.

'We believe that it is your husband, Robert. He was found in his vehicle, and he was carrying identification. However, his identity will need to be confirmed with further forensic examination.'

Breaker allowed her a moment, and then offered her a tissue.

She took her hand away from her mouth and reached out for it. 'How?'

'A gunshot wound.'

'Someone killed him?'

'It is the most likely explanation at this time.'

'Jesus.' She dabbed at her eyes. 'I knew he was dead. That detective seemed confident that he was still alive, but I just knew he wasn't.' She buried her head in her hands.

He allowed her another moment.

Breaker knew that *if* she was innocent, the next step could seem rather callous, but there really wasn't much choice. She wasn't being level with them. She'd been in Weeton that day, and she had lied about the alibi. *You reap what you sow*, Breaker thought, knowing he couldn't beat himself up about his next move.

'Is it okay if we continue this interview later?' Mrs Brislane said.

'I'm afraid not.'

'Why?'

'For the reasons we discussed earlier.'

'I told you already, I went to Weeton to meet my husband, to tell him the truth about my relationship with Eli, but he never showed up at the station. I waited a couple of hours and then headed home.'

'Yes, you did,' Breaker said. 'And you also said you didn't share this with the police because you figured you would be made a suspect in his disappearance.'

'Yes.'

'And you admitted to lying about having counselling on that day ...'

'Yes.'

'I'm going to level with you, Mrs Brislane. Before I took that phone call, your argument was weak. Most would say *desperate*. I think you did meet your husband, and I think that meeting ended in his death.'

'That's not true.'

'Right now, Mrs Brislane, that small patch of woodland that your husband drove into is a crime scene. It's being picked clean. You know that the evidence they find will identify how he died, and hopefully, who is responsible. We sit here with a small window of opportunity. I'm not lying to you when I say that once that body is formally identified, you'll be a major suspect. You've obstructed justice already by lying about your whereabouts, and we now have confirmation that you were in the area where the murder occurred. We'll take a DNA sample from you. You could then argue that your DNA will be on his car and his clothes because he's your husband. But your husband had been in Leeds for several weeks, *without you*, and I suspect his clothes will have been washed in that period. Do you see where I am going with this, Mrs Brislane? The evidence will build and build. If you are responsible for his death, the facts will lead us there.'

'Do I need a solicitor?'

'In every eventuality, you will require a solicitor. Time is short now, Mrs Brislane, and I would like to offer you an opportunity. Tell me what really happened. Confessing now to these events allows you to demonstrate remorse and that goes a long way with a judge.'

AFTER PHONING AND UPDATING GARDNER, Yorke approached Rosset, who'd just finished a conversation with the Exhibits Officer.

'He's recovered a USB drive from the victim's pocket,' Rosset said.

Yorke's eyes widened. 'I need access to it, sir.'

'Any idea what we're going to find on there, Mike?'

'Brislane was in Leeds looking for Mark Topham. He claimed to have found him. Let's hope these are the details.'

'Say you're right, and this isn't just a collection of family photos, then what?'

'Then, sir, I politely request to be the one to take Mark in.'

Rosset smiled 'Now you're asking for a favour?'

'I'm asking because it's the right thing to do.'

'Probably. Except ...' he ran a hand through his hair, 'There could be information regarding Dr Louis Mayers on that drive. You said yourself, if Mark Topham was in Leeds, he must have been looking for Mayers. What if the poor bugger in the boot of that car found them *both*?'

'You could be right. This could fall under your investigation. Just assign me the task of investigating that USB. Then, all the information comes to you first-hand. Just allow me the arrest if we find Mark.'

Rosset thought about it and then nodded. 'Okay, but you'll need a couple of officers to assist you.'

I have Gardner ... He kept his mouth shut. That would go down like a lead balloon. He nodded.

'Yes, thanks you, sir. Could you please arrange for the USB to be taken back and logged into evidence now, and then have the files sent over to me encrypted, so I can start looking over them? Then, I can get in touch with you with my initial findings and what I need.'

Rosset nodded.

Yorke was surprised. He expected Rosset to suggest he looked at the files at HQ, which would have been fine, but then he wouldn't have been able to involve Gardner.

He didn't want to involve Gardner out of obligation. He wanted to involve Gardner because no one else knew Mark

Topham like she did and, depending on what was on that USB, she might be the most valuable resource he had.

He said goodbye to Rosset, nodded his respect to the multitude of officers and SOCOs, and retraced his steps down the dirt road, and back onto the field.

The snow fell thickly now, slicing the air.

Moments after giving a DNA sample, Helen Brislane asked to speak to Breaker again.

'Your solicitor isn't here yet,' Breaker said.

'It's like you said, you'll find my DNA. Are you telling me the truth? If I tell you what happened, will it help me moving forward?'

'Confessions which save time and resources are always looked on more positively.'

'I'm pregnant.'

'Congratulations.'

'I didn't shoot Robert.'

'Can I restart the recording?'

Helen nodded. Breaker restarted the video recording and introduced the session. Then, he nodded at Helen to begin.

'I did meet Robert,' she sighed and leaned forward. 'Contrary to what I told the other detective a couple of days ago, our marriage was a mess. Counselling wasn't helping either.'

Not surprising, if you have an affair with the counsellor.

'I know what you're thinking, but things didn't start happening between me and Eli until I was absolutely convinced that me and Robert were over. I want to make *that* crystal clear. While Robert was up in Leeds working, we had arguments on the phone. We agreed to meet to have some *clear-the-air* talks and we'd been to Harewood House before, when we were much younger, so Robert suggested there. I arranged to go to Weeton, where he would pick me up from the station. Except ...' she paused to have a mouthful of water from her paper cup. 'I'd already planned to end it. I wanted to be with Eli. They were polar opposites, Eli and Robert. Eli loved children and wanted them.' She rubbed her stomach. '*Whereas* Robert didn't want to know, despite all the promises he'd made me before we married.

'We were at the stage in our relationship, where we couldn't go longer than a minute without an argument. So, we were already at it before he'd driven us out the station carpark. We made it about two miles down the road before I told him to pull in. He did, and I told him we were done, and I would get out and walk back. He lost it completely. Where he'd stopped, there was a turn off onto a dirt path. It was overgrown with brambles and whatnot, but you could see it. Before I could get my seatbelt off, he had driven onto it and was accelerating.' Helen put her head in her hands. 'Just give me a moment ... it was bloody scary.'

'I understand,' Breaker said. 'Take your time.'

She took a minute to collect herself, lifted her head from her hands, sighed and continued. 'The dirt road continued through a patch of trees. I remember it suddenly getting a lot darker, the further we went. I was crying at this point, pleading with him, but it didn't stop him. The track narrowed and became cluttered, so he was forced to slow down. At this point, I was shouting at him to turn the car around to take me back to the station. He ignored me and then stopped by a fallen tree.

'I was surprised by how calm he seemed. Our

arguments would often be very fiery, but since I'd announced that we were over, he'd been silent. Surely, he must have known that things weren't working between us? I tried to reason with him by telling him that we could still be friends, but he just kept staring straight ahead, and not responding. Then, he asked me if there was someone else.' She stopped to reach for the tissue she'd used earlier which was still on the table. She dabbed at her eyes. 'I ask myself, thousands of times *every single day,* if things would have ended differently if I'd lied? Told him there was no one else?'

She took another mouthful of water.

'But there's nothing I can do now. I told him about Eli. At the time, I *thought* it best just to get everything out in the open. And then ... *Jesus* ... he took a gun out of the glove compartment,' she touched her forehead, 'and put it to his head. I screamed for him not to do it ... shit ... his eyes. They were all scrunched up. He was going to do it. There was no doubt ... so ... I did all I could think of doing ... I reached over and grabbed the gun.

'He was far stronger than me, but I managed to force it downwards. I almost got it to his lap, but then he yanked back and ...' She pressed the tissue to her eyes. 'A moment please.'

'Of course,' Breaker said, reaching over and refilling her paper cup from a jug of water.

'The gun went off, but I didn't shoot him ... I was trying to stop him ... that's the truth ... you have to believe me.'

I do, Breaker thought.

'It was in his stomach. He was in a lot of pain, and there was blood everywhere. He was calling me a bitch over and over. I told him it wasn't my fault, over and over. But he just kept yelling at me, calling me awful things! *Dreadful things.*

He said he couldn't believe that he'd married me. And then he said something that made everything worse ... he'd had a vasectomy the month after he married me. That he'd always known that I wasn't fit to have children with.

'Everything had been a lie. *Everything*. For years he'd told me that he didn't want children, but we'd never stopped trying. *Never*. I just kept believing that he would love any child that was his anyway. But the coward had strung me along. He was wasting my life ... such a fucking coward ...' She stared at the wall behind Breaker. He realised that she was about to get to a part in the story that she was ashamed of.

'I want you to know, Detective, I wasn't thinking straight. The journey into the woods, the gun, his abuse ... I was struggling to make sense of anything ... I really need to make that clear in this interview ...'

'You are doing,' Breaker said.

'I told him to get in the boot of the car.' She gulped and looked down at the table. 'I told him to get in the boot or I wouldn't take him to hospital ... that I couldn't bear to hear his abuse any longer ...'

Breaker allowed her a minute to collect herself. 'What happened then?'

'I got out and opened his door for him. He stumbled out and worked his way around the side of the car. Then, I opened the boot for him, and he climbed in.' She paused to think. A glazed look passed over her eyes. Then, she flinched. 'His howl. It was awful. Loud, like an animal. But he made it in, and he made it onto his back. He was pale, in a mess ... he told me I was his only chance ... I closed the boot ... Oh, God, what's going to happen to me?'

'What did you do next, Mrs Brislane?'

'Am I going to jail?'

'What happened next?'

'Nothing.'

Breaker remembered Yorke's words. *There were claw marks and bloody handprints on the inside of the boot.*

'I walked away. I followed the dirt track back to the main road.'

You left him to die.

'I think I was in shock. In fact, *I know*, I was in shock.'

You could have saved him.

'I was confused. All the abuse, those years of lies, and in that moment, I just couldn't get past it. I sat in a café near the station for hours.'

'Didn't you have blood on you?'

'I never touched him. After he shot himself, I climbed out of the car so he couldn't touch me.'

'What happened in the café?'

'Nothing really. When I started to feel able to think clearly again, I realised it was too late. I knew that if I went back to the car, he would already be dead. Then what, face this? Face what I'm facing now? He lived a life following people who didn't want to be followed and finding people who didn't want to be found. I thought that my only chance was that you'd think it was someone else – someone he'd pissed off. I haven't heard from you in eight months.' She touched her stomach again. 'I thought it was okay to start a family. Please, Detective, tell me, I made the right decision, that everything is going to be alright?'

IT HAD BEEN an exhausting day for Alan and Eddie, so the Conduit treated them to steak and new potatoes with a perky pepper sauce of his own devising. They ate it in the dining room, rather than the kitchen, because meeting Mark the dog might have been one step too many for Eddie. He'd been subjected to visualisation after visualisation and his mind would be sore.

The Conduit had ventured out earlier to buy Eddie a green floral dress. Not being certain what size to buy, he'd opted for several larger ones. Fortunately, one of them had fitted.

When Eddie had consented to wear the outfit, the Conduit had patted Alan firmly on the back, and his protégé had glowed over his achievement.

The dining room looked reasonably festive because the Conduit had hung the cards given to him by members of his faculty, and some of his patients from the Roundhay practice, on the wall. He couldn't abide Christmas music, so he'd opted for some gentle piano music in the background.

The Conduit sat at the head of the table, and to his right, Alan ate slowly and thoughtfully. To his left, Eddie had used his steak knife to cut the meat, but he'd yet to take a mouthful. The Conduit had poured himself, and Alan, a glass of wine, but had given Eddie water. He already had enough chemicals in his system.

'Drink some water, Eddie, cleanse the pallet,' the Conduit said. 'Often that is enough to spike the appetite.'

Eddie didn't look up. He moved the meat around his plate. 'Saskia, please. Call me Saskia.'

The Conduit looked across at Alan. They didn't need to say anything. Their eye-contact spoke volumes. *Remarkable progress. Simply remarkable.*

'Well, Saskia,' the Conduit continued. 'I appreciate the day that you've just had and, so, if you wish to leave your meal until later, no offence will be taken.'

'Thank you.'

'But I would suggest trying to eat. Tomorrow does promise to be another long day.'

'I understand,' Saskia said.

The Conduit looked at Alan again. 'Do you mind?' He gestured at Saskia with his hand. 'She's your patient.'

Alan shook his head and continued to eat, happy to allow the Conduit to probe today's progress.

'So, tell me Saskia, how're you feeling now?'

'Different.'

'Can you elaborate?'

'Lighter ... younger.'

'Happier?'

'Yes. Like a burden has been lifted.'

'Because you can now feel female?'

'Yes, but not just feel, but rather *know* that I am.'

'This calls for a toast.' The Conduit raised his glass.

Alan followed suit, but Saskia moved her eyes between them still looking dazed.

'To new beginnings,' The Conduit said.

'To new beginnings,' Alan said.

'And tomorrow, I am going to head to the shop, my dear young lady, and buy you some lipstick,' the Conduit said.

With this, Saskia's bewildered expression intensified. She moved her head left and right repeatedly as if she was some kind of robot that'd just malfunctioned.

Alan started to stand up. The Conduit held a hand up to gesture him to stop. *This is part of it. This is how we test.*

Saskia stopped moving her head. 'It's already—' She pinched her thumb and forefinger together and drew them over her lips. 'I don't understand ... Dad—' She moved her pinched digits up and down her face.

Alan tried to stand again, but again the Conduit gestured for him to stay.

Watch her. Watch her re-live the visualisation!

Saskia scribbled on her forehead. She leaned her head back, so she was staring up at the ceiling.

The Conduit looked at Alan. He was nodding. He understood now. In Saskia's head, at this moment, her father was yanking her head back and covering her face in make-up.

Saskia squealed, fell silent, and then looked down at her plate as if suddenly deactivated.

The Conduit was disappointed, and he showed this in his expression to Alan. That was some show, and he would have loved for it to continue.

He took a mouthful of wine and had an idea. He winked at Alan, stood up and pointed down at Saskia. 'You want to wear make-up, gay lord, you wear it. All over your fucking face.'

Saskia snapped back into life and looked back up at the Conduit. 'I will wear make-up, Dad, but I'll wear it how I want to,' she lifted the steak knife in her right hand to her cheek, 'and not all over my *fucking* face.' Starting from beneath her eye, she split her entire cheek open.

The Conduit's eyes widened.

Saskia drew the sharp, serrated blade down her face over and over again, tearing ragged lines into her skin. 'I don't want you to call me your son anymore. I'm your *daughter—*' She pushed herself backwards and the chair went over. She went with it.

That was the moment she was slapped, the Conduit realised.

Lying on her back, Saskia was now working the blade into the flesh on the other side of her face.

'Shouldn't we stop her?' Alan said.

'Why?' The Conduit said. 'We must watch, and we must learn. Everything we do is about learning.'

As she went to work on her forehead, Saskia shouted, 'Don't deny it, Dad. You've known for a long time. I dare you to go back to work and tell your friends that your child no longer identifies as male—'

'Another slap from her father,' the Conduit said, quietly to Alan. 'It's perfect.'

They sat back and watched Saskia carve her face to ribbons.

AFTER HIS PHONE call with Breaker ended, Yorke shared the news about Robert with Gardner.

'What a horrible way to go,' Gardner said, looking down at the floor.

Yorke put a hand on her shoulder. 'At least you know it wasn't because of your case.'

'If I hadn't put him on such a stressful case, he could have been working on his marriage.'

'From what I just heard, Emma, I don't think that marriage was salvageable.'

For a brief moment, Yorke thought of his own marriage, but then reassured himself. Robert and Helen's marriage had been rotting for years. Any issues that he and Patricia were experiencing were in their infancy. After this investigation, he would ensure these problems didn't worsen. He would even try and accept that ridiculous little dog, Rosie, into their lives.

After this conversation, it took a few hours for Yorke's email to ping. His hand was sweating as he clicked on the encrypted zipped folder recovered from the USB and downloaded it to his laptop. After extracting it, he saw that there were over a dozen named folders.

Two jumped out at him immediately.

Mark Topham.

Dr Louis Mayers.

He started by opening the 'Mark Topham' folder. It was stuffed full of files.

As he delved, Yorke imagined climbing into the late Robert Brislane's mind. It was a disorganised, and messy place, and Yorke wondered how the private investigator had managed to weave it all together and locate Topham.

There was everything from scanned images of Topham's handwritten school reports to five years' worth of itemised phone bills. There was also a copy of crime scene report on the murder of the male prostitute, Dan Tillotson. Yorke shuddered over the ease by which someone operating outside the law could access this kind of information. He listened to audio files of friends, colleagues and relatives, Robert had spoken to, and recorded on his mobile phone, probably without consent. Finally, he read copies of Topham's personal emails.

'It's remarkable,' Gardner said, who was looking through the files on her computer. 'You could write a fully fleshed out biography of Mark's life from all of this information.'

'Isn't it creepy that, when all is said and done, our entire lives can be reduced to fact-packed files, and anecdotal recounts, on a single USB drive?'

He left Gardner to read, and listen, her way through the files again, while he accessed the second folder on Dr Louis Mayers.

Obviously, Rosset and his team would be panning for gold in this folder too, but this wasn't a problem. He had

Rosset's promise that he could arrest Topham if he was alive, so it was completely irrelevant who sieved out that nugget first.

A lot of the information that Robert had gathered on Mayers was very similar to what Yorke's team had accrued on him back during the investigation. Mayers' education, his background as a private psychiatrist treating insomnia, the tragic shooting at his practice, and his time with Dr Martin Edwards supporting with HASD. Unsurprisingly, it all stopped dead on the day that Christian Severance went into custody, and Mayers disappeared into the ether. There were no audio recordings in this folder. Yorke wondered if Robert had recorded interviews with people who knew Mayers, in the same way he had done with Topham, but had never got around to uploading them. He paused to quickly email Rosset, asking if any audio files had been recovered from Robert's phone which had also been on his possession in the boot.

Yorke and Gardner ordered pizza and continued relentlessly into the night. Scribbling notes, drawing arrows between pieces of information, and pausing regularly to bounce ideas off each other. Rosset emailed back to report that there weren't any audio recordings.

It was late before Yorke finally admitted. 'I'm starting to worry that the information that led Mark to Mayers, and then Robert to Mark is not here.'

Gardner didn't respond. Her eyes were wide as she stared at her laptop. Then, her fingers danced over the keys at lightning speed. She stopped, snapped her fingers and then pointed at the screen. Yorke wandered over to the small desk she was working on at the foot of his bed.

She was pointing at a photograph of the front cover of a

book by Dr Louis Mayers. *Ending insomnia – begin your new sleep cycle.*

'Yes, I saw it before. Robert must have cut the image out from somewhere on the internet and saved it onto a word document. He was probably planning to make some notes underneath it after he read it perhaps, but never got around to it.'

Gardner pointed at the bottom left corner of word document. 'Small font, but can you see the number he's typed underneath the cover? It's easy to miss.'

'7. An accidental click of a button perhaps?'

'Or ...' She clicked on the internet tab at the bottom of the screen. She'd already found the book online. 'These are the first few pages available as a sample. She clicked forward several times. And this is page 7.'

There was one line of writing on the page, about a third of the way down.

To Frederick Lancer – my one true and constant friend.

'Bloody hell, Emma, you genius.'

SHE SPENT the evening with one of her favourite letters from him. This letter was a meditation on free will. It was her favourite because of the situation she was currently in.

A small white cell. No windows. No natural light.

Not *her* world. A world designed by *them* to take away her free will. A barren, white, *frozen* hole.

She read the final quotation used by her admirer in his letter. It was from Epictetus in The Discourses. *Man, what are you talking about? Me in chains? You can fetter my leg but my will, not even Zeus himself can overpower.*

And that was the truth. This world was *their* world. Her

world belonged only to her, and she could retreat to it at any time.

Any time.

That was the true power of free will.

She read her admirer's name at the bottom.

Milo A Russey.

But that wasn't his name. Not really. Although what was in a name, really? She thought about another letter he'd written to her in which he'd meditated on the idea of identity.

Milo A Russey was an anagram of his real name. Louis Mayers.

How else would a letter from her new friend, the infamous Conduit, make it into this barren white frozen hole?

She left the letter and approached the cell door. There was a single peep hole. They used it to ensure that she was on the other side of the room before they opened the door.

She looked through it. At first it was dark, then it was light, someone had been watching her.

'Come in if you want, doctor. Freedom isn't out there.' Lacey Ray pointed at her head. 'It's in here ... and my God, is it ever so blue.'

15

DECEMBER 28TH

F REDERICK LANCER, MAYERS' *one true and special friend*, was also a psychiatrist. Or, at least, had been. He'd retired his partnership last year at the age of fifty-six. Looking at his plush living conditions, it'd been a rather lucrative partnership.

Yorke had been over the moon to discover Lancer was alive. He'd been less than over the moon to discover they had a two-hour journey ahead of them. Lancer had opted to see out his twilight years in the Welsh seaside town of Llandudno.

Gardner had also been particularly irritating on the last stage of the journey. She'd stayed in Llandudno every year throughout her childhood, so she completely succumbed to nostalgia. 'That's the pier in which we used to watch Punch and Judy. That's the longest pier in Wales ... That artificial ski slope used to be the Happy Valley. Open air theatres and miniature golf-courses ... We used to get on that tram, all the way to the top of the Great Orme.'

When Gardner had pointed out her favourite Fish and Chip shop, Yorke had told her that enough was enough.

Lancer offered them tea and they gratefully accepted. It had been a long drive. Especially for Yorke.

The retired psychiatrist was a robust, healthy looking man with a full head of hair, stylishly parted at the side. Yorke made a mental note to start planning for an early retirement.

'You know this will be my third visit in a year from people asking questions about Louis,' Lancer said.

'Can you remember the names of the other two people?' Yorke said

'Not by name, but one was a detective, and the other was a private investigator looking for someone who was missing. Actually, the private investigator left a card. You want me to dig it out?'

Yorke showed Lancer photographs of Topham and Robert. He also gave him their names. Lancer nodded for each. 'I remember the name Brislane well. I remember thinking that I had a friend with a similar surname.'

'The first one who came to see you, DI Topham, disappeared.' Gardner said.

Lancer sat back on his sofa. 'I hope you don't think I'd anything to do with that.'

'No, sir. That is not why we are here.' Yorke said, throwing Gardner a look to try and remind her that she was supposed to a passive observer.

Yorke showed Lancer the picture of the book cover on his phone. 'We believe it was this book which led both Mark and Robert here ... to you.'

Lancer nodded. 'Yes, it did. *That* is the most ironic dedication ever! I hated that book and I told Louis so. We were both specialists in sleep and I found his suggestions too fanciful and not backed by science. It drove a wedge between us, and we never spoke again. I certainly did not remain his *one true and constant friend*. There was an element of truth to it though, I suppose, in that I was his only friend. You know, I'm surprised he never changed that dedication. He probably just kept it to rile me! This must have been over five years ago now.'

'And you're aware of what happened next with Dr Louis Mayers?'

'Of course. I watch the news. I tried to contact him after he was nearly killed in that shooting at his practice. He flat-out refused my peace offering. There's a man who could hold a grudge.'

'And you know about his role in the Salisbury murders?'

'Yes.'

'And?'

'I was surprised.'

'Why?'

'Well, when you train to be a doctor, you want to help people, don't you? Mind you, he did always champion the idea of sacrifice in order to serve the greater good. That individuals are expendable in the search for the great truth. Maybe he started to believe his own hype?'

'We believe that whatever you told Mark Topham and Robert Brislane may have led them directly to Mayers,' Gardner said.

The colour drained from his face. 'You think that's why the detective disappeared?'

Before Gardner shattered the retired doctor with another comment, Yorke got his reassurances in. 'We don't know that, but if it was, you can be sure he was driven enough to find him anyway.'

'Yes, he did seem desperate ...' he looked down, and then up again. 'And the private investigator, is he okay?'

'I'm afraid not,' Gardner said.

Lancer gulped.

Shit, Gardner, not again, Yorke thought.

'But, it had nothing to do with Mayers.' Gardner said. 'We have the killer, and it's unrelated.'

Yorke said, 'The reason we're here, Dr Lancer, is because you may be able to help us put everything right. It is possible that something you told these two men revealed the whereabouts of Louis Mayers.'

'But that's impossible because I don't know where he is.'

'I understand that, but maybe there's something in your history together, something in your friendship.'

'Okay, I understand. We met at Oxford University. You want me to start there?'

'As good a place as any,' Yorke said.

BOTH THE CONDUIT and Alan came to Saskia's bedside when she started moaning that morning.

Her face was bandaged. There were patches of blood blooming on the bandages. She would need her dressing changing soon. Tiny, quivering eyes peered out between swathes of cloth.

Alan knelt, took Saskia's hand, and gently soothed her with a hush. Meanwhile, the Conduit knelt too, and gave her a shot of morphine.

Saskia's eyes stilled and glazed over.

'Are you ready for his next session?' The Conduit said, standing up.

Alan tilted his head back and looked up at him. 'Will she not be in too much pain?'

'The morphine will help. You did some good work yesterday, Alan. I would not like to see it go to waste.'

'I'm ready then.'

The Conduit felt a rare moment of sadness. He would miss Alan when he was gone.

But they all had to go eventually - that was the name of the game.

Still … four days … just didn't seem very long at all.

FREDERICK LANCER's tale was long, and Yorke's fingers burned from taking notes.

"Thick as thieves" was not a strong enough idiom to describe the friendship between the two psychiatrists. At university, and early in their professional careers, these two had been completely inseparable.

But the divide did come.

'It was strange. He went to bed one night and woke up with a whole different belief system. I won't indulge myself by exploring the complexities of his beliefs except to say that our conventional approach to therapy, our *scientific* based approach, CBT, just wasn't enough for him anymore. He no longer wanted to modify thoughts regarding poor sleep, such as *if I don't sleep well, I'll get ill; I'll never sleep again; I cannot sleep without medication.* So, he wrote this book on building a new sleep cycle which allows the patient to retain maladaptive thoughts. Ridiculous, I know! So, alas, our relationship went in different directions. Earlier in our relationship, we'd vowed never to let this happen. Our favourite book was Jekyll and Hyde. Read it?'

Yorke shook his head. 'No, but I know what it's about.'

'Well … Jekyll's approach to science is mystical, almost supernatural; while his close friend Dr Lanyon's approach is grounded in what was observable and measurable, i.e. real science. It drives a wedge between them. We vowed never to allow that to happen to us. To let radically different approaches destroy our relationship. However, we failed in our plan. Dr Jekyll and Mr Hyde, eh? Quite fitting when you think about what Louis has become. A monster.' At first, Lancer looked proud of his analogy, but then his expression quickly turned forlorn again.

Yorke flicked back through his notebook. This was a lot to consider, but he still felt there was something significant missing. Topham and Robert would have both heard something that sent their minds racing and pointed them quickly in the next direction.

Knowing that Lancer's recount was quickly coming to an end, he tried other questions and ideas to stimulate him into revealing more. 'Can you think of any connection to Leeds?'

'When I first met him, he loved rugby. Used to support Leeds Rhinos. Bloody passionate. Even used to drag me along to the games.'

Yorke wrote it down. Topham and Robert could have headed down to some home games to look for Mayers. He pictured them flashing around a photograph to the fans. He made a note to contact Rosset immediately and get officers, armed with photographs, down to the stadium to speak to staff.

It was the best they had so far, and potentially, the route by which Topham and Robert had travelled.

The interview ran its course. At the door, Yorke thanked him.

'It's funny though. His life could so easily have gone in a totally different direction,' Lancer said.

'How so?' Yorke said, still in the process of shaking Lancer's hand.

'Well, when I first met him, he didn't actually want to be a psychiatrist. He wanted to be a teacher. He had this romantic belief in helping young people achieve their potential when their minds were most open to influence. Our relationship led him to psychiatry, so in a way, maybe all this is partly my fault. If he'd never have met me, he may have ended up helping rather than destroying.'

'I guess ambitions change,' Yorke said. 'I wouldn't hold yourself responsible.'

'Yes, but his ambition never really did change. I remember him telling me once, much later in his life, that he regretted his decision. He started to look into lecturing. I don't know if it ever went anywhere.'

As they approached the car, Gardner said. 'A lecturer, eh? Jesus, that'd have been bad news. Imagine letting that monster loose on young minds.'

Yorke stopped. Gardner did too.

'It makes sense now.'

'What does?'

'The photograph of Mark that you found. Where he was sitting.'

'Leeds University?'

'Yes. Don't you see? Mark was looking for him. He suspected Mayers was lecturing.'

'Surely he isn't?' Gardner said.

'I don't know. I hope not. I'll get in touch with Rosset. With the Leeds Rhinos angle, and this, we have a fair bit of work for them to do.'

WHEN LACEY RAY was led into Dr Stewart Holden's office, she managed, as always, a quick glance at her reflection in his window. She winked at herself, admiring the tattooed jaguar on her neck peering out from beneath her lengthening hair.

A large guard forced her into the chair and chained her hands to the table.

Holden looked up at the guard and nodded at him.

'Do you want to be alone with me, Doctor?' Lacey said. 'Is that correct procedure? Aren't you putting yourself in jeopardy?'

The guard left the room.

'You're no danger to me, Lacey.' Holden looked down and made some notes. His glasses slid to the end of his nose.

Lacey laughed. 'Forgive my laughing, but no one else has ever said that to me before!'

Holden looked up, pushed his glasses back and smiled. Middle-aged wrinkles clotted around his eyes. 'I think I said that last time and, if I remember correctly, the time before too.'

'I said *"no one else"*, I didn't say *"no one"*.' She took a deep breath. 'I have a request to make.'

'Go on.'

'A new doctor.'

'Why?'

'I want one that doesn't spy on me.'

Holden stopped smiling. He rubbed his stubble. She could hear the scratching sound. 'Lacey, it has been a week since we last spoke. How've you been?'

'Fantastic. I went for a walk along the beach and stopped in at a wine bar with some old friends.'

Holden nodded. 'We get an hour a week. If you don't want the support offered to you, then it really does not bother me.'

Lacey leaned forward in her chair. 'Now, now, Doctor

... let's not pretend! You're fascinated by me. Dare I say, besotted? You'd sit here and listen to my nonsense all day long if you could. I see you at my door most evenings, or rather, I *see* that little eye.'

Holden sat upright and adjusted his slipping glasses again. 'That's ridiculous.'

Lacey couldn't move her hands freely from where they were locked down to the table, but she could raise an index finger. 'Don't speak for a moment. Be silent and listen.'

'Why?'

'Indulge me ... There it is!'

'There's what?'

'The distinctive whistle of the air through a bent septum. Did you break your nose when you were younger?'

Holden glowed.

'If I listen really carefully when you're at my door, I hear that same noise.'

'Most people make a noise when they breathe.'

'Except your sound is unmistakable! I've heard it every night at my door for seven weeks. And, every night since you began your perverted observations, I've taken you into my *Blue Room*.'

Holden's eyes widened and he started to take notes again.

'I've told you many things about my Blue Room, Doctor. I've told you it physically mirrors the world that I am meditating in apart from the colour, which is, as the name suggests, blue. The darkest blue you can imagine. It is also very cold in there. Ever so cold. Did I also tell you that it was a place of judgement?'

Holden nodded. 'You did. So, you are saying that I need to face judgement?'

'We all need to face judgement … just some sooner than others.'

Holden chewed his bottom lip for a moment before replying. 'Lacey, we do not need to discuss your diagnosis again. You're more than aware of what malignant narcissism entails. To be mindful of it is the main approach in our strategy. Right now, you're attempting to control the conversation. You're trying to intimidate and strike fear into me—'

'And is it working?'

'To recognise your thirst for attention and your feelings of supremacy is the cornerstone of the treatment.'

'I already do recognise them! In fact, I positively fucking revel in them.'

Holden nodded and made some notes. 'And the medication? We increased your dosage three weeks ago. You are seeing no reduction in obsessional thoughts and delusions?'

'You might as well unchain me now, so we can run around this table again … and again. Do you like being stuck in a circle? That's one of the reasons I decided to take you into the Blue Room. It just cannot go on like this forever.'

'But it can, Lacey, you can be in this institution forever.'

'I left this institution a long time ago, and I took you with me. We went into a place that has no limits. Would you like to hear what happened there?'

He wouldn't be able to resist. Incessant curiosity was part of his nature. That's why he watched her through that peephole every evening.

'I'm offering you the chance to really look in now. Come away from the door, and the peephole you cower behind, step inside a world that you fantasise about seeing.'

'Okay.'

'Good. Come this way. Close your eyes if you will. No? Okay ... I understand. We all start somewhere. After all, in its infancy, the Blue Room wasn't what it is now ... You came in one night, Doctor. You came from behind your barrier, and you came to me in my room while I slept. You came with intentions not just to understand me, but to *know* me in every way you could. To dominate me. To show me, what we both already know, that you too are a narcissist. But the worst possible kind. One that skulks and hides away in the shadows ready to bend people to your will. I know another doctor like you, but he doesn't skulk, he rejoices in his grandeur, while you scurry around in the dirt with the other rats, feeding and shitting, and waiting for vulnerability. So, you stood over me in my sleep, and started to undo your belt, except you underestimated me, and when I showed you my capabilities, and rose up to hit you over and over, you scuttled to the corner like a cockroach. I could've squashed you there and then, but instead I decided to spend some time with you. A long time. Days, possibly weeks, if you could endure that much suffering. I've read many of my reports. I know you all think that I have little regard for human life, but you are wrong. I care deeply for human life. It can be so glorious. But you are not the glory, Doctor, neither are many of the others who have been unfortunate enough to come into my Blue Room. To preserve the garden, you have to pick out the weeds. But I offered you something, when I tied you up in the cell, something that you never offered to me when you incarcerated me here. I offered you free will. The ability to make your own decisions. So, on that first day, I gave you a choice. I showed you my secateurs and asked you to choose between a finger and your eyes. That is more freedom than I've ever been afforded by you. You chose your finger. The next day, I gave you the same choice. Again, you wriggled a finger for my blade. This continued for many days, and although you grew weaker and paler, you retained your sense of self. I fed you painkillers to help with the discomfort and you actually started to thank me for them! The free will I afforded you made you feel like a human being, so you continued to behave like one. You engaged me in conversation, you talked about your family, your hopes and dreams. You even laughed at one point. But, then, one day, you ran out of fingers. Alas, there was no more free will, and I cut out your eyes. The change in you was sudden. You could argue that it was the blindness, but it was more than that. You became forlorn, beaten, and distraught. You begged me for death, over and over. To the extent that I almost gave it to you just for some peace and quiet. I told you that this was the effect of taking away freedom, choice, and our own sense of self, but you struggled to comprehend this, instead becoming more and more like an animal with every passing day. There you still are, Doctor, in my Blue Room, and there you will stay as my prisoner.'

Holden was pale as he frantically made notes. 'The medicine really should be helping with these delusions ... I'm going to increase the dosage further.'

'I have another choice for you to make now, Doctor.'

'I'm not playing your games.'

'Milo A Russey has been writing to me for months.'

Holden ignored her, and continued to make notes.

'Milo A Russey is an anagram for Louis Mayers.'

Holden stopped writing.

'That got your attention! Here's your choice, Doctor. I need you to make a phone call. You make the phone call and you can have my letters, which you can take anyway I guess ...'

He looked up at her.

'So as an added bonus, I'll resist the urge to make what happened in the Blue Room a beautiful reality.'

16

G ARDNER HAD PARKED her irritating trip down memory lane following the interview with Lancer. So, after Yorke had placed a call on his car speakerphone to Rosset to get him onto the Leeds Rhinos angle, he welcomed the silence in which to think.

Unfortunately, this was short-lived.

'What are you thinking about?' Gardner asked. A line of inquiry which always cut short the constructive thinking process!

His scathing retort never found airtime because Rosset rang him back. 'No home games for the Rhinos for a while, I'm afraid. I've got someone contacting all staff with our modified photograph of Mayers. I'll let you know if we get a hit.'

Yorke thanked him and hung up.

Gardner said, 'Is it worth emailing all season ticket holders with an image of Mayers? If he does go to the Rhinos' games, someone has to sit next to him.'

'And if Mayers receives the email himself under his new identity?'

'He gets spooked and runs.' Gardner opened Yorke's glove compartment and took out her tic tacs.

Yorke realised that the two of them were practically living out of each other's pockets. 'It's still an option though when we exhaust all of the other options,' Yorke said.

'All of the other options?'

'Yes … the ones I was working on before you interrupted my thought processes.'

They chewed through a large chunk of the journey in this 'thoughtful' silence before Yorke voiced the narrative. 'So, Mark was drawn to Leeds because he discovered Mayers' interest in the Rhinos. While there, Mark started to suspect that Mayers had undergone an identity change and was lecturing. Because Robert also saw Lancer, he ended up on the same path, and sighted Mark outside the University of Leeds and contacted you. Unfortunately, he never managed a face-to-face with Mark because the incident with his wife got in the way. Agree, so far?'

'Yes,' Emma said.

They were interrupted by another call. This time by an unknown number. Yorke moved into the fast lane to overtake someone hogging the middle lane and answered. 'DCI Yorke?'

'Yes. Who is this please?'

'My name is Dr Stewart Holden. We've never spoken before, but I work at the Princeholm psychiatric hospital in Bristol.'

Yorke's blood ran cold. He only knew of one patient. He glanced at Gardner, whose eyes were as wide as his.

'It's about Lacey Ray.'

There was the confirmation. Feeling the surge of adrenaline, Yorke asked for a moment to move across into the slow lane and reduce his speed. 'Go on.'

'She's asked me to call you. Normally, I don't indulge patients' whims, but this seemed rather important. She wanted me to read this to you, and then tell you how she can help with the current situation.'

'Current situation?'

'The search for Louis Mayers, the doctor responsible for the massacre at *Rose Hill*.'

Yorke indicated off onto the hard shoulder, stopped and hit the hazards. He took a deep breath and listened.

'Dear Lacey, I want to introduce today's letter by reflecting on the process of regeneration. The human body's remarkable capacity to heal itself has always been of great interest to me. Take the liver, for example. If part is lost through disease, it can grow back to its original size. I know my own father wasn't thinking about these regenerative properties when he drove himself into an early grave with his single malts, but I digress, the point is, our bodies can, if we allow, heal themselves. Yet, even when the body regenerates, it can never be truly the same as it was before. Did you know that the liver can heal to the same size, but not to the same shape? Now, consider the mind, my dear Lacey. It too can be destroyed, torn, figuratively, to pieces, and then the process of regeneration can begin. Many of my peers would rather allow those maladaptive thoughts to fester in one's conscious and unconscious minds like a cancer, debilitating the host. But my alternative, to allow those thoughts to overwhelm and destroy the mind, is the true path to healing. Destroy the mind. Then, rebuild. Regenerate. *They* say you destroy, Lacey. But do *they* ever mention what you have built? What you have regenerated? You cleanse the world of its scourges, Lacey, by destroying, and then you allow it to grow, newer, and healthier.'

Holden stopped reading. Yorke opened his mouth to

speak, but his mind fell momentarily blank. He glanced at Gardner. Judging by her expression, the letter had been just as jarring to her.

'DCI Yorke?' Holden said.

'I'm here.'

'That's what she wanted me to read to you.'

Two psychotics in conversation.

'Are her incoming letters not checked?' Yorke said.

'Yes, of course.'

'So, why did no one realise that Mayers was making contact?'

'He signed off with a different name.'

'Really? Isn't it clear as day that someone not of sound mind is making contact with your prisoner?'

'We like to refer to them as patients here, not prisoners ... we feel it aids the healing process.'

'You've not answered my question.' Yorke's car shook as a lorry streaked past.

'Do you know how many letters Lacey Ray receives?' Holden said.

'No.'

'Hundreds, Detective. Hundreds of letters. She's famous.'

'Jesus.' Yorke looked at Gardner again, who was shaking her head. 'She's a killer.'

'So, was Charles Manson, it didn't stop him being revered.'

'Do you read her fan mail?'

'Yes.'

'And?'

'She is a woman who takes pleasure out of murdering abusive men. Sadly, this has quite an appeal to many women in this country.'

'Did the letters from Mayers not stand out then because they were from a male?'

'No, she has a fair share of male fans too. Some men enjoy the idea of aggressive, dominant females. We are also inundated with visitor requests.'

'And?'

'We deny them all, based on the fact that she is in fragile mental health. We cannot control what will be said to her. At least with the letters, I can check them first.'

Not well enough obviously, Yorke thought.

'Are you keeping a record of all these fans?'

'Of course. We can share this information with you. They are mainly letters of adoration, and philosophical ramblings, like the one I just read you. If anyone claimed to be about to commit a crime, we would report it immediately.'

Yorke sighed. 'What else do you know about this situation?'

'She has given me all the letters from Mayers. Fourteen in total.'

'I need you to put them to one side for trace evidence.'

'I will do.'

'What do they say?'

'More of the above. He discusses identity, change, rebirth – many such similar themes.'

'Personal information? Location?'

'Nothing I could see.'

'Okay, we need to see them. I'll have an officer come to collect them in your area. They will bag up the evidence and scan it in for us to look at. Obviously, we need to speak to Lacey Ray – she may have an idea where Mayers is.'

'She will only speak to you, DCI Yorke.'

Yorke looked at the time. It was almost two, and he was

shattered from the four-hour round trip from Leeds to Llandudno. Bristol must have been another three-hour journey, but what choice did he have?

'Traffic permitting, I'll be there for around six.'

'We'll make the arrangements.'

As Yorke completed his return journey to Leeds, he checked in with Rosset. The Detective Chief Superintendent was starting to sound a lot perkier now. He was obviously getting over being kept in the dark regarding Yorke's search for Robert, and clearly appreciating the regular updates.

At the hotel, Yorke asked Gardner to stay focused on the University angle.

'I'll see how I feel after seeing Lacey,' Yorke said. 'If I'm too knackered to drive back, I'll book into a hotel there.'

Gardner nodded, and got out of the car. 'I know you don't, but I really think Mark is still alive.'

'I hope you're right, Emma.' He pointed at the communal glove compartment. 'Don't forget your tic tacs.'

OVER THE LAST HOUR, the moans had been persistent and loud.

Alan was no fool. He knew that Saskia needed a hospital. She'd practically taken her face off. If the pain didn't kill her, infection or sepsis was surely on the cards.

Dr Harris had his eyes closed on the sofa opposite him. It was common for the big man to do this when he was deep in thought. It wasn't advisable to interrupt him. These were the moments, *the only moments*, in which the psychiatrist could become snappy. It wasn't pleasant to see this sudden change in demeanour. Alan wondered how he was managing to endure Saskia's moan; maybe there was a rhythm to the sound of pain, rather like white noise.

Alan adjusted his seating position on the hard-backed chair in the corner of the lounge. He forced back his own groan as his curved spinal column was forced into a manoeuvre. He reached behind himself to ensure the thick cushion was in the small of the back where his spine curved drastically inward, offering little support for his upper body. The cushion took some of the weight and kept the aches at bay for a short time.

A sudden howl from Mark in the kitchen made him jump and the cushion fell away. Dr Harris' eyes snapped open.

Alan expected rage. Instead, the doctor rose to his feet, gave him a gentle nod and left the lounge.

He was just replacing the cushion in the small of his back when he heard a louder, more pained howl, which quickly subsided to a whimper. Harris spoke loudly to Mark, but Alan could not tell what was said.

Seconds later, Harris was back in the lounge, holding the two-metre pole with the pruning saw at the end. Its jagged teeth were wet with blood.

'It's only an hour since we fed him the leftovers from your gift yesterday.' Harris pulled a handkerchief from his pocket and cleaned the blood from the saw.

Alan could hear Mark crying.

'It's getting rather noisy in this house. I can barely think.' Harris sighed. 'The trouble is, I worry that if I give Saskia any more morphine it may kill her.'

As Harris thought about it, Saskia's moaning continued, and Mark's crying worsened. 'Back shortly.' He took his trusty pruning saw with him.

Saskia fell silent. Moments later, so did Mark. Harris must have decided to give him some morphine too.

Harris returned with a small jewellery box, sat down, closed his eyes, and took a deep breath. 'Silence.' He then patted the sofa next to him. 'Alan, please come and sit.'

Alan obliged. While keeping his eyes closed, Harris passed the jewellery box over.

'I'm not one for sentiment, Alan, but when you showed me your mud figurines the other day, it made me realise that trinkets can have a powerful presence in our lives. So, for that enlightenment, my dear boy, I would like to offer you up some of my own memorabilia in return.'

Alan opened the box and looked at the three twisted lumps of metal. He looked up. Harris had opened his eyes and was now staring straight at him. 'The three that ended me.'

Alan reached into the box and moved the bullets into a line to try and give it some order. The misshapen nature of the metal disgusted him. It reminded him of his own body.

'You didn't die,' Alan said.

'Not physically, no. Alas, I was destined to keep this hulking, clumsy form.' He smirked. 'When my patients came in shooting that day, I felt what anyone else would feel. Mind-numbing fear. The kind that makes you climb under a table and shake with not a single clue of what to do. When they found me, I pleaded with them not to kill me, because that's what you do, isn't it? That's what everyone does.' His smile grew. 'If I'd known then, what I know now, I'd have told them to jolly well get on with it! When I opened my eyes in hospital, well ...' he paused and looked away.

'Well?'

'Do I need to go on? You've experienced it too. After

that Chinese businessman raped you and then fell to his death. It's not just the sudden change, is it? It's more a realisation of the change, that you are something more than just meat and matter, and the mind can take you beyond the limits imposed by it. Many people can have these defining moments. But they didn't know how to *realise* them, *harness* them, and then the change destroys them. Eddie? Mark? They just couldn't accept. They couldn't *realise*.'

'So, you made them realise?'

'Yes, but with Mark it was too late, and he had to be *reduced*.'

Harris looked down at his hands. 'It's sad that in these times of discovery we have to lose people, but that is how all innovation, and achievement comes about. People will not understand what I am doing until my discoveries are part of the unquestionable fabric of science. Until then, they will seek to stop me. Until then, we must learn and then eradicate any traces that may stop the progress.'

Harris stood and went over to the fireplace. He picked up a box and brought it over to Alan.

'Another trinket?' Alan took the box.

Harris shook his head. 'Tomorrow, we will begin the final part of your journey, Alan. I would like you to familiarise yourself with the contents of this box.'

He opened it.

'It is time for you to harness the great change you have experienced.'

Alan stroked the pistol inside.

17

'M OST PEOPLE BEGIN with a pleasantry, DCI Yorke. You could ask after my health or my happiness. You could *even* remark on how good I look.'

'That's not why I'm here, Lacey.'

'A shame. I really thought you'd appreciate my new hair. Took a while to grow out. I don't really miss the shaved head. It was rather boyish. And it showed too much of my tattoo. Made me look quite aggressive.'

Yorke couldn't resist a sardonic grin. 'A gentle creature such as yourself?'

Lacey returned the smile. 'How's Jake?'

'Let's stick to why I'm here.'

'Dr Louis Mayers ... yes, he's quite a card, isn't he?'

Yorke looked around Dr Stewart Holden's office. At first Yorke had thought that Holden had been very hospitable by allowing him use of his office at short notice. But, after arriving, Yorke had realised that the good doctor had only offered the room so he could hang around and rubberneck. Yorke had quickly sent him packing, leaving him alone with Lacey and one guard. The guard had also wanted to stay, but Yorke had repeatedly pointed out the unbreakable chains around Lacey's wrists, until the guard had relented and given them some breathing space.

'I've had a long day. A lot of driving. I know how you love to beat around the bush, but could we please get right down to it? Why is Mayers writing to you?'

'I'll forgive your tone of voice. You're clearly fatigued. But, if you recall, it was me that reached out to you. Some gratitude would be nice.'

Yorke nodded to pacify her. *Don't try to pretend that you asked me here out of the goodness of your heart, Lacey. What do you want?*

'Why is he writing, Lacey?' he asked again.

'He admires me.'

'It seems a lot of people admire you. I've heard about the fan mail. It must really feed your narcissism.'

Lacey smiled. 'Well, it gives me something to do. I try to write back.'

'But not to Mayers?'

'You should already be aware that the doctor is not providing an address.'

'Yet, you claim to be able to help?'

Lacey nodded. 'I know how to find him.'

'Please share.'

'Maybe.'

'Why the games? Are you trying to protect him?'

'Don't be silly. He fits my MO perfectly, doesn't he? Remember Susie Long, the innocent young girl he brainwashed into killing your officer's boyfriend? Regardless of what Louis says, what he *claims*, he's just another monster. A monster I'd have no hesitation in putting down.'

Yorke nodded down at the chains that looped through

the table. 'Well, as that is not going to happen any time soon, you could just tell me what you do know, and I could bring him down for you.'

'You know, Michael, you always did talk common sense. So, so different from Jake. Boring, yes, but very sensible.' She winked. 'Don't take offence, but that was why I always did prefer Jake. He's so fucking edgy! What's he up to these days?'

'No offence taken, Lacey, but please refrain from using my first name. So, if I'm talking common sense, why not just tell me what I need to know?'

Lacey tutted, and turned her head from side to side as she spoke. 'Boring ... boring ... by-the-book ... Detective Chief Inspector Michael Yorke ...'

Yorke could feel himself becoming more agitated, but she wanted him to bite, so he forced himself not to. Instead, he looked at his watch. 'I'm becoming less and less convinced that you can be of any use. If you've only asked me here to bait me in some way, I'll take my chances, and go and study the letters. Try and work out where he is myself.'

'Don't be so touchy! You get results, don't you? Your approach works. The team player. The leader. That's what Jake respects in you. He wishes he could be just like you rather than the maverick. The impetuous outlaw. On the night he killed Simon Young, I saw that fire in his eyes. He's a born killer—'

'You killed Simon Young.'

'I did, did I? Have you bought into the lie too?'

He looked at his watch again. 'You have less than a minute to convince me to stay ...'

'I heard he killed again. I also heard he saved your life. How does it feel, Detective, to be indebted to everything you're not? A bent cop, a fugitive ... a killer?'

Yorke stood up to leave.

'Do you know why Mayers admires me? Because he thinks I'm just like him. I chose that letter that Dr Holden read to you for a reason. He believes that I destroy only to bring forth regeneration. I guess there is some truth to what he says. I pluck out the diseased cells, and the world around it flourishes. It is newer ... healthier.'

'Do you really believe that bullshit?'

'It doesn't matter what I believe. It's what *he* believes, and he will fail because of those beliefs.'

Yorke put the palms of his hands on the table. 'What do you mean?'

'He'll fail because he believes I have the capability to admire others and that I can be trusted. But you'll fail, Detective, because you believe that you'll find him with those letters. He sent eighteen letters in total. Holden has fourteen. I flushed four of the letters down the toilet – the ones that specifically told me where he was.'

Yorke leaned forward. 'Tell me, Lacey. Help me put an end to this madness. You said yourself that he was a monster. I know you would take some pleasure in seeing him fall.'

'Yes ... I probably would ... But that is not enough.'

'Do you want me to beg?'

Lacey smiled. 'Not enough.'

'*What do you want?*'

'One thing. It is non-negotiable. Yes, while you go away and ponder whether you can do what I'm about to ask in good conscience, Louis may strike again. Another care home may fall as a result of his murderous spells, or worse still, a school ... but, you see, I do not care, *Michael*, because there is only one thing left in this world I truly care about. Only one thing.'

'What?'

'My son Tobias. I just want to see Tobias again.'

Yorke could hardly believe his ears. 'Tobias Young?'

'*Ray*, Detective. Tobias *Ray*.'

IT WAS SNOWING HEAVILY, but when Patricia saw his car come into the driveway, she burst out the door, darted across the garden and, with her bare feet freezing in the snow, embraced Yorke.

When they kissed, it felt like they'd been apart for months, rather than days.

Yorke pulled away. 'Let's get inside. You're shivering.'

'This is the warmest I've felt all day. I've missed you. Why didn't you tell me you were coming home?'

'I didn't know myself. I was going to spend the night in Bristol. I've been driving all bloody day.'

'Why?'

'Let's get in first.'

Inside, Yorke was mobbed by Rosie the dog.

'Seems very pleased to see me, despite hardly knowing me.' Yorke knelt and stroked the cockapoo. Her tail wagged and she launched up. The long tongue swept over his face. He stood back up and wiped his face. 'I'm really not sure about that.'

'Takes some getting used to, I admit.'

'So, it's going to carry on? Bloody hell. How's the housetraining?'

'So, so.' Patricia pointed at the gate at the bottom of the stairs which shut off upstairs. 'Beatrice's stairgate has come in handy.'

'Good, because I'm looking forward to our own bed

tonight, and I don't want any surprises. How are the newly engaged couple?'

'At the cinema.'

'Good. Better than touring wedding venues.' He opened the lounge door. 'Do you think I'm boring?'

Patricia followed him into the lounge. 'What makes you ask that?'

'Ah, nothing really. Do you?' He turned back to face her. She noticed that he looked quite serious about the question.

'Well, earlier this year, we had a Russian hitman in our house, so I'd say life with you was anything but boring.'

'Not really the reassurance I was after.'

After Yorke had been upstairs to kiss Beatrice's sleeping face, Patricia gave him a pint of Summer Lightning, poured from a bottle.

After several long mouthfuls, he told her everything he'd experienced today, right up to Lacey's ultimatum.

'That boy has had enough,' Patricia said. 'How old is he now? Seven? I'm not sure he, or his mother for that matter, could cope with that. She abused him. Taught him to kill for pity's sake.'

'That's what I said to her.'

'And?'

'Well, her response was odd. Not what I expected at all.' Yorke took another mouthful of beer.

'Go on.'

'She started crying.'

'Crocodile tears.'

'Yes, I know, but it still took me by surprise. Then, she started to talk about regeneration again. In particular, change. All that stuff that Mayers had been spouting about in his letter. She claimed that Tobias had changed her. That she wasn't the same person anymore. That she could see outside herself now.'

'And?'

'And ... nothing. That was her demand. She wants to see Tobias again, or she won't tell us where Mayers is.'

'And you told her where to stick it?' Patricia turned Yorke's head to make eye contact.

Yorke pulled his head back. 'Of course!'

'Good.'

'Although, we are kind of desperate. Mayers is out there, and what he's managed to do with Rose Hill is truly frightening.'

'Don't you waver, Mike. We're talking about a seven year-old boy.'

'I know ... I know ...' Yorke had another mouthful. 'I'm going to look at those letters he sent her in jail. They'll be scanned in by now. I have to hope she was bluffing about the letters she destroyed, that the answer she claims to have found is still in those letters.'

Patricia sighed.

Yorke looked at her. 'Are you disappointed?'

'Why?'

'No reason ...'

'No, go on.'

'I think you were expecting us to spend some time together.'

She smiled. 'Yes ... but this is so important, I understand.'

'There's nothing I want more, Pat, than to be with you. That's why I came home ... It's just ...'

She put a finger to his lips, '... that there's a cold-hearted psychopath out there?'

'Yes.'

'So, stop thinking, and go and do what you need to.'

Yorke drank his beer quickly. Patricia could only imagine the anxiety her husband was currently enduring. She hoped the alcohol would soothe him. 'Are you okay?'

'I think so ... All this talk of change! I'm just wondering when it is my turn! I feel like I'm on a hamster wheel going around and around. No matter how many of them I stop, they always seem to keep on coming back, and each time, no matter how many times, I can't seem to satisfy this hunger to stop them.'

She held him tightly.

———

AFTERWARDS, as heavy winds flogged the night, Yorke sat by a small light in the office, reading Mayers' letters, wondering how one mind could become so twisted in on itself.

Then after that, he turned out the light, closed his eyes and listened to hailstones beat a cadence on his window and wondered how long it would be before he too was finally consumed by everything he'd seen and experienced.

And following this, Yorke fell asleep and dreamed of the woman he'd loved for so long, even after her death, and spoke her name out loud several times in the darkness.

Charlotte.

Charlotte.

Charlotte.

18

DECEMBER 29TH

GARDNER LIFTED HER head, rubbed sleep out of her eyes and looked down at her notes on the desk in front of her. She'd drooled on them and some of the words were smudged.

She went to the toilet, splashed water on her face until she felt like she could string a sentence together, and then returned to the desk to phone Yorke.

'Morning, Emma.'

'Jesus, Mike, you sound worse than me.'

'The world according to Louis Mayers didn't make for easy reading. I didn't sleep too well afterwards. I did make notes on the letters, but Lacey was right, I'm afraid, there was no indication of his whereabouts. I'll send the notes and the letters over this morning, so you can start looking over them yourself while I make my way back up.'

'You should get a train, Mike. You must be burned out.'

'I'll be fine when I get some caffeine in me. I have some Pro Plus in my car.'

She looked down at the empty packet by her own notes. 'You did. Sorry about that, Mike.'

'Well, I guess this is what happens when you practically live together. With no caffeine then, you'll have to wake me up with what you've found out.'

'Not a great amount, I'm afraid. I researched the universities. If Mayers had an ambition to lecture, then surely, he'd opt for his passion – Psychology? I can't see him at the University of Law or Leeds Art University, can you?'

'No.'

'So, the three universities offering Psychology are: Leeds Beckett, the University of Leeds and Leeds Trinity. I'm going to try and contact the admin departments today, but we are smack bang in the middle of the Christmas holidays, so I hold little hope. Using the internet, I researched the professors working in Psychology across the universities. Most of them had photographs online, so it was easy to whittle down the possibilities to three. Have you got a pen, Mike?'

'Yes.'

'Here are three male professors of Psychology, without online photographs, all in their mid-fifties.'

Gardner read them out and Yorke wrote them down.

'So, if you get their addresses from HQ, Mike, I could visit this morning?'

'Nice try, Emma. There is only one place these three names are going right now, and that's to Rosset. I'd have to be insane to let you go alone, when Rosset has that small army at his disposal.'

'Mike—'

'*Roles reversed?*'

Gardner sighed. 'I'd make the same decision.'

'Sit tight, Emma. Read Mayers' letters that I send to you. I'll text the password for the encrypted file.'

'Okay.'

'I shall be there in four hours or so. Try and get some sleep.'

'How's Patricia?'

'Patient, Emma.' Yorke sighed this time. 'God help me if she wasn't.'

ALAN PILED up the four beermats on the corner of the oak table and pushed the pint he wasn't really drinking to the other corner of the table. He then reached into his rucksack at his feet and pulled out his four Chinese Mud Men and a ruler. He lined them up, so they were exactly four centimetres apart. He wondered, briefly, what his collection would look like with the fifth fisherman holding the long spear if it hadn't been used in the murder of a Chinese businessman and sealed away in an evidence box.

As always, when staring at his figurines, he experienced a pleasant loss in time. When he did, eventually, pull himself from his reverie, he recalled that he was in the Campus pub – the *Old Bar*. It was the first time he'd been here. Watering holes aren't the best of destinations if you've no friends to drink with. Unless you were a drunkard, that is, but such an uneven, chaotic state of being repulsed him.

It was New Year's Eve. The shift from one year to the next represented order, so he saw the logic in their celebrations. He took a mouthful of craft ale and winced. He didn't, however, see the logic in poisoning the natural order of the body with this junk.

The music wasn't to his liking either. Anything involving singers in groups really jarred with him. He despised the clash of voices – male or female. A solo singer sat better with him, but no vocalist, and a simple electronic beat was best of all. Chaotic music was cluttered and made him flinch whereas a perfect cadence, fast or slow, soothed him.

The occupants of this bar, of which they were many, didn't seem to mind the chaos. Around the tables, they clustered in both small and large groups on this raised platform. Despite the cold weather outside, women opted for little clothing; men, at least, had some order by opting for similar attire. Dark jeans, shoes, and buttoned shirts.

On the lower platform, along the bar, students scurried like rats under a stinking alcoholic cloud.

As much as Alan tried to find order in the chaos around him, he knew there was very little. There was no other way, really, than *his* way. He pulled his rucksack onto his knee and placed a hand inside. It was up to him to restore order.

The music stopped. Time for the countdown.

Two young women stood behind his table, looking down at him. They both wore low-cut red dresses, and both had long blond hair. They could have been twins. It was a fleeting flash of order. A tease. An attempt, from a source unknown, to prevent the unpreventable ...

'Ten ... nine ...'

The countdown had begun. Alan didn't hear the next numbers because one of the pretty women was speaking, 'Can I see your figurines?'

'No,' Alan said.

'Six ...'

She swooped one off the table. Both women started to grin.

'Four ...'

'Why the bowtie, freak?'

'Two ...'

'Weirdo! I'm talking to—'

'*Happy New Year!*'

Alan shot the woman holding the figurine in her chin, and the lower half of her jaw swung loose.

The music to *Auld Lang Syne* flared up. Everyone around him, including the woman with the ruined face, started to sing, but the lyrics were different. They didn't match the music. It was the most extreme, grating example of disorder that Alan had ever experienced.

'*Alan Sants, wets his pants.*'

He stood up and shot the other woman point-blank in the forehead. She flew over the banister running alongside the raised platform.

'*Alan Sants, wets his pants.*'

He leaned forward and tore the woman-in-red's jaw from her face.

'*Alan Sants, Alan Sants.*'

He shot aimlessly into the crowd around him. People started to fall. No one screamed, they just continued to sing.

'*Alan Sants wets his pants.*'

He carried on killing, until he couldn't see for all the blood and bodies.

———

'ALAN?' The Conduit stroked his face. 'Alan?'

He bought him back gently. He was really starting to love this boy. More so than any who had gone before. Even Christian Severance.

Alan cried, but he smiled too. They weren't tears of happiness. They were more than that. So much more. They were tears of realisation.

The Conduit led him through to the kitchen and sat

him with his back to the dog, who was sleeping. He put a glass of water to his lips and let him drink. 'Not too fast.'

He took a sip and stopped crying. He looked up. 'Thank you, Conduit.'

'Don't thank me.'

'I saw how it could be. I saw *what* could be. Thank you for showing me.'

'You saw it. *You*, Alan. I didn't put it there. You did.'

'I love you.'

'I love you too.'

The Conduit pulled up a chair beside Alan. Alan leaned to his side, so his head rested on the doctor's lap.

As the doctor stroked his hair, he closed his eyes and sighed. Success came with a cost, and the loss of Alan would be the greatest yet. 'You'll burn for eternity, my dear boy.'

'Thank you, Conduit.'

'The idea of you, the memory of you, that is the fire that will always burn. I'm so proud of you.'

Alan didn't respond. He was already asleep on his lap.

The Conduit heard the rattle of a chain, and his dog's head appeared at his side. He licked the back of Alan's neck.

The Conduit took his hand from Alan's hair and stroked his dog's pitted scalp. 'Good dog.'

The dog nuzzled his master's hand.

———

YORKE WAS in the fast lane, and well into his journey back to Leeds when he received a call from Rosset. 'We know who he is, Mike.'

Yorke felt his adrenaline surge.

'The first two professors checked out just fine,' Rosset said. 'The third professor ... Dr Alexander Harris ... well, this is where it gets interesting. On record, in all the databases, Harris exists just fine. Where he was born in Cumbria, his parents, his education – right up to his employment at the University of Leeds as a Psychology professor. He is also a practising psychiatrist at a clinic near Roundhay. It was his passport photo which gave us an almighty shock.'

'It was Mayers, wasn't it?'

'Yes.'

'So, he's acquired a fictional identity. Not cheap. But it can be done.' Yorke thought of the shady syndicate dubbed *Article SE* by the South East Regional Organised Crime Unit. Its tentacles spread far and wide and tightened around many criminal enterprises throughout the South East of England. They were responsible for Yorke's experiences earlier this year. He wouldn't be at all surprised if they were responsible for knocking together fictional identities for the right fee.

'What's his address?'

'Again fictional. He lives on eighty-two Edgemont Drive. Edgemont Drive stops at 80.'

'So where does the University and the psychiatry practice send his employment correspondence?'

'He has a Post Office Box in a Royal Mail sorting office.'

'Have you been?'

'Yes, with a warrant. There's a large build-up of correspondence. He hasn't been there in a few months, so none of the staff we spoke to can recall him.'

'What about other mail? Junk mail? Election information? What happens when the postman realises eighty-two doesn't exist?'

'Harris redirects *all* his mail to the PO box. Nobody has any cause to look for the missing house.'

'But if this house is registered to Harris on the electoral register, he can vote?'

'Yes. It's a solid identity as I said.'

'Your thoughts?' Yorke said.

'I've got many,' Rosset said. 'Where do I start? Other than it begins with a lot of officers. The University of Leeds is about to get a surprise when it's asked to open its doors for Christmas. We need to pull apart their CCTV and try to get a starting point. We need to speak to all his colleagues, and his students. He's been coming and going from the University daily. Someone will know something. Your take?'

'I'm not suggesting you don't throw a lot at this, sir. But I'm playing devil's advocate when I say that if we go in hard now, then he may get wind and then we won't be able to collar him when the university reopens in January.'

'So, what do we do, Mike, drag our heels and wait for another of Dr Death's patients to open fire in a confined area?'

Yorke bit his bottom lip and took a deep breath through his nose. Rosset was clearly fired up, and his nerves were worn. Yorke empathised. In fact, after glancing at his speedometer dancing around 90, he realised he was just as charged up.

'No, sir ... I'm just suggesting a more measured approach. We *know* who he is. So, right now, it feels like we've almost got him. That we have one hand on his shoulder. But we don't. Without knowing where he is, we're playing with false confidence, and the only thing we can say with any certainty right now is, if he runs again, we know he can change his identity. Then where are we? Back at square one.'

'I need you here, Mike. You're part of this team. I want you involved in the game plan.'

'I'll be there within an hour.'

It was early evening. Yorke and Gardner were swilling their third pints of northern swamp juice. On another occasion, Yorke would've admitted he was starting to enjoy it and, as with all good beers, it just took a while to fully acquire the taste. He was in no mood to discuss beer though, only to drink it.

It took most of the three pints to go through Rosset's plan of action which, in the early afternoon, had already started firing on all cylinders.

'And you were there? It doesn't sound like any plan of action you'd be involved in!'

Yorke swallowed a mouthful of beer. 'It seems the subtle approach is a collection of dirty words up here. The station practically turned into a call centre, and every employee of the university, *including the canteen staff*, were dragged kicking and screaming from their Christmas celebrations.'

'Jesus. Is Rosset not worried about the press getting involved?'

'They're trying to gag them as we speak.'

'That never really went well for us in the past.'

'On deaf ears, Emma.'

'Louis Mayers won't be back.'

'Again, on deaf ears. They seem to think he'll walk right back into their hands.'

'The man is a ghost.'

'Guess what I'm going to say?'

'Something involving ears?' Gardner finished her pint. 'What about the Lacey Ray situation?'

'I can't even begin to imagine the process involved in getting a seven year-old boy in a high-security psychiatric hospital, never mind in front of an infamous serial killer.'

'I can't imagine there is one.'

'Precisely. She was adamant that she wasn't giving up anything without seeing him.'

'Is it worth another run at it?

'Maybe in a couple of days when Rosset's gung ho approach crashes and burns.'

'You look knackered, Mike.'

'Yep. At least I got to see Patricia last night. These round trips around England are a nightmare. It doesn't help that it's *here*. I never thought I'd get to this neck of the woods again. A lot of bad memories here.' *And good ones*, he thought, *depending on which way you look at it.*

'Because of your best friend, Brandon. The one that died?'

'Among other things.' He finished his pint. 'I think we should head to bed now, Emma, the bar is calling me, and with what we've got on, I don't think that'd be such a good idea.'

'Mike, after our last conversation here, I did some research on the internet. I know what happened to you while you were at university ... I'm sorry.'

Yorke took a deep breath. He wasn't at all surprised. He'd given a lot away in the last conversation. She was ex-police after all, and she wouldn't have gone to sleep on a mystery like that.

'Are you angry with me?'

'No. I'd have done the same. I'm at fault for drinking too much and letting too much go.'

'Why are you at fault, Mike? Why's it so wrong for you to talk about these things? You did nothing wrong.'

'Not spotting something clear and obvious in front of me before people died is considered wrong in my book.'

'You were in love.'

'Not an excuse.'

Gardner leaned over the table and put her hand on his. 'You were also a kid. Does Patricia know?'

'Yes. No secrets. We work in a world of secrets ... we don't want them at home.'

Having lied, he looked away. Patricia had kept secrets from him, after all. Her father, Douglas Firth, had been mixed up with organised crime, and she'd almost died in a car accident as a result of that. It was a secret that had come to light earlier this year. A bloody revelation that had wreaked brutal havoc on their lives. But that was it now. No more secrets. She'd promised him, and he believed her.

Yorke pulled his hand away from Gardner's. 'This is long in the past. Over half my life ago. I'm a different person now. Also, it's not relevant to our current situation.'

Gardner nodded. Her expression was full of sympathy.

'I'm exhausted,' Yorke said. 'And need an early night. Me and you start early. We need to find Mayers before he gets wind of the manhunt Rosset is leading. Are you in?'

'You need to ask?'

'So, no distractions?'

'No distractions.'

LACEY ALWAYS DREAMED VIVIDLY, and often woke up disorientated. It took her a few moments to realise that she was still in her cell, or her 'Convalescence Room' as the founders of Princeholm hospital termed it, and that something was wrong.

Very wrong indeed.

When she tried to lift her head from her pillow, and couldn't, it dawned on her that she was paralysed. Not one to hit the panic button, Lacey simply considered why this might be. She'd heard of sleep paralysis, so it could potentially be this, which meant movement could be restored any second. Of course, there was the more serious possibility of a stroke, and if the damage was permanent, locked-in syndrome. But there was *still* no panic. If necessary, she possessed the capabilities to retreat inside herself, and live out the rest of her natural life in her Blue Room.

Her eyes were working, so she scanned her Convalescence Room. The lights were dimmed in the evening, and only a slight glow slithered through a strip above her door—

Her eyes fell to the man sitting in the corner of her room.

Again, no panic. It wasn't in her nature. But knowing that this predicament couldn't be good, she did try to move again.

Nothing.

She wasn't able to speak, but did manage to produce a groaning sound, which at least gave her some indication that some parts of her were still working.

'You are conscious then, Lacey?' It was Dr Stewart Holden. 'I'm sure you're not panicking, but if you are, I'd like to reassure you that this condition is temporary. I've given you a combination of drugs, one of which is a neuromuscular-blocking agent. It prevents nerve impulse transmission. There's a risk of respiratory failure, which is why I've been keeping an eye on you and have brought some equipment.' He pointed down at the duffel bag at his feet. 'I'd like you to know that you'll not die tonight because I don't fear you reporting me.' He rose to his feet. 'There'd be no fun in that for you, Lacey. No fun at all. You've already told me of your intentions to trap me in your Blue Room. So, I see no reason why you'd deviate from your original plan regardless of what comes to pass in this room tonight.'

He walked over to the bed. The ration of light from the corridor outside accentuated the sharp, bony angles of his face. He looked down at her. Lacey expected him to smile, to revel in his new-found dominance. Instead, he stroked her face.

She *felt* it and tried to move away but remained frozen.

'You'll realise now that some sensation remains.' His hand moved into her hair.

She considered retreating into her Blue Room, but then she would miss out on Holden's play. She wanted to know his intentions, because that would fuel what would come later. And there would be a later. *Of that, Dr Holden, you can be sure.*

'I'm a narcissist just like you, and I wish to dominate, as I'm doing right now. But you knew that, didn't you? It's easy to recognise kindred spirits. One of your suggestions riled me, and it brought me to your door this evening. What did you call me? A rat scurrying in the dirt, feeding and shitting, and waiting for vulnerability?' He pointed at his belt. 'Didn't you describe me undoing this? Preparing myself to fuck you? You think I would soil myself with your juices,

Lacey?' He took his hand from her hair and stepped back. 'And then, what came next? A cockroach, I believe? Scuttling in the corner, kept alive to endure your sadistic ways?' He smiled for the first time. 'You said I underestimated you. Do you think it's now possible that you underestimated me?

'You planned to offer me free will in your Blue Room, so in the interests of fairness, I'm going to offer you the same. As you cannot speak, I'll ask you to move your eyes. Tonight, I prepared my resignation letter, effective immediately. I am financially secure enough to walk away from this job. Your choice is this. Blink once if you want me to resign. Then, you'll never have to see me again. Sounds like a dream come true for a victim, doesn't it? I'm offering to walk out of your life forever. Never to be seen again, never to be taken into your Blue Room. Now for the second choice. Blink twice, if you want to endure what I've brought with me tonight.' He pointed at the door. 'Outside this room.'

Lacey knew that what awaited her behind that door would be particularly nasty, but the prospect of her losing her grip on Holden and never having her special time with him? That was something she *could never* endure. She blinked twice.

'Predictable,' Holden said.

She wanted to say, '*Predictable* will be the first word I carve into your chest.' Instead, she moved her eyes to the door to see where the decision had taken her.

Holden left her bedside and went to open the door.

The tall guard who'd escorted her to the office yesterday for her meeting with DCI Yorke came into the room. This hulking meat sack usually swaggered around the hospital full of confidence. In this moment, he looked nervous. As he came into the room, he looked back and forth between Holden and Lacey several times. Holden closed the door behind the guard and sat back in his seat in the corner.

The guard approached Lacey's bed and then looked back at Holden again. 'Do you have to stay?'

'Would I really put you off?'

'Maybe.'

'Judging by your red face, Stan, you've taken the tablet I gave you. There'll be no problems.'

Stan turned back, took Lacey's blanket and pulled it off. She felt the cold air settle on her. It would be nice if that was a sign that the paralysis was going to rapidly alleviate and allow her movement, but she knew that was wishful thinking.

As Stan slipped her pyjama bottoms off, she realised that she still had an option. The Blue Room had always been a good place to retreat when she was having sex with repulsive clients back in her days as an escort, and tonight, it could offer the same sanctuary. She could easily disappear, and when she came back, Stan would be long gone. But there was a cost. Not experiencing what Dr Holden was subjecting her to would be a wasted opportunity to fuel the fire, and the more intensely that fire burned, the more pleasure she would derive when her turn finally came with the doctor.

Seeing Stan take off his trousers, slide on a condom, and then lubricate himself with Vaseline, was particularly disgusting, but it only served to make her more resolute. Her eyes moved to Dr Holden's. He sat in the corner with his arms folded, smiling. She thought about the choice she would offer him between his eyes and fingers, and how much joy would come from his decisions. Then, Holden was blocked from view as Stan clumsily mounted her.

She made eye-contact with the pulpy mass of filth as he drove inside her. She hoped the creature could read the intentions in her eyes as he raped her and see the fate that awaited him too. The sweat running into his eyes made him blink, and he broke eye-contact, lowered his face, and increased his tempo. She turned her eyes to Holden's smiling face. He would know that despite incapacitating her, he'd left her capable of some sensation. He *knew* she would be feeling every single one of this pig's vicious thrusts. As the pain intensified, she made the only noise she was capable of. A deep, *hollow* groan.

She fought a growing urge to take a break in her Blue Room. She'd chosen blue because she was a fan of Chinese methods. They use blue light to soothe illnesses and treat pain.

Another Chinese method she was a fan of was Lingchi. One day, she would subject the meat sack on top of her to death by a thousand cuts. She tried to smile; whether it actually materialised on her paralysed face, she wasn't sure. After ejaculating, Stan climbed from her. Now empty of his sexual drive, he looked apologetic. Without removing the condom, he hoisted his trousers up.

Again, Lacey wanted to smile. *For putting yourself inside me, you will apologise after each and every cut. Your last words on this earth will be a thousand apologies.* She watched Dr Holden stand. *Whereas you, Doctor, won't be able to apologise, because I'm going to reach down your throat and tear out your vocal cords.*

Holden opened the door. 'You can leave now, Stan.'

Stan skulked towards the door, still fastening his belt. Lacey noticed him duck slightly as he exited to avoid clipping the top of his head.

Holden closed the door and laughed. 'He feels guilt

now, Lacey, but give him a day to recharge, and his uncontrollable and dysfunctional drives will return. But hey, who are we to judge? Aren't we all victims of our drives? In your fantasy, you were going to offer me the same painful choice every day. I, now, will repay your graciousness. Every night, I'll come back to your room with Stan and offer you the same choice I gave you today.'

He opened the door to leave. He paused in the doorway for a moment and then turned back. 'Every night until you beg me for death.'

He left and closed the door.

How nice of you, Doctor, Lacey thought, *to take time out of your busy schedule to play a little game with me ...*

19

DECEMBER 30TH

CHARLOTTE WHISPERED HER goodbyes, took a step out into the empty air, seemingly hovered for a moment as if to defy gravity, and then disappeared. Yorke, who had reached out merely a moment ago, closed his fist around emptiness, shut his eyes, and listened for the final sound of her existence. He heard nothing. Maybe he was too high up to hear anything? Maybe he was in shock? He took a deep breath, tried to recover control of himself, and then the screaming from below began. He could hear that alright. The sound of those poor people stumbling across the incomprehensible. He clamped his hands to his ears; he bit his bottom lip to hold in his own screams and he ran back over the rooftop to the fire door. How could you do that? How could anyone do that? Of course he knew the answers to these questions already, and all the subsequent questions which came like swift bee-stings. He knew because he'd seen the answers in those eyes. In the emptiness, in the blackness, in the hollowness of those eyes. But how had I not seen those answers before this moment? They always tell me how sharp I am. How keen my eye is for detail. Detail. The devil is in the detail. Below the animal-like screams intensified. They were looking for their own answers through a guttural cry of distress and disgust. Finally, away from the screams and through the fire door, Yorke slid to the floor. He fought back tears. Gone. A brief candle. A mere flicker of eighteen years. Extinguished forever. He couldn't fight back the tears much longer. They came in full force and he bled his heart out at the top of the stairwell ...

... Yorke sat up in the hotel bed, and let the duvet fall away from his damp body. He reached over to his bedside table for his glass of water and drank it all. Naked, he climbed out of bed, and went into the bathroom. His eyes were puffy, and he wondered if he'd been crying in his sleep. Tracing his damaged face in his reflection, he thought of Borya with his boxcutter. He thought of Lewis, Terrence, Christian and all the other monsters who'd crawled out from the heart of darkness.

He thought of Charlotte.

Thought of their intimacy, their bond, their love.

A lie. She'd felt nothing. She hadn't been capable. She'd told him so before she'd left this world.

He loved Patricia, but never had he loved so passionately, so *devastatingly*, as he'd loved Charlotte.

And she'd been another monster like all those other monsters. Reginald, Mayers, Lacey.

Yet, he still wanted to see her again. Look on her beautiful face. Those feelings never went away. Ah, just to see her, just the once ...

He went through to the desk, logged on to his laptop, and typed her full name into the search bar. The first hit ...

Killer student falls four floors to her death. Suspected suicide.

He clicked. There was a picture of the building on the university campus. The building he'd been standing on in his dream, minutes ago, and for real in 1994.

There was a picture of her in a cocktail dress at their halls of residence for the *Boddington Hall Valentine ball*. It had been one of their first dates. They'd kissed all night.

He traced her face. Young, beautiful, seemingly innocent. Then he closed the laptop. He'd just wanted to see her. Just remember her for a moment. Now, he could feel himself coming back to reality. Patricia was the person he loved now. Charlotte was a different time, and he'd been a very different person...

Lacey Ray. *'My son ... Tobias ... I just want to see Tobias again.'*

Could this have been all Lacey wanted?

To see?

Would a photograph suffice?

It took several phone calls, but Yorke was able to get the phone details for Jane Young. The first part of their conversation was predictably explosive. She recognised Yorke's name and, even though he was not at fault, she associated him with the darkest times in her life. The kidnapping of her son by Lacey Ray, and the murder of her husband, Simon Young, by the same person. She wasn't impressed by Yorke's request for a recent photograph.

'He's still broken, you know.'

'I'm sorry to hear that, Mrs Young.'

'Do you have children?'

'Yes.'

'Do they respond when you talk to them? Do they look you in the eyes?'

'Yes, Mrs Young, they do.'

'Do they become excited when they're happy? Do they cry when they're sad?'

'Yes.'

'So, can you even begin to understand how insulting this request is. You want me to give something sentimental to the person who ruined Tobias, and ruined my life?'

'I won't pretend to understand the pain that you're in, Mrs Young. What you've experienced, what you're still experiencing, is unacceptable. We tried our best to stop all of those things happening—'

'Not hard enough.'

'—and we're there for you in any way we can be in the future.'

'I'm all alone, Detective. Do you know that? All alone with a boy who can no longer function in society.'

'I'm so sorry.'

'She killed my husband.'

Who was a very bad man, and the main cause of your suffering. 'I'm sorry.'

'Occasionally, Simon's colleagues give me money. Why do they do that? Do they care?'

'I don't know,' Yorke said.

'Are they trying to buy my silence?'

Yorke saw this crack in the veneer of the organised crime outfit, Young Properties. It was a crack which Yorke should, as a law enforcement officer, be peering into. But it was also a crack he had no time for right now. He made a mental note to report it back to SEROCU, the South East Regional Organised Crime Unit. Would she turn against those her husband used to lead?

'I believe that if you send a recent photograph, Mrs Young, you'll save lives. For that, you'll not only have my gratitude, but the silent gratitude of all those families who won't be torn apart by this criminal's future actions.'

'And that's all you can offer me?'

It sounds like a remarkable offer for the average moral individual, Yorke thought, *but then I guess that anybody who was married to Simon Young, and clearly aware of his moral bankruptcy, would probably be in deficit herself.*

She sighed. 'Okay, I'll send it. She can see how hollow my boy looks. If she claims to love him as much as she does, it will hopefully bring her much discomfort. I'll take the photograph on my phone and email it. Give me an email address, please?'

As Yorke gave her his secure police-issued email address, he felt the juices in his stomach start to boil.

———

AFTER SEVERAL EXHAUSTING morning sessions with Alan, the Conduit took some time out to sit with Saskia. He noticed that her facial bandages were damp with blood, and in dire need of change, but he needed a moment's rest before doing that.

Saskia wept and muttered to herself, and the Conduit acknowledged her state of extreme shock. She would require some extensive work, but at least she'd survived the night, and had now acclimatised to a safer dosage of painkillers. He sat beside her with her head on his lap. He stroked her hair as he'd done with Alan the previous day.

'Aristotle once said friendship is a help "in performing noble actions, for *two going together* are better able to think and act". Tomorrow, is a big day for my friend, Alan. His actions will be noble and, although I won't be physically there, I'll be mentally with him to help him better think and act.' He paused. 'But then he will be gone.' He looked at the fire he'd built earlier raging in the fireplace. He was succumbing to a rare moment of extreme emotion. He fought and choked it back. 'But I'll still have you, Saskia. And I hope that we two can go together into a new chapter. My ideas, my philosophies, continually evolve, and I believe that you're exactly what I'm am looking for.' He pointed over to the desk in the corner of the room. 'Those books over there, Saskia, contain everything. Every moment since my rebirth as the Conduit. Experiences, learnings, hopes, dreams ... everything. One day those works will inspire a generation. Rather than fear my discoveries, they will embrace them. They will learn from them, and everything will change. In the same way Freud, Kraepelin, Bleuler did ...'

He closed his eyes, slept and dreamt of greatness.

LACEY RAY SPENT the morning feeling nauseous and, as she sat behind the desk in Dr Holden's office, staring at the little turd, she considered projectile vomiting. Then, hopefully, Stan, the rapist standing behind her, would come to the doctor's aid, and she'd be close enough to lurch forward and bite his nose off ...

'You seem a little off-colour Lacey. Are you menstruating?'

'I didn't sleep so well, doctor. It is important to sleep well. You should enjoy your last few nights doing so. Especially while you're still *intact*.'

Holden smiled and slid something over the table to Lacey. 'This might make you feel a little less sick.'

She stared down at the printed photograph of Tobias.

Last night, Lacey remained calm throughout an ordeal that would have destroyed the minds of most because she'd never been at the mercy of emotion. Yet, right now, she felt her heart surging.

My boy. All grown up. Seven! How wonderful ...

She stroked his pale face. *My handsome boy ...*

'Dead behind the eyes,' Holden said.

Lacey ignored the irritant and continued to stroke her boy. Her chains jangled.

'Are you crying?' Holden said. 'Jesus, are those tears real?'

Lacey looked up. 'Michael Yorke is a man of integrity. There are few of them in the world. Have you got a pen, Doctor? You'll need to write this down and deliver it word for word to him.'

YORKE WAS in the car with Gardner when the call from Dr Holden came through.

'It worked, Detective. She crumbled.'

Yorke glanced at Gardner with widened eyes. She, too, wore the same intense expression.

'She wants me to read this to you: "In the letters I destroyed, he spoke of a favourite café in which he sometimes wrote his letters. Although he didn't name the café, he provided details of some of what he could see. In one letter, he described a skate park. In another, a duck pond and some botanical gardens. I used Google Earth during my internet time. There's a place in Roundhay park which fits the descriptions. It's called Swan Café". That was all.'

'Internet time?' Gardner said.

Yorke glared at Gardner. She really couldn't help herself!

'Who's that?' Holden said.

'My partner. It's fine.'

'Yes, our patients are given internet time. Similar to library time. They can use it for news, research, entertainment. There're strict controls and they're always observed. For example, they don't use social media and make contact with anyone.'

This didn't concern Yorke. The only thing that concerned Yorke right now was the fact that Dr Louis Mayers frequented Swan Café. It was the biggest lead to date. After thanking Holden, he contacted Rosset to tell him.

'Jesus, well done, Mike.'

'I'm going to head there right now to talk to the staff and the owner,' Yorke said. 'I suggest that you ask some of your team to start identifying CCTV spots in the vicinity. At some point, recently, Dr Louis Mayers strolled into that café. Catch him on CCTV, potentially track him to his vehicle, and with ANPR, we could have him before sundown.'

After hanging up, he pulled over to put Roundhay Park into the SatNav. He noticed his hands were shaking slightly. The adrenaline was coursing through him.

Twenty minutes.

His phone rang again. It was Patricia. As he was stationary now, he put the mobile phone to his ear. 'Hi Pat.'

She was crying.

'Pat? Are you okay?'

'No, Mike. It's Lexi ...'

'What's happened?'

She coughed on her tears. 'Terrible—'

'*Pat, what's happened to Lexi?*'

'Her father, the fucking monster, beat her. Her and Ewan both went to tell him about their engagement, and he just lost it.'

'Where are they both now?'

'Ewan is okay. He pulled him off her, but ...' She started to cry again. He'd never heard her like this. He felt the familiar cold in his neck. *No ... no ... not that. Please, not that.*

'He fractured her skull. She's in intensive care.'

'Jesus ... and?'

'They don't know. They're about to operate on her.' She cried again. 'Mike, please, I need you.'

'I'm coming. It'll be hours, but I'm coming.'

'Thank you.'

'Keep me updated. I love you ...'

He explained what had happened to Gardner, forcing back his own tears. 'Her father's a religious nut, and dangerous. He probably thought that Lexi was abandoning him and their religion for heathens!' The shaking Yorke was experiencing prior to the phone call had now intensified.

'Mike.' Gardner clutched her arm, 'Are you alright to drive?'

'I'll be fine. I need to drop you off. Can you catch a train or bus back to the hotel?'

'Roundhay is near where you jump onto the motorway, Mike, just drop me there. I can get a head start on interviewing the owner and the staff at Swan Café before Rosset has even briefed his team.'

'You're not a police officer, Emma.'

'Bullshit, I'm not. When this is done, I want back in.'

'It's good news ...' He could still feel the tears threatening. 'But it's not legal—'

'Drop me off, Mike. You've got enough on your plate. Besides, I'd just get a taxi there anyway.'

———

GARDNER WONDERED why Mayers had chosen Café Swan as a place to reflect and write his letters. The small, circular shack really wasn't anything special. The place didn't even feel centrally heated, and Gardner felt no warmer after leaving the snow outside.

There were about seven small tables around the café. Each one festively decorated by an unlit candle in a 'Merry Christmas' holder. There was no one else in the café, but it was still early, and it looked as if it was only just opening.

Leaving her ski jacket on, she took a seat by a bookshelf. She took a quick look and grabbed a copy of Wuthering Heights by Emily Bronte. Someone came to the counter from the kitchen. It was a young girl at the counter, late teens, early twenties at a push, and so probably not the owner.

'You order at the counter, Miss,' she said.

'Ah, okay.' Gardner stood back up and walked to the counter. 'How much for this book?'

'Up to you. Just a donation. I read that for my A-levels. I found it unnerving. Heathcliff, especially.'

'Cruel men often have that effect,' Gardner said. 'Can I get a Cappuccino please? My name is DI Emma Gardner. Do you know when the owner is in?'

'That'd be my parents. Neither are here today. I take on most of the shifts during my holidays ... Chocolate on your Cappuccino?'

'No thank you. So, you're on break from Uni?'

'Yep. Would you like anything else with your coffee?'

Gardner pointed at the flapjacks. 'One of those please. What do you study?'

'Philosophy Major, Psychology Minor.' The young lady said lifting the plastic dome and taking a chunk of flapjack out with tongs. 'These are lovely. I helped Mum bake them.'

'And gluten free,' Gardner said. 'Which means they will agree with me. What's your name please?' She took out a notebook from her bag.

'Lyra Cross.'

'Your mother and father?'

'Lydia and Malcolm Cross.'

Gardner wrote it down. 'Your family had this café long?'

'Since I was ten.'

'Living and working together. I bet you're very close. They must miss you when you're away.'

'I'm never away. I go to the university here.'

'The University of Leeds?'

She nodded.

Gardner's heart fluttered. She unzipped her ski jacket and reached in for the photograph of Louis Mayers. She put it on the counter. 'Do you recognise him?'

Lyra stared at the photo. Gardner watched her. Her eyelid twitched, and she chewed her bottom lip. It was difficult to read into this though because she'd been awkward to begin with. Most nineteen-year-olds often were when in conversation with the police. 'No ... sorry.'

'Look again, Lyra. We think he works at your university and we think his name is Dr Alexander Harris.'

Lyra obliged. 'Maybe ... there're a few older professors. This could be one of them I guess, but he doesn't lecture me.'

'We have reason to believe he sometimes comes to drink

coffee in here. Stands to reason. It's a stone's throw from the university.'

'I'm sorry, I've never seen him here.'

Gardner slipped the photograph back into her inside pocket. 'You'll be at University studying during term time. I assume that's when he comes in, during his lunch hour perhaps? Is it okay if you contact your mother and father, Ms Cross? It really is important that we try and find this particular man.'

'Of course ... what's he done?'

'We don't know that he has done anything. We just need to eliminate him from our inquiries.'

'I'll bring the coffee and cake over to you and then head into the kitchen to phone Dad. Is that okay?'

'Of course.'

'And you'll keep an eye on the café in case anyone comes in while I'm out back?'

Gardner nodded.

At the table, Gardner chewed on her flapjack and stared out of the café window. A small family were feeding the ducks despite the sign instructing them not to do so.

Suddenly, for no explicable reason, Gardner didn't just feel cold, she felt very alone too.

YORKE KNEW he was exploiting his position by breaking the speed limit, but he'd given everything he had in the name of justice over the years, so now with a family emergency, he'd forgive himself for this lapse in responsibility.

If a camera caught him, or if he was sighted by a fellow officer, his plate would be run. They'd identify him as a DCI, and no chase would ensue, although he may be questioned on it later. Still driving at past ninety for the best part of four hours was not something he was relishing or enjoying. He was already exhausted from a whole week of bloody driving.

Fortunately, the weather was on his side, and the roads weren't congested. Patricia was phoning in regular updates, but they offered very little because Lexi was still in surgery. They were trying to relieve some swelling on her brain.

He was glad Lexi's father was in custody. For all of his religious pretence, Art Franco was nothing more than a cruel and violent bully. Yorke would love a run at him in the interrogation room, but correct procedure would prevent that from ever happening.

Now, as he drove, he felt swamped in guilt. Hadn't he also responded with shock, or rather, *horror*, when Ewan and Lexi had announced their engagement? Okay, he may not be a vicious, aggressive bible-basher, but had it not demonstrated a certain narrow-mindedness?

He gritted his teeth, stabbed at the accelerator, and prayed to God that Lexi would be okay.

LYRA CROSS FELT FUNNY. She closed the door which separated her from the café floor and leaned against the kitchen sink.

She *knew* Dr Alexander Harris. Not only was he a popular lecturer at her university, but he also came in regularly to drink coffee. Often, if the café was quiet, and she herself was between lectures, or on a day off, they would sit and chat.

He was enigmatic and charismatic, full of anecdotes, and wisdom. He seemed as passionate about philosophy as he was about psychology, so they could spend many hours discussing Plato and Aristotle.

Why had she lied? He was an older, very experienced man, who could take care of himself. If the police came looking for him, there should be nothing to prevent her from doing her duty ... nothing. Why was she suddenly feeling *protective* of him? He could be dangerous ...

She picked up the phone and dialled a number she knew, but had no recollection of ever learning, or using before. It felt suddenly right. This was her duty to Dr Harris. He needed to be *protected* from the police officer who had just come into the café. He was the one in danger.

Yes, it felt right ... yet illogical ... what was she doing? Was it possible to stop herself?

'Hello?'

'Dr Harris?'

'Yes, who is this please?'

'Lyra at the Swan Café?'

'Ah, my dear. I guess someone has come looking for me then.'

'Yes, Doctor, a police officer. A woman.'

'Inevitable, I guess. Is she alone?'

'Yes.'

'She thinks you're phoning your father, does she not?'

'Yes ... Doctor Harris?'

'Yes, dear?'

'I'm not sure what I'm doing.'

'You know what you're doing. Close your eyes for the moment and remember that warm day in June, when we confronted Descartes' philosophy. You remember?'

'Yes. I think therefore I am.'

'Do you still feel warm, Lyra?'

'Very.'

'Good. Here is what I want you to do.'

'Anything you say.' She listened carefully to his instructions.

Afterwards, he said, 'And if anyone else comes into the café, you must tell them you do not know who I am. Do you understand?'

'Yes.'

'Bye, Lyra.'

'Bye, Doctor.'

Despite the cold, Lyra did feel warm now. She could feel the sweat on her brow. She took off her jumper and opened the door out of the kitchen.

The detective was just finishing her coffee.

Lyra Cross didn't know why she was feeling this way, but she did know that Dr Harris made her feel ever so safe. And right now, she really didn't want to let him down.

OUTSIDE LEXI'S HOSPITAL ROOM, Yorke and Patricia hugged. It was a harder embrace than it had been the previous evening when they'd been reunited following several days apart. In fact, partway into the embrace, Yorke realised that Patricia was using him to keep her upright.

'Her face, Mike ... before they took her into surgery. Her face—'

'The doctor just told me it went well.'

'—It was so pale. Like the bodies I see.'

'Stop thinking like that—'

'The ones I see day in day out.'

He came out of the embrace and held Patricia by her shoulders. He looked into her bloodshot eyes. 'She'll make it.'

'He practically knocked the life out of her.'

'And now she will heal.'

Yorke kissed his wife on her forehead and then went into the hospital room to see Ewan and Lexi.

COMING OUT OF THE FOG, Gardner hoped that what she'd just experienced was a nightmare. But as the fractured pieces glued themselves together in front of her, she realised it was wishful thinking.

The face of Dr Louis Mayers carved itself out of the chaos, and a hand closed over her face to stifle her scream. Her obsession with finding Topham had led her straight into hell ...

... Gardner had headed straight for the Cross household after Lyra had provided the address. It took half-an-hour on foot from the café to Chapel Allerton using her mobile phone for directions. On route, she considered contacting Yorke on the way to update him but decided against it. He'd looked completely traumatised by the news about Lexi and was driving at God knows what speed. It was safer to give him some space.

When she reached the road where the Cross family lived, she saw that many residents had decorated their houses with Christmas lights. The Cross residency itself had erected a twinkling reindeer in the front garden.

After she'd rang the doorbell several times, she heard a young man's voice from behind the door. 'Is this DI Emma Gardner?'

'Yes. Who's this?'

'Matt, Lyra's brother. Could you come around to the

back? I don't have the key for the front door, and Dad's just put some coffee on in the kitchen.'

'Yes ... no problem.'

The snow had built up high around the side of the house, and Gardner was pleased she'd opted for sturdy boots. It was proving to be a particularly cold close to the year, and Gardner was glad, more than ever, of her job at Marks and Spencer's. The sizeable employee discount had allowed her to restock her winter wardrobe.

In the back garden, Gardner noticed the two oak trees at the rear. They stood side-by-side like a pair of sentries. Their twisted, snow-covered branches seem to reach out, tense, and ready to strike. She shivered.

Behind her, a patio door slid open. She assumed that the lanky young man wearing a bow tie and a brown tweed jacket was Matt. 'Please come in.' He said, tucking his black curtained hair behind his ears.

'Lyra didn't say she had a brother,' Gardner said.

Matt took several steps back to allow Gardner access through the door. 'Ashamed of me, probably.' His smile was awkward. He clearly wasn't used to attempting humour.

As she stepped in through the patio door, she asked. 'Your father?'

'In the kitchen. He wants to know if anyone else is coming? He's only made enough coffee for three.'

'No, just me.' Gardner looked around the room. It was an office of some kind. 'Is your mother not here too?'

'No. Dead I'm afraid ... last year.'

Two things bothered Gardner about this. While he slid the patio door closed behind them, she quizzed him on the first thing. 'I'm sorry ... Lyra didn't mention that.'

'Didn't she?' Matt locked the patio door and slipped the

key into his pocket. He turned. 'She has struggled to come to terms with it.'

The second thing that bothered Gardner was Matt's matter-of-fact way of reporting his mother's death. It lacked emotion.

Her heart rate increasing slightly, Gardner looked around the office. A desk, computer, a long sofa and blank walls. The décor revealed little. 'Does your father work in here?'

'Yes.'

'Just thinking some pictures might be nice.'

'He hates distraction.'

'Okay, can we go and talk to him, we really need to press—'

There was a loud whine from somewhere in the house. 'What was that?'

'Our dog.'

'It didn't sound like a dog.'

'It was.'

Gardner's heart beat even faster now. 'What breed?'

'Not sure, a big dog. You'll have to ask my father.'

'You don't know the breed of your own dog?'

Matt shook his head but didn't respond.

She heard the whine again. She felt a surge of adrenaline. *It wasn't a dog.*

Gardner opened the door to the office.

'You can wait in here ...' Matt said from behind her.

She ignored him and walked into the hallway. More non-descript décor. Where were the Christmas decorations? Had the reindeer in the garden been a ruse?

Again, the whine ...

Tasting bile in her mouth, she headed towards the sound and opened the door barring her way.

For a moment, everything looked normal. The kitchen had a boisterous Christmas tree in the corner; a large dinner table in the centre of the room with placemats and a pepper grinder; a TV mounted on the wall playing a *Toy Story* movie; and a large man with his back to her, down on his knees, petting his dog.

But she couldn't yet *see* the dog, and then came that whine again.

A human arm slipped around the big man's waist. Her breath caught in a throat. The man's head turned to look at her, a large smile dripping from his face. He looked so different without a moustache, but it was him. She desperately looked around for a weapon as he rose to his feet. She dived for the pepper grinder. Her hand closed around it as Mayers stepped to one side to reveal what he'd been petting.

She felt her world burning.

Curled on the floor, naked, with the arm that had embraced Mayers' waist still stretched out in front of him, was what was left of her friend, Mark Topham. His hair was gone, and he'd lost over half his body weight. To others, he may have been unrecognisable, but not to Gardner. When you had shared so many of your sorrows with one person, who in turn had shared so many of their sorrows with you, there was no mistake. A bond was forged out of emotion, which could not be disguised by any physical appearance.

Too stunned to cry, Gardner emitted a single gasp, which seemed to die even before it left her mouth. She wanted to go to him, hold him, comfort him, protect him, help him … but now, Matt's hands were holding her back. The pepper grinder smashed on the floor.

'Leave her,' Mayers said. 'Let her go to her friend. Let her see.'

Unconcerned with her own safety, Gardner went to Mark and knelt in front of him. His face was lined with scar tissue, and his shaved head was covered in white dints. He didn't look afraid of her, but neither was there any recognition in his eyes. There was only curiosity.

For fear of hurting him further with her pity, she held back her tears. She showed him her hand, and moved it slowly towards him, so he could see that she meant no harm, and only wanted to touch him.

Her palm settled on his cheek, and she felt her insides melt.

He whimpered again, and she worried he may pull back. But she persisted, and held her hand there until he calmed, closed his eyes and sighed.

And then, despite her best efforts, the tears came. 'Mark ... I'm sorry ... I'm so sorry ...' *I'm too late ... I'm too late. I failed you.*

She looked down over his mangled body.

Apart from despair, a newer emotion began to rise within her when she saw the twisted lumps of flesh where his genitalia should have been. Rage.

She glared back at Mayers and Matt. '*You monsters!*'

'He's happier now than when he came to me,' Mayers said.

'I'm going to kill you. *Both of you.*' She bared her teeth and started to rise to her feet.

She noticed, too late, the extended pruning saw in Matt's hands. He swung and everything dissolved ...

... on that small bridge between consciousness and unconsciousness, Gardner listened to her captors talk. They spoke of violence and death. They spoke of a place called the *Old Bar*, and the tide of blood that would wash in a new age of discovery. She listened to the monsters talk, and realised that here, in the heart of darkness, true evil and true depravity, found a pedestal. And from this pedestal, the voices took on a form of sensical clarity that did not exist outside this black heart. She wished so much to be outside of it, but feared that when you were truly inside it, as she was right now, you could never again leave it …

The hand slipped from her mouth.

'Glad you could join us again, DI Emma Gardner,' Mayers said. 'I'm not overly surprised by your presence here. I suspected Lacey would betray me at some point. You could say it's the nature of the beast. Fortunately, once I'd realised my error in revealing too much to her in my earlier letters, I put a contingency plan in place. I expected an army, Emma. I thought I'd have to run again. But it seems lady luck is all mine. You came alone.'

Gardner narrowed her eyes. 'But more will come. You're insane. Nothing you've done, or will do, makes any sense. What you've done to Mark is senseless, what you did in *Rose Hill* is senseless, what you plan to do is senseless. You're imprisoned somewhere dark, Mayers. So dark, it takes on a light of its own. But outside of that prison, you're simply crazy—'

Mayers held up the palm of his hand. 'Please stop there, Emma. I've given you a particularly high dose of lysergic acid, so you are making little sense. I want you to conserve your energy, so you are able to act when I need you to act. In much the same way, I had Susie Long act when she met Mark's lover, Neil.'

'You bastard. You *absolute fucking bastard.*'

'Experiments are the name of the game, Emma. And today, I wish to put you at the heart of a new one. So, are you ready?'

'No.'

'Exactly as I thought, but I do need your compliance. Alan?'

The young man who had called himself Matt came into the room. He was holding a gun and, beside him, Topham crawled on all fours.

'Put the gun to his head, Alan.'

The gaunt young man put the gun against the back of Topham's head.

'Now, Emma, are you ready?'

'Yes .... you bastard ...'

'Good. My name is the Conduit. I am a channel. I become the piece that is missing from inside people, and I allow the thoughts, feelings and behaviours to move fluidly through me and within them. Do you understand?'

Gardner didn't respond.

'Alan, are you ready to pull that trigger?'

'Yes, Conduit.'

'*Do you understand, Emma?*'

'Yes! Fuck you ... I understand!'

'Okay. Your darkest memory. Let's go.'

SEEING a seventeen-year-old hooked to machines was never a welcome sight. It was even less so when the person involved was someone you were extremely close to. Yorke really struggled to fight back tears, but did so because his adopted son, Ewan, was broken, and needed a pillar of strength, not a crumbling adult.

During the entire time Yorke was in the room, he stood behind his son with his hands on his shoulders. A few times, Ewan reached up to put a hand on one of Yorke's.

The doctors had been positive. Surgery to relieve

swelling seemed to have gone well. It hadn't been as bad as they first thought. There was reason to be optimistic, but seeing a young lady with her head bandaged, completely out for the count, did little to alleviate Yorke's anxieties.

His mind constantly flicked between three concerns. The first was the religious nut, and Lexi's father, Art Franco. He hoped his Salisbury colleagues were doing enough to build a case that would lock this bastard up. His second concern was his response to Ewan and Lexi's announcement. It had been immature and was now twisting him up inside. He'd vowed to always be there for Ewan, and now, by extension, Lexi. During that announcement, he'd not been there for anyone. His third concern was the investigation in Leeds. What had Gardner found out? He'd checked his phone a few times but was yet to receive an update. It was also getting very late.

When evening arrived, they were ushered out of Lexi's room. Patricia walked together with Ewan to the carpark. As he followed, Yorke texted Gardner.

ALAN TAPPED the Conduit on the shoulder, forcing him to pause his treatment.

'You need to see this,' Alan said, pushing the detective's phone into his hands. Part of a text message from Michael Yorke was on the lock screen. *Lexi out of the woods. How did ...*

The Conduit took Gardner's hand. He'd already induced hypnosis, so she offered no resistance. He pressed her thumb against the home button on the phone. It recognised her print and opened.

The Conduit read the message in its entirety.

Lexi out of the woods. How did it go at Swan café? Update?

Michael Yorke. The detective who stopped Christian Severance. *Was it him that Lacey contacted? Why then did he not come? Was this Lexi important to him?*

The Conduit read a few of Gardner's sent messages to pick up a feel for her style. He then replied.

So glad to hear about Lexi. Disappointing on investigation front. Café owners overseas for New Year, and staff do not recall seeing Mayers. I've left messages for owners to contact, and I will let you know when I hear something. Rest now.

He read it back carefully. He added a kiss at the end as the detective did on all her other messages, and he hit send.

The Conduit knew that his time in Leeds was coming to an end now. He could never return to the university, and it was only a matter of time before they found this house. Before, when Emma Gardner was unconscious, he'd contacted his source in Southampton. They were processing another new identity. They were quick, and they were thorough, but they charged a fortune. They had access to his money because they would move his finances from one identity to another and take their cut during the transference. Dr Alexander Harris, just like Dr Louis Mayers before him, would simply disappear. But not before he went out with a bang ...

Hopefully, this message to Michael Yorke would buy him more time. Tomorrow was New Year's Eve, and both he and Alan had prepared extensively for the celebrations.

He turned his attention back to Gardner.

'So, tell me Emma, what do you see in Tezcacoatl's temple?'

GARDNER STOOD alongside Mayers in the old barn. The interior was lit by a hearth at the back. Black smoke billowed out, but a hole had been cut out in the roof just above it to allow most of the smoke to escape.

'Why have you brought me back here?' Gardner looked at Mayers.

He pointed at the carnage before them. 'To see the Repenting Serpent.'

The serial killer, Terrence Lock, who believed himself to be an Aztec priest, had erected six stone steps in his makeshift temple. They rose to an altar presided over by a metre-high golden statue of a man dancing. Lock knelt over twelve-year-old Ewan. The killer had already carved open the boy's chest.

Gardner started to move forward. Mayers took her by the shoulder. 'Watch ... wait ...'

Gardner's eyes fell to DI Iain Brookes, Ewan's natural father, who was dead in a pool of his own blood at the bottom of the steps. 'Ah, Iain.'

Next to Iain, Michelle Miller, mother of one of Lock's victims was in a wheelchair. She was conscious but wore the glazed expression of dementia.

Gardner again tried to move, and Mayers again held her back. 'Patience, Emma. Here you come.'

A younger, weightier version of herself, was the first through the barn door. A younger-looking Yorke, following closely behind her, announced their arrival. 'Police! Terrence. It's over. Step away from Ewan.'

Lock held up a scalpel. It glinted as it reflected the fire burning in the hearth.

Yorke said, 'Armed response is approaching, Terrence.

If you do not put the weapon down, and step away, you will be shot.'

Lock leaned closer to Ewan.

Gardner glared at Mayers beside her. 'I don't know why you've brought me here you prick! I made peace with what I did a long time ago.'

'But I didn't choose this memory, Emma. *You did.*'

Yorke raised his voice. '*This is your last warning, Terrence. I'm telling you to put that down and step away ...*'

'It's your memory,' Mayers said. 'Tell me, Emma, what's this Lock doing?'

'He's about to cut out Ewan's heart.'

'Why?'

'Because of his beliefs. He thinks he can appease deities. Bring change ...'

'Interesting approach.' Mayers smiled. 'And who's the old woman in the wheelchair?'

'Michelle. She has dementia. He has brought her here to represent *his* late mother. He believes he betrayed his mother and is now repenting for his betrayal. He wants her to watch the repentance.'

Gardner turned back. While Yorke continued to reason with Lock, her younger self knelt over Iain's body. She recalled the cold touch of his skin, his dead eyes, his blood, and the gun she found in his hands.

'I've seen enough,' Gardner said to Mayers. 'I remember everything, I can—'

'But why, Emma? These are the experiences that define us. This one defined you.'

Yorke was shouting up at the killer. 'You watched your mother die, Terrence. Someone who brought you into this world, loved you and you sat there, and you *watched* her die.'

Lock stood up. His eyes were so wide he could have torn all the muscles in his face. '*Shut up!*'

'Are we close, Emma?' Mayers said to her. 'Does your defining moment come as a result of that gun I see in your hand? Is that what changed you?'

'*Fuck you!*' Gardner said.

'I am not the enemy, Emma, merely the channel ...'

A hideous loud moan tore through the barn. Ewan's back arched. He smashed his head from side to side as froth spewed from the corners of his mouth and his eyes rolled back. Yorke had made it to the first step, but he was still too far away.

There was a loud series of thuds.

'It's Michelle, the mother substitute,' Gardner said. 'She's stamping her foot, distracting the prick.'

'And where're you going?' Mayers said, pointing at her younger self, now moving towards Yorke and the foot of the stairs.

'Ah God,' Gardner said, 'Please ... not again ...'

Michelle opened her mouth. 'Stoooooop!'

Lock's eyes were wide and unflinching as they looked at the woman whom he considered his mother.

'Stop!' This time Michelle's use of the word was short and sharp.

Lock looked down at Ewan and then up at Michelle again. He pulled his hands from Ewan's chest and said, 'But mother, I'm doing this for you.'

Gardner wanted to close her eyes but was unable to.

'The price of admission I'm afraid,' Mayers said. 'You're here for the whole—'

There was a loud bang and Lock seized his throat in both hands; the scalpel slipped from his grip and clattered against the top step. He stood up as blood squirted out from the cracks between his fingers. Still looking confused, and unable to take his eyes from the woman he believed to be his mother, he reached out to her with one of his bloody hands. There he lingered on the sixth step, until he couldn't stand any longer, and then he plunged. His bones cracked as he bounced from one unforgiving step to the next before his head finally burst on the bottom one.

'Good shot, Emma,' Mayers said.

Gardner didn't speak, feeling again the force of the moment. She watched Lock's twitching form grow still underneath a snake-embraced urn. It was the only time that she'd ever killed anyone.

'I've made peace with it,' she said.

'I believe you.'

'Accepted it.'

'I've no doubt.'

She turned to face him. 'So, why are we here?'

'Because of the energy here ... can you feel it?'

'You are insane.'

'The air practically crackles with it!'

'What do you want?'

'To use it. To harness that power. To make you do what I want you to do.'

'You are deluded. It doesn't matter how many drugs you give me. I'll will never do a single thing you say.'

'By the time this night is through, I won't have to say anything. Are you ready to hit rewind, so we can go again?'

20
DECEMBER 31ST

WHEN YORKE WOKE on the sofa, he cursed and fumbled around for his mobile phone. He'd passed out ridiculously early. He wasn't surprised to see that Rosset had tried to call him three times last night. He'd knocked his phone onto silent in the hospital and then forgotten to switch it back on.

He was also disappointed to see no contact from Gardner. He reread her message from last night. She'd obviously not heard from the holidaying café owners yet. He tried ringing her. No answer.

He texted her: *Bloody hell, Emma. I can't usually get shot of you. Don't go AWOL on me now. Ring.*

He then phoned Rosset. He began with an apology for knocking his phone on silent.

'Don't apologise, Mike. You sound like you went through hell yesterday.'

'Where're you up to?'

'When you rushed back south, we got the contact details of the café owners, Lydia and Malcolm Cross.'

Yorke stood up and stretched. He was expecting to hear

the same as he'd heard from Gardner, that the owners were overseas for a New Year break ...

'We went around to speak to them.'

'*Sorry?*' Yorke's blood ran cold.

'Yes, but they couldn't identify Harris, unfortunately. So, then, we went to the café and spoke to the daughter, Lyra Cross, who works in the café several hours every day when she's not attending the University of Leeds. And, believe it or not, despite studying psychology, she didn't recognise him either. She said the name was familiar, but he wasn't lecturing on any of her modules.'

Yorke was pacing. *Think, think, Mike, think ...*

Why would Emma have sent that message?

Think ...

Jesus ...

He steadied himself against the wall.

She didn't send that message.

'Mayers has got my friend, sir.'

'Your friend? What are you talking about?'

After, he'd finished explaining who Gardner was, and that dodgy text message, he prepared himself for both barrels.

And received them. Twice.

Then, he said, 'I know, sir. Throw everything at me later, but right now we have to find Emma.'

'Well we've been searching for Mayers based on this location, but we're no closer. CCTV has thrown nothing up. We're struggling for witnesses ...'

'Emma was in the café, *yesterday*, just before you. She was on foot. She probably walked. How did she find Mayers? Or how did Mayers know she was there? Wait a minute ... of course ... this girl, Lyra, she knows *something*. She must do.'

'She's a nineteen-year-old girl—'

'He's probably in her head, like he's in everyone's bloody head. She let Mayers know we were on to him, and he took Emma. You need to pull Lyra in now.'

After ending his phone call to Rosset, Yorke spoke to Patricia.

Her hand flew to her mouth when he explained the danger Gardner was in.

'I'm so sorry, I'm going to have to go again. I hate to leave you in the middle of all this.'

She held out his car keys. A tear formed in the corner of his eye. She embraced him.

IN THE INTERVIEW ROOM, Rosset felt sorry for Lyra Cross. She could barely get through a sentence before having to pick up a glass of water with a trembling hand. He'd had to refill it three times already and they were only a couple of questions in. But there was no time for sympathy, not now that Emma Gardner was missing, and potentially, in the company of a monster.

Yesterday, Lyra had told Rosset that she didn't know Harris, and he'd smiled and walked away. Today, trusting Yorke's intuition, Rosset pressed and pressed, almost aggressively. He told her about hypnosis, showed her Harris' picture repeatedly and explained how the doctor was a very dangerous man.

Eventually, her eyes widened. '*I do know him!*'

Rosset felt a rush of adrenaline. 'How?'

She thought for a moment and grew pale. 'This isn't right ... why did I forget? *How could I forget?* He came in weekly during term time. We had many conversations. What's he done to me?'

'Manipulated you. Maybe hypnotised you.'

'Yes ... I can feel him in my mind ... it's so hard to describe. It's horrible.'

Rosset showed her a photograph of Gardner. 'Do you recognise this police officer?'

Her hand flew to her mouth. 'Oh God, yes. She came in, looking for him, like you did.'

'And what happened?'

'Shit! I think I contacted him. It's blurry ... but I *think* I did.' Lyra started to cry. 'I warned him.'

'What then?'

'Oh no, *I sent her to him!* Have I put her in danger?'

'Where did you send her?'

Lyra closed her eyes and was silent for about a minute. Eventually, she said, 'I'm sorry, I just can't remember. It's like I'm watching it on a television screen. I *know* it's me, but it seems to happen separate from me. I can see myself hand her paper with the address written on it, but I cannot see the words.'

Rosset sat back in his chair and held himself back from sighing. 'How did you feel while you were doing what he wanted you to do?'

'Hard to explain ... kind of like I was safe from harm.'

'Why might that be? Are you worried about anyone hurting you?'

'No.'

'Have your parents ever harmed you?'

'No, of course not.'

'So, what has Dr Mayers, sorry Dr Harris, made you paranoid about?'

She rubbed tears from her eyes. 'I don't know. I only know that he makes me feel safe from it.'

Rosset continued the interview for some time, but when it became clearer that it was going nowhere, he refilled her water, patted her on the arm and asked her if she was prepared to see a psychologist to try and uncover more. She agreed.

As he was leaving the interview room, she said, 'There is one thing.'

He turned.

'It's stupid really.'

He started to walk back to the table.

'There's a dream I keep having. No ... sorry, it makes no sense.'

'Please, Ms Cross, go on.'

'I go into this house.'

Rosset nodded.

'It's like I'm drawn to it. The front door is open for me.'

This is something, Rosset thought. *This is really something.* 'And?'

'And the next thing I know I'm sitting in a dark room.' She paused for a mouthful of water. Her hand was trembling more than ever.

'Then?'

'That's it. Nothing. I told you it made no sense. I just sit there. In the dark. Alone.'

'How do you feel then?'

'Vulnerable. Paranoid. Like something might happen.'

'Until?'

'Until I wake up.'

Mayers could have put that experience in her head to create the paranoia, but still, it did not tell them where

Mayers was. Unless ... did he actually take her there in reality?

'Could you describe the house?'

'Yes ... but you could go there if you want.'

Rosset's eyes widened. 'You know where it is?'

'It's a real house. It's on Hyde Park Road near the pub.'

Rosset's throat went dry and he reached for his glass of water.

THE CONDUIT RELISHED A DIFFICULT PATIENT.

Most were so badly damaged by their PTSD that they came willingly, but occasionally, there were those, like Detective Emma Gardner, who liked to drag their heels. It made the outcome even more rewarding.

Despite working on her throughout the night at the expense of any sleep, he wasn't tired. The adrenaline kept him focused. He was lucky to enjoy his work so much when many did not.

It'd also been a welcome distraction following an emotional evening in which he'd bid farewell to his finest subject, Alan. The young man was to spend his last twenty-four hours alone. This had been a necessary decision. Alan was experiencing some hesitance in the grand plan because he idolised the Conduit and didn't wish to leave his side. Twenty-four hours apart should break the reliance and allow Alan to really find his independence. Then, the world would be gifted the most extraordinary New Year it'd ever had.

So, aided by his drug therapies, hypnosis, and good old-fashioned bullishness, the Conduit had driven Gardner into the heart of her trauma again and again, and changed the narrative.

Now, the detective sat in the kitchen, her head lowered, a thin line of drool reaching from her bottom lip to the oak table, while he knelt beside his loyal dog and stroked his pitted head for the last time.

'For all of your failings as a human being,' the Conduit said, 'You really have been man's best friend.'

The dog nuzzled his master's hand.

The Conduit looked back up at Gardner, who was starting to stir. The thin line of drool snapped, and her hand closed around the gun that the Conduit had placed there for her.

───────

As HE NUZZLED his master's hand, Topham felt both awe and repulsion; contentment and emptiness; protection and threat. The world had suddenly become a kaleidoscope. An exhausting mix of *everything*. A storm of emotions.

He *needed* his master yet *hated* him. And despite hating him, loved him too.

Topham realised that before now, *long before now*, he was something else, *someone else*. But the truth was so shrouded by darkness that he just couldn't reach it. He could also sense pain in the black. A pain so great, so unfathomable, that to journey back into that darkness may be the end of him.

This woman was part of that truth. She'd come from that dark place.

When he'd first seen her, he'd felt little, but when she touched his face, he'd felt *everything*. That kaleidoscope, that mix, that storm ... but rather than being thrown about by this tumultuous tide of sensation, he was *soothed*.

And he realised that not everything in that darkness was bad. That there had been goodness there too.

Then a name crawled from the void, like the hand of a long dead loved one.

Emma.

THE CONDUIT WORKED some moisturiser into his pet's neck underneath the metal collar that was chained to the D-ring on the wall. The animal's skin often became irritated and sore. 'Goodbye, Mark.'

The Conduit stood and turned to face the detective. Her eyes were now open, and she had the gun in a two-handed grip.

It was time. She was ready.

Using hypnosis, the doctor took her back to the night that she killed someone. Except, the Conduit had significantly altered the memory.

In this new narrative, the Aztec mythology was no more. Neither were statues and the wheelchair-bound elderly lady. But the crème de la crème of the new version was that the original killer, Terrence Lock, had been replaced by a new foe. A twisted and bitter bent copper, who had spent years in the employee of the Young family, supporting their sinister web of organised crime. This bent copper had been exposed by DI Iain Brookes who had paid for the truth with his life. He lay dead, while his son, Ewan, was being carved up by the copper in some twisted form of revenge.

DI Mark Topham had certainly not counted on DCI

Michael Yorke and DI Emma Gardner interrupting his bloody swansong.

In the new narrative, Gardner had her gun trained on Topham. She couldn't allow Ewan Brookes to be diced beyond recognition. So, she had given him two warnings, and when he'd refused to back away, she'd been forced to shoot him dead.

Now, back in reality, feeling like the ultimate puppeteer, the Conduit started the narrative again, except this time, he moved to one side, so Gardner's glazed eyes could fall on his dog, who was staring at her from beside the Christmas tree.

Gardner rose to her feet and pointed the gun at the Conduit's pet.

'Drop the knife, Mark,' Gardner said.

It was the first of the two warnings, and the Conduit almost clapped. The night had been long, she'd been difficult and resistant, but as always, he was the victor.

Goodbye Mark, he thought and smiled. *My loyal and best friend.*

THE BMW X5S FILED IN, and the end of Hyde Park Road quickly felt like a military zone. A firearm had been used in the *Rose Hill* massacre, so there'd been no opposition when he'd requested Armed Response.

Many of Rosset's officers moved to clear the area. The sky was dark, and the snow thick, but that didn't deter rubberneckers from coming out of their houses to see what was happening to one of their neighbours. This was far from an everyday occurrence on Hyde Park Road.

Armed officers took up strategic positions, while a pair

of their colleagues closed in on the front door of the red-bricked terrace that Lyra Cross had pointed out on Google Earth and said, 'That's the house I went into in my dream. I can't remember what it looks like inside. I just remember sitting in darkness. Suffocating, cold darkness ...'

Rosset watched the armed officers knock and deliver their warnings. When there was no response, they crashed through the door.

Please, Rosset thought, *let this be an end to it all...*

His phone buzzed. He saw that Yorke was calling him. He ignored it, waiting instead for the sound of gunfire, or the protests of an insane doctor as he was dragged kicking and screaming from the house. Finally, one of the armed officers appeared back at the smashed entrance.

Rosset took a deep breath. Here he comes. *Merry Christmas, you murdering prick ...*

The second armed officer emerged from the house making the all-clear gesture with both hands.

Rosset kicked a wheelie bin over.

'Drop the knife, Mark!' Gardner said.

Topham understood enough to know he was about to die, but he didn't feel scared. Light had perforated through the cloud of darkness that had clouded everything that had come before this place, this house, his master... and although, he *still* couldn't really see much in the cloud, he *felt* something. Something he'd not felt for a very long time.

Friendship.

This explosive realisation showered him with fragments of experience. Her warm embrace, her warm lips against his forehead, her warm hand clutching his ... no one had been there for him like Emma Gardner had. *No one.*

'*For the last time, drop the knife, Mark!*'

Topham smiled. 'You're the best of us, Emma.' A tear ran down his face.

GARDNER SAW Topham slicing Ewan's chest, yet something was wrong. His words didn't seem to match with his actions, and his voice sounded different somehow ...

'*You're the best of us.*'

Again. Topham's voice was broken, more beast-like than human, but it was *definitely* him. She tightened her grip on the trigger.

'*You're the best of us.*'

She swayed. She could *see* him murdering Ewan, but ... those words. *Those words.* They meant something ...

... He'd phoned her. After, he'd made the biggest mistake of his life. After he'd lost control and killed that young man.

'I'm sorry, Emma.' There'd been no force in his voice. He loved her. He always came to her.

'What for?'

'For not listening.'

'Mark, what's wrong? Where are you?'

'Goodbye, Emma.'

'*Don't you do this, don't you say this to me, Mark Topham! Where the hell are you?*'

'*You're the best of us ...*'

He kept repeating it. It became clearer, less coarse, each time. It was as if he was using the words to clear his throat.

Ewan was gone now. Topham was hunched on the floor, naked, emaciated, and trembling.

Gardner put the gun down on the table. She got to her feet. She was drugged up, and unsteady, but she was here. Pulled from that nightmare. She steadied herself against the table and looked at Topham. Her friend.

He was *coming* back too. His eyes were widening. *Realising.*

She stumbled over to him, slipped to her knees and put her arms around him. 'I've missed you.'

'Emma.' His voice remained hoarse, more like a growl. 'Be *careful.*'

And then she remembered who else was here with her, but it was too late. She felt the tightness around her neck and was yanked away.

'SHIT,' Rosset said. 'Shit!'

Yorke held back his own frustrations. He was probably less calm than anyone else in this situation, but if experience had taught him one thing these last years, it was that blind panic got you nowhere. 'You've tried.'

'I thought we ... *Shit, shit!*'

The car speakers vibrated. Yorke reduced the volume down on the dash. 'Do you think he's been there?'

'Don't know yet. It's just full of dust and covered furniture. The house was repossessed over a year ago, and the house has been vacant and on the market since then. I expected to find him squatting there. *Fuck!* If he's been there, we'll know soon enough. I practically kicked forensics through the door.'

Yorke looked at his Sat Nav. 'I'm there in thirty. I'm hanging up now in case she phones.'

He phoned Gardner's phone again and left another message. He'd lost count of the amount of times he'd done this, but he still did it again, two minutes later.

THE CONDUIT HAD LEFT it rather too long to strike. Stunned that his replacement narrative had failed, and bursting with scientific curiosity over the fact that the both of his subjects were connecting, he'd hesitated in making a move. Eventually, he'd swooped and managed to get the pole of the pruning saw over the detective's head and against her neck.

Despite being large and strong, the Conduit tended to avoid situations like this. Deep in the recesses of the mind, there was no one deadlier, but in a physical confrontation he was largely untested.

However, he seemed to be faring quite well. He'd yanked her tightly against him. Her hands were on the pole, trying to pry it loose, but his grip was solid.

His dog barked and pounced. There was a clank as the beast was pulled back by his chain, and a thud as he hit the wall.

The detective continued to pull at the pole, and the Conduit was impressed by her resilience and strength, but the doctor was confident that his hold was unbreakable.

His dog was back on his feet, bounding around, tugging at the D-Lock on the wall.

He spoke between gritted teeth. 'Be still, dog, your time is soon.'

When the Conduit noticed a drop in the detective's

resistance, he sensed victory. A smile spread across his face; he was going to enjoy these last moments. He opened his mouth to speak—

He wailed in pain.

Without him noticing, the slippery bitch had dropped a hand from the pole, reached behind herself and grabbed him by the balls. For the Conduit, everything glowed white.

He knew she was sharply turning but, trapped in this sudden explosion of pain, he failed to resist turning with her. At least he still had the pole ...

He felt Mark's arms around his legs. *His dog.* Then he was falling.

GASPING FOR AIR, Gardner watched Mayers wrap his arms around the Christmas tree to steady himself. It didn't work. Both him, and the tree, fell backwards towards Topham.

Topham, who was thin and wiry, scurried to the side as the overweight doctor's feet left the ground. Gardner, still struggling to catch her breath, dived towards the table to retrieve the gun. When her hand settled on it, she heard an ear-piercing shriek. She looked back.

Mayers had managed to cast aside the Christmas tree, but only to receive Topham, who had pounced on top of him and sank his teeth into the doctor's hand.

'Get off me.'

Growling, Topham shook his head from side-to-side. Mayers shrieked again.

Topham pulled away with a chunk of flesh in his mouth. Grimacing, Gardner readied the gun to threaten

Mayers, but then her friend reared up and drove into the doctor again, this time closing his jaws on his face.

For fear of hitting Topham, Gardner lowered the gun.

Mayers writhed, but this only seemed to help Topham get his teeth deeper into his face. Again, he was shaking his head like a real dog playing tug-of-war with its owner. Gardner watched Mayers' skin stretch as Topham edged backwards. Then, came the sound of ripping.

'Mark!' Gardner said.

Topham turned and looked at his best friend. Mayers' cheek slipped from his mouth. 'Emma,' he growled. He bared his bloody canines, turned back and went for the jugular.

———

Topham trembled in Gardner's arms.

It wasn't the cold because he was used to being naked. He shook because of the *onslaught* of experience. After Emma had perforated the cloud of darkness, his memories had started to trickle out; now that the puncture had widened, everything streamed out. 'No, Emma, no ...'

He was curled in a ball, and she held his head tightly against her chest. 'It's okay.' She stroked his head. 'It's okay ... I have you now.'

Topham gulped when Neil, the only man he'd ever loved, walked back into his consciousness. He whimpered as a spotlight fell on the moment when Yorke said that Neil was dead. He cried as the despair, the drinking, the prostitution and the self-pity tore into him like a sandstorm. He wailed when he heard Dan Tillotson's skull break open as he landed the final blow.

Afterwards, he slipped his head from Gardner's grip

and turned to look at Mayers. Blood was still weakly pumping from his torn neck. 'You destroyed everything. You made me destroy everything.'

He looked down at his own naked body. Mutilated, and glistening with the doctor's blood. 'You destroyed me.'

He looked at Gardner. He'd covered her clothing in blood too. She had tears running down her face now. He stroked her face. 'Happiness or pity, Emma?'

'Happiness.'

Liar. How could you not pity the freak you're holding?

He curled up against her and let her hold him tightly for a while longer.

Later, he said, 'Thank you, Emma, for coming to find me.'

'You'd have done the same for me.'

He looked up into her eyes. 'I can't go back Emma. You know that.'

There was a pause. He expected her to argue. She didn't speak.

'They'll put me in a cage.'

Still no reply.

'I need you to do one more thing for me.'

This time there was no silence. 'Anything, Mark. I'll do anything you ask me too.'

THE DRUGS in Gardner's system were playing havoc with her. Her vision blurred and twisted. Thoughts, both surreal and razor sharp, circled each other in her mind. Her emotions shot up and down extreme gradients.

Yet, through all of this, she tried, for her best friend, to stay focused on what he wanted.

She'd taken off his metal collar with the key hanging beside the back door; dressed him in some of Mayers' clothes which she found in a wardrobe upstairs; driven him in the doctor's car, which she'd done slowly and cautiously as she struggled to interpret the straight lines which made up a road; removed some cones which blocked off the entrance to an old brickworks site near Wakefield; and headed down a snow-covered dirt track to the quarry's edge.

Topham leaned over and nuzzled his head against Gardner's shoulder. 'Thank you, Emma.' His voice sounded less damaged now, and more like the voice she knew, and loved.

'Mark—'

'I love you, but I need you to go now, Emma.'

'But, there can—'

He lifted his head from her shoulder. 'Please ... leave, drive away and don't look back.'

'There's always another—'

'I should already be dead, Emma.'

'*I just can't!*' She said, shaking.

'Emma, you promised.'

She looked out of the window at the snow-tipped quarry. It looked peaceful and must have looked so welcoming for Topham. Someone who had experienced so much trauma over the last couple of years and would only be destined for more.

She turned, leaned over and kissed his head. 'I promised.'

She rubbed tears from her eyes, hoping he hadn't seen them. She wanted to be strong – for him.

Topham smiled. 'It's been a ride, Emma.'

She turned away, unable to stop her tears.

'Drive away, Emma. Don't watch. I don't want you to watch.'

She nodded but was unable to speak. She heard the car door open, and the sound of him climbing out.

'No wait,' she said, turning back.

He leaned in through the open door.

'Bye, Mark.' She smiled.

Topham smiled, and for a moment, with the help of the drugs plying her body, Gardner saw the strong, commanding detective, whom she'd spent the best part of her career alongside. His perfect hair, his perfect teeth, and his perfect suit.

Topham closed the door. She switched her car lights off, turned the vehicle and drove away, content to remember DI Mark Topham as the proud, strong, albeit sometimes vain man, that had never had a bad word for anyone.

GARDNER FOUND SOMEWHERE TO STOP. Her mind was whirring uncontrollable and she feared losing consciousness.

She phoned Yorke. 'I'm safe, Mike.'

'Oh God, Emma ... thank God ... thank God ...'

'If only you were always so pleased to hear from me.'

'Where're you?' He sounded close to tears.

'In a field somewhere.' She closed her eyes. 'Feeling groggy.'

'Why? What's happened? Where's Mayers?'

'Dead Mike. Mark killed him.' She laid her head against the steering wheel.

'What? You found him? You found Mark?'

I did. And now he's gone again ... forever. 'Yes.'

Everything was really swimming now. Exhaustion seemed to have got a sudden grip on her.

'Are you okay, Emma? You don't sound okay. *Where are you?*'

'With Mark,' she lied. Gardner gave Yorke the address. 'Go there. You'll find Mayers.'

'You sound sick.'

'I'm fine. I'll phone an ambulance after you ring off. He just gave me *stuff* ... lots of junk ... but it's over now, and I'll be fine ...'

'You sound anything but, Emma. You're slurring. Please tell me where you are. I'll get the ambulance—'

'No time, Mike, you need to know that there's someone else.'

'What?'

'Someone helping him.'

She stopped and realised she was no longer holding the phone.

She could hear Yorke's voice somewhere in the distance. 'Emma ... Emma ... are you there?'

With her eyes closed, she reached down to the floor to get the phone back.

'Emma ... Emma?'

She fell into the darkness.

THE DOCTORS WERE hopeful that Gardner was out of the woods, so her husband, Barry, had opted to rest and installed himself in a nearby hotel. Yorke, on the other hand, was a glutton for punishment and sat alone in the hospital waiting room, waiting for her to wake, ready to ask her where Topham was so he could prepare the arrest.

Yorke looked up at the clock on the waiting room wall. It was past eleven o'clock and so almost New Year. He'd be contacting Patricia bang on twelve. Full of apologies, as usual - it wasn't the New Year party he'd promised her when the Christmas holidays had begun.

Yorke drank his fifth coffee. It'd been almost eight hours since Gardner had been spotted in a field by a couple of ramblers. He was beat, and the caffeine in instant coffee was not providing enough of a wallop to sustain him. He paced the waiting room, wincing at the tinsel and other tacky decorations. This was one Christmas he'd want to forget in a hurry. He stopped by a wall of cards, hand drawn and sent in by local school children to the NHS workers. It was a nice touch.

One of the cards was fronted with a picture of Santa Clause. The creative young person had gone to town on him with red crayon. He thought back to Rosset's description of Mayers' body.

Topham had done that. He didn't need to wait for DNA results for confirmation. There was no way Gardner had done it.

Rosset hadn't ordered Yorke to attend the crime scene but had tried to encourage him. If Yorke had still been worried about Gardner's warning that someone was helping Mayers at that point, he'd have gone to assist in any way possible.

But this person Gardner had been referring to had already been found at the crime scene. He'd been another "patient" of Mayers and had been disfigured by the cruel psychiatrist. Saskia McLarney was biologically male but identified as female. Rosset's team were still struggling to get much sense from her. She'd been pumped full of morphine.

'DCI Yorke?'

Yorke turned from the Christmas cards. A doctor had got within a metre of Yorke without him even noticing; he really was running on empty.

'Emma is awake, and she wants to speak with you.'

'Shall I contact her husband, maybe she wants to see him first?'

'Normally, that would be appropriate. However, she says its urgent she talks to you. She thinks a crime is going to be committed.'

ALAN SANTS, wets his pants.

Alan Sants, wets his pants.

Alan Sants, Alan Sants.

Alan Sants wets his pants.

It was a song that forever stayed with him. He stroked one of his mud figurines. Like the fingerprints of the sculptor. *Forever burned into the fired clay.*

He heard the Conduit in his head: 'Is this experience a stain on you, or is it something you could use?'

He checked his Chinese Mud Men were four centimetres apart and replaced the ruler in his bag, alongside the gun.

He looked at his watch. It was almost half-past eleven. His eyes swept the *Old Bar.* The clientele differed from his repeated visions he shared with the Conduit, and the music wasn't quite as loud, but the themes remained the same.

Uneven. Chaotic.

Disordered.

'If it isn't Mr fucking Bowtie!'

Alan looked up. Not the two pretty women from the

other narrative. Instead, two of Eddie's sheep. They'd been there the night that he'd been pushed to the floor. The night that the Conduit had first held a hand out for him.

'You seen Eddie?' Knuckle-dragger one asked. 'We haven't seen him in days. Maybe you're meeting him here?'

'We've seen the way you look at him.' Knuckle-dragger two said.

Alan smiled.

'Why are you smiling?' Knuckle-dragger one said.

Saskia. You mean Saskia. And you should see the way he looked at me when he cut off his face.

Knuckle-dragger two pushed over his figurines. 'Stop fucking smiling.'

It was still too early, so Alan let his smile fall away, but inside he was laughing. 'I don't know where he is.' He stared deep into Knuckle-dragger two's eyes. *At twelve o'clock, I'm going to kill you first.*

GARDNER WAS out of bed when Yorke came into the room. She was arguing with a nurse while pulling wires from her body. There was a twitchy officer stationed at the side of the room, edging forwards. Gardner had still not been spoken to since the death of Mayers, so she had to stay in police custody.

Yorke said, 'Hey, Emma, what's—'

She turned her wild eyes onto him. 'It's twenty-to-twelve.'

Yorke nodded.

'We have to go, Mike, you don't understand—'

'Make me understand.' He went to her, put his hands gently on her shoulders, and eased her backwards onto the bed. She was pale and had a thin sheen of sweat over her face.

'There's another person ... someone helping him. They were planning something awful.'

With his hands still on her shoulders, Yorke said. 'It's okay, Emma. You told me. We got the accomplice.'

'Really?'

'Yes. They were at the house. Rosset called me.'

'Thank god.'

Yorke removed his hands, and Gardner started to shuffle back up the bed, until she was in a sitting position. The officer stepped back. The nurse sighed with relief and started to reconnect the wires.

'I heard them talking,' Gardner said. 'They had a gun and were planning to go to the Old Bar at the University of Leeds to see in the New Year! Jesus. Imagine? So close to another disaster.'

Yorke felt sick. Something didn't sit right. Rosset said Saskia's face was a mess – how would he have got into the bar unnoticed? Why would Mayers risk his plans by mutilating the gunman?

'What's wrong, Mike?'

Yorke was back on his feet. 'Describe this other person to me, Emma?'

'Hair in curtains. Pale skin. Angsty teenager look. Bowtie.'

'Was there anything wrong with their face?'

'Gaunt.'

Yorke could feel the scar tingle on his face, he could feel the cold at the top of his chest. His senses were going haywire. 'I think there's someone else, Emma. The person we found is too badly damaged to do anything like this.'

Gardner pushed the nurse away.

'No,' Yorke pointed at her with a trembling finger. 'You're in no state. We're a stone's throw from the university. I can go.'

He looked at his watch. He still had twelve minutes but, by the time he negotiated his way out of the hospital, it would be a lot less.

'It'd be faster to go on foot,' the nurse said.

'I know,' Yorke said, sprinting for the door. He shouted over his shoulder. 'Phone for back-up Emma and then try to get in touch with the bar.'

THE LAST PART of the sprint was uphill. He wasn't wearing the right footwear for this. He slipped and skidded on snow. His shins burned. He felt old injuries reemerge.

At least he had a clear route. Most New Year revellers were already in their chosen drinking establishment. As he ran, his eyes rarely left the clocktower which towered above Leeds.

It was three minutes to twelve when he reached the Parkinson Building, the base of the clocktower. He recalled the photograph that had brought them to Leeds only a week ago. *Mark Topham. Dishevelled. Sitting on the third step leading up to the building.*

Yorke realised that in all the chaos which accompanied Gardner's reawakening, he'd not asked her one of the most crucial questions. *Where was Mark?*

As Yorke flew into the University campus, the burn in his legs seemed to spread up and over his chest. He'd not run as fast for years. He hoped it was a stitch and not his heart preparing to explode.

Two students were in his way. One was staggering

every which way but forward, while the other was vomiting down their front. From the bottom of the steps leading up to the campus drinking hole, the Old Bar, a large doorman was shooing the drunken pair away.

Yorke swooped past the students and finished up next to the doorman. 'DCI Michael Yorke.'

The doorman's hand shot out and barred his way. 'ID?'

'This is an emergency.' Yorke rustled in his pocket for his badge. 'Have you not been contacted?'

'No one has said anything.' the doorman held up his radio.

'There must have been a phone call?'

'Maybe, but who'd answer it? Busiest night of the year in there, mate!'

Yorke showed his badge. 'I have reason to believe that someone has a firearm in your bar. We need to evacuate—'

A loud voice boomed from inside the bar from the speakers. 'The moment we've been waiting for ... ten ...'

He was too late.

'Ten.'

Alan pulled the gun from his backpack and covered it with his jacket.

'Nine.'

He nodded farewell to his Chinese mud men.

'Eight ... seven ... six.'

He was on his feet and moving down the stairs at the end of the raised platform.

'Five ... four ... three.'

Alan was barging past people to get to the bar.

'Two.'

He was facing knuckle-dragger two.

'One.'

He let his jacket slip to the floor and pinned the gun to his target's head.

'*Happy New Year!*'

There was a loud cheer.

'Courage is fire.' Alan pulled the trigger.

The staff behind the bar were sprayed with blood and brain.

'And bullying is smoke.'

'Nine.'

Yorke slipped past the doorman and bounded up the steps, two at a time.

'Eight ... seven.'

Yorke hit a corridor leading to the bar entrance. He heard the doorman shouting after him.

'Six ... five.'

Some students were gathered in the corridor, so rather than slow down, Yorke threw himself against the left-side wall and slid by them. He wondered if the doorman was chasing him. He didn't have time to look back and see.

'Four ... three.'

He was through the open doorway into the bar. There was a thick river of students between him and the stairs which led to a raised platform overlooking the bar area.

'Two.'

How was he going to get through?

'One ... *Happy New Year!*'

A gunshot.

Screams.

Yorke waded through the river of students. 'POLICE! LET ME THOUGH!' Several students clashed with his firm shoulder. Some spun off him, gasping for air. 'LET ... ME ... THROUGH!'

Another gunshot.

Yorke was on the stairs now. Squeezing himself between the short banister, and the descending students, he made it onto the raised platform.

Another gunshot.

He kicked away a stool, stood beside a table littered with glasses, gripped the banister, and looked out. The gunman was about six metres away, standing with his back against the bar. He was wiry and wore the bowtie mentioned by Gardner. Several bodies lay around him. Space was forming around him as the students scattered in all directions.

'POLICE! PUT THE GUN DOWN!' Yorke's demand was blunted by the screaming.

The gunman fired into the crowd. Students fell. Yorke picked up a pint glass and threw it as hard as he could in the bastard's direction. It smashed against the bar behind him. The killer stopped firing while he scoured the crowd for the source of the projectile.

Yorke threw another. This one smashed next to the gunman's feet. He looked up towards Yorke and their eyes met.

'PUT THE GUN DOWN!' Yorke launched a bottle this time, which hit the gunman's shoulder and then shattered on the floor.

The gunman raised the gun. Yorke lobbed the last bottle on the table. It missed the killer's head by an inch. The bastard was about to take his shot—

The doorman stood up behind the bar, reached over

and grabbed the gunman by the hair and yanked him backwards. The bullet hit the ceiling above Yorke's head. He felt the sprinkle of plaster.

The doorman banged the back of the gunman's head off the bar and let him fall to the ground.

Clever boy ... Now, the gun ...

The man of the hour clambered over the bar and kicked the gun away.

Good ...

He knelt over the gunman to incapacitate him.

Careful ...

The doorman slumped backwards. He was clutching his eye.

Shit ... the glass ...

Yorke looked at the stairs to his left; there was still a build-up of students around the bottom of them. No good. He hoisted himself over the banister and dropped down. Pain shot through his knees and his lower back.

Ahead, the doorman, on his backside, was using his feet to slide himself away. He clutched his face. 'My eye ... *my fucking eye.*'

The killer was also sitting on the floor, but he wasn't going anywhere. He was smiling and holding a bloody, smashed bottle.

A bottle Yorke had thrown.

Yorke held up his hands, showing the smiling killer that he was unarmed. The screaming was subsiding, but it was still noisy, so Yorke moved closer and spoke loudly. 'Listen. I'm police. It's over—

'*My eye! He's taken out my fucking eye.*'

The killer flinched. Yorke looked at the doorman with narrowed eyes. He felt devastated for the man, but he desperately needed him to be quiet.

'Listen. You're not in control of yourself.' Yorke edged forwards, his hands out. 'Mayers, Harris, the Conduit, whatever you call him, has brainwashed you.'

The boy smiled. 'Brainwashed? The world did that to me long before Harris found me.' He nodded his head to indicate the bodies on the ground behind Yorke. 'He was simply my conduit to this.'

Yorke chanced another step. 'He's dead, son. The Conduit is dead.'

It broke the killer's smile. 'Liar.'

'He's dead, and I'm sorry for what he's done to you.'

'I am Alan Sants. *No one else is responsible.*' The boy turned the bottle and put the jagged glass to his neck. '*The world will remember that.*'

'There's been enough pain, enough death.' Yorke took another tentative step. 'All because of the man in your head.' He held out his hand. 'Let me help you.'

'*Remember me.*' Alan pushed the glass into his neck.

Yorke lurched forward, slipping to his knees. As he did so, he reached out towards Alan, hoping he'd not misjudged the distance. He hadn't. He took hold of the boy's wrist and yanked backwards. The bottle slipped from Alan's hands and clattered on the floor. Yorke brushed it away.

Alan slipped backwards. The collar of his shirt was already painted red with blood.

'You don't get to do this.' Yorke leaned over the boy. 'You don't get to do what you've done and just leave.'

Alan smiled.

Yorke reached behind Alan's neck and untied the bowtie. He then used this to mop at the blood on the wound to try and gauge the damage. It was messy, and was bleeding a reasonable amount, but it wasn't pumping out. With both hands, he pressed the bowtie to the wound and applied pressure.

The screaming had stopped. There was just moaning from Alan's conscious victims, including the doorman, and the murmurs of anguish from those who'd come back in to help.

'You're too late,' Alan said.

Yorke kept the pressure up, keeping his eyes firmly on the killer's eyes. There was still life in them.

He could hear the emergency services flocking in.

He felt a hand on his shoulder. 'We'll take it from here.'

Yorke turned his head and looked up at the paramedic, who was standing alongside a uniform. The police officer had an old and rugged face. He also spoke with a growl. 'This is the bastard who did it. You might want to give this prick a miss.'

Yorke let go of the bowtie, stood up and turned to face the paramedic. 'Save him.'

The paramedic nodded.

Yorke then looked at the officer and narrowed his eyes. 'No one gets to make decisions on who lives and who dies.' He pointed behind him at Alan Sants. 'Not him ...' he raised his bloody finger to the officer's chest '... and not you either.'

THREE WEEKS LATER

MADDEN DRUMMED HER fingers on the table as she read the psychologist's report.

'Says you're fine to come back.'

Yorke nodded. 'Always was, ma'am.'

Madden guffawed. 'After all of that?' She raised an eyebrow. 'Many would have crumbled.'

Yorke shrugged. 'Probably did, for a while, in my own way, but some quality time with Patricia and my family helped. And then there's Rosie.'

'Who's Rosie?'

'Don't ask.' Yorke looked down at the tooth marks on his left brogue.

'I heard your son's girlfriend was seriously ill.'

'She's much better now, ma'am, thank you.'

Madden rose to her feet and looked out of the window. Yorke rolled his eyes. She always did this when she was about to get philosophical. 'Gunmen rarely survive shootings of this nature.'

'I know, ma'am.'

'They are either shot, or commit suicide.'

Yorke nodded.

'Yet, Alan Sants survived, because of you.'

Yorke flinched. 'The wound wasn't deep.'

'Modesty, as usual. You got to him, Mike. You also paid attention in your first aid course – you helped stem the bleeding.'

'It was the right thing to do.'

'Yes, it was, Mike.' She turned back to look at him. 'Even though he killed four people.'

Yorke took a deep breath. 'Your point, ma'am?'

'No point, Mike. You did the right thing.' She sat back down. 'Emma Gardner has reapplied.'

Yorke knew this already, but he didn't say so. Just nodded.

'Your thoughts?'

'She's one of the best officers I've worked with.'

Madden nodded, and leaned forward. 'Is that why you took her with you to Leeds?'

Yorke had to be careful here. He couldn't lie. That is what had happened. All he could do is try and mitigate the bad feeling around it.

'I've been reprimanded already, ma'am. I've conceded it was poor judgement. I put her in danger.'

'Now, now, Mike. She put herself in danger. It seems you are both very good at doing that. Putting *yourselves* in danger.'

'Once again, sorry ma'am.'

'Yet, there's something about you two, together again, that appeals to me.'

Yorke nodded. 'She's an effective part of my team.'

Madden nodded. 'Something still bothers me though.'

Yorke met her eyes. He knew what was coming next.

'Mark Topham?'

'Tragic,' Yorke said. 'Despite what he did, he was still one of us.'

'Yes.' Madden nodded. 'I was referring to the nature of his death though.'

'Suicide, wasn't it?'

'How did he get to that old quarry, Mike?'

'I really don't know, ma'am.'

'Emma Gardner spent all of this time trying to find him, and when she finally did, she lets him go,' she clicked her fingers, 'just like that.'

'He jumped out of the car at a traffic light and ran, ma'am.'

Madden took a deep breath through her nose. There was a whistling sound. 'Yes, Mike, I've read the report. I'm bringing her back.'

Yorke forced back a smile. He was trying to appear contrite.

'You can go now, Mike.'

'Thanks, ma'am.'

As he was leaving, Madden said. 'Well done on stopping Mayers, Mike. He was a twisted bastard. Again, you've made the world a better place.'

It was the first time she'd congratulated him. She turned to her computer and started to work.

Yorke stood there, thinking of a reply. Failing to do so, he simply left the room.

THREE MONTHS LATER

L ACEY OPENED HER eyes.
'Ah, there you are,' Holden said.
Here I am.

'So, you know the drill in *my* Blue Room.' He smiled.

A drill ... now there's an idea.

'Blink once Lacey if you want me to tender my resignation.'

One day, after I cut off your eyelids, you will crave the ability to blink as I do.

'Blink twice if you want to endure what I have brought with me tonight.'

Lacey blinked twice.

Holden shook his head and smiled again. 'So stubborn, but credit where credit's due. Your capacity for suffering is impressive.'

I can't wait to test yours out.

Holden opened the door and let the rapist into the Convalescence Room.

As always, Lacey endured the process. It never weakened her. It only strengthened her. Oh how wrong was

Dr Holden? His fallibility gave her more pleasure than he would ever know.

After the guard had left, Holden closed the door. Usually, he laughed, and mocked her from the door. Today, he decided to come back over to the bed.

She wriggled the fingers on her right hand.

Oh! Welcome sensation!

She tried to move her other hand. No joy.

He leaned close to her. She could smell the stink of his breath.

It's unfortunate that your drugs can do nothing about that!

'I don't care how strong you are, or *think* you are, Lacey, you will fail. Like everyone before you has failed.'

There have been others?

'It will be a glorious moment when you are sitting across from me in the office asking for death.'

I'm afraid that will be a moment that only exists in your mind.

She wriggled the fingers on her left hand.

Ah, here comes mobility ...

'See you tomorrow Lacey. Stan has talked about bringing a colleague tomorrow. I'll try to accommodate him.'

Holden turned from the bed. Lacey lifted her arm and reached out. She was sure she brushed the small of his back.

He strode across the room.

She moved her other arm and turned her head.

Almost there ...

She heard the door slam and the clunk of the lock.

The muscles on her face twitched, and she managed a smile.

Ah well ... maybe, next time.

SIX MONTHS LATER

W HEN KENNY SAT down opposite him in The Wyndham Arms, Yorke put down the postcard and drank his Summer Lightning faster. It was said that the only way to fully comprehend the old man's Irish slur was to join him in inebriation.

'Long time no see, fella.'

'Been a busy year, Kenny.'

Kenny pointed at his own cheek – he was referring to the scar on Yorke's face. 'Finding the bastard who did that to you?'

Yorke shook his head. 'That was a while back.'

'Never understand how you folks do it.' He paused to take a mouthful of ale. 'Catching crooks.'

'It's like any job, really, you just get up and get on with it.'

'But you catch one, only to have another pop up again. Must feel like you're chasing your tail sometimes.'

Yorke laughed. 'Something like that.' He finished his pint.

Kenny pointed at Yorke and nodded his head. 'One thing I always had figured out about you.'

'Go on.'

'You're not a loner. Me?' He turned his palms in the air. 'I thrive as one.'

Yorke smiled. 'Your point Kenny?'

'People rely on you. They need you. Thrive in your presence.'

'Kind words, Kenny, but you need to be switching back to the session ale and pace that drinking—'

'Why're you sitting alone, Michael?'

'Just fancied it.'

'People like you weren't born to sit alone. Now, that other fella, on the other hand ... the one I usually see you with ...' he clicked his fingers ... 'Jake ... now, he's someone I can see sitting alone. He doesn't relate as easy as you, do you know what I mean? Where is the big man anyway?'

Yorke struggled to respond.

Kenny's eyes widened. 'He's not—'

'No,' Yorke said, looking down at the postcard. 'Nothing like that.'

Yorke slid the postcard over to him.

Kenny pulled down a pair of spectacles from his forehead.

He squinted as he read it. 'Slow down, old friend.' He looked up. 'What does it mean?'

'I used to drive him crazy by driving too fast. Despite a rugged exterior, Jake's the most careful driver out there. Ponderous, if you ask me.' Yorke shrugged and pointed at the card in Kenny's hand. 'Received it this morning.'

Kenny turned over the postcard and looked at the white lighthouse on a craggy cliff edge. He read out the name of the place. 'Bass Harbor Head Light, Mount Desert Island, Maine. Far afield ...'

'Yes,' Yorke said, nodding. 'New England.'

'Holiday?'

Yorke sighed. 'I don't know, Kenny. He's been gone a long time now.' He stood up. 'Stay here, Kenny, while I go and grab another pint. I don't want to drink alone.'

Kenny nodded. 'Yes, sir.'

Continue the journey with DCI Michael Yorke as he is reunited with his old friend, Jake Pettman, in Better the Devil ...

Scan the QR to
READ NOW!

FREE AND EXCLUSIVE READ

Delve deeper into the world of Wes Markin with the
FREE and **EXCLUSIVE** read, *A Lesson in Crime*

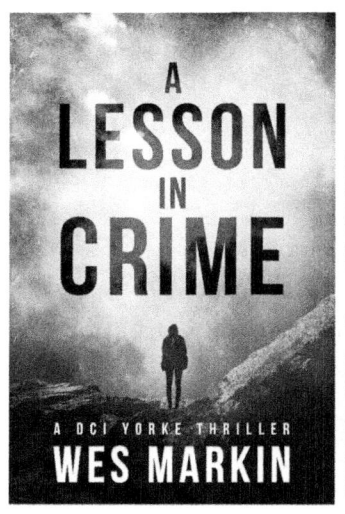

Scan the QR to
READ NOW!

JOIN DCI EMMA GARDNER AS SHE RELOCATES TO KNARESBOROUGH, HARROGATE IN THE NORTH YORKSHIRE MURDERS ...

Still grieving from the tragic death of her colleague, DCI Emma Gardner continues to blame herself and is struggling to focus. So, when she is seconded to the wilds of Yorkshire, Emma hopes she'll be able to get her mind back on the job, doing what she does best - putting killers behind bars.

But when she is immediately thrown into another violent murder, Emma has no time to rest. Desperate to get answers and find the killer, Emma needs all the help she can. But her new partner, DI Paul Riddick, has demons and issues of his own.

And when this new murder reveals links to an old case Riddick was involved with, Emma fears that history might be about to repeat itself...

Don't miss the brand-new gripping crime series by bestselling British crime author Wes Markin!

What people are saying about Wes Markin...

'Cracking start to an exciting new series. Twist and turns, thrills and kills. I loved it.'

Bestselling author **Ross Greenwood**

'Markin stuns with his latest offering... Mind-bendingly dark and deep, you know it's not for the faint hearted from page one. Intricate plotting, devious twists and excellent characterisation take this tale to a whole new level. Any serious crime fan will love it!'

Bestselling author **Owen Mullen**

Scan the QR to
READ NOW!

ACKNOWLEDGMENTS

Before I name and shame the many wonderful people who have supported me on this journey thus far, I would just like to stop, take a breath, and consider what a wild ride this has been! I never imagined Yorke would find as many readers as he has done, and I am extremely proud of what he has achieved in his seven adventures. Although Christmas with the Conduit is the final DCI Yorke thriller, I would certainly never rule out the return of this great detective, and hopefully, one day, he may return in another series. The biggest thank you must go to my wife. Jo makes all be possible. It is her support, and encouragement which really keeps me focused and on track.

I would also like to say thank you to other members of my family, Janet, Peter, Ian and Eileen for supporting me during my 'creative holidays' which can descend, without warning, at any moment of any day and leave me rather distracted. Thank you Hugo and Bea, who keep reminding me how important it is to enjoy every single minute of every day.

Thanks, as always, to Jake, who is always there to challenge and criticise (constructively!). Huge appreciation again to Debbie at *The Cover Collection*, who hit it out the park again with the front cover. Thank you to Aubrey Parsons who continues to breathe life into Yorke and co on the audiobooks.

Thank you to Jay Arscott, Kath Middleton, Jo Fletcher,

Karen Ashman and Jenny Cook for ruthlessly editing. Thank you to all my Beta Readers who took the time to help put Yorke on track – Keith, Carly, Russ, Donna, Holly and Alex. Thank you to the bloggers who remain behind me – Shell, Susan, Dee, Caroline and Jason.

I hope you enjoyed Yorke's Christmas special, and I hope you all join me and Jake Pettman when he stumbles upon a strange pit in a small town called Blue Falls in New England ...

STAY IN TOUCH

To keep up to date with new publications, tours, and promotions, or if you would like the opportunity to view pre-release novels, please contact me:

Website: www.wesmarkinauthor.com

facebook.com/WesMarkinAuthor

instagram.com/wesmarkinauthor

twitter.com/markinwes

amazon.com/Wes-Markin/e/B07MJP4FXP

REVIEW

If you enjoyed reading ***Christmas with the Conduit***,
please take a few moments to leave a review on
Amazon, Goodreads or BookBub.

Printed in Great Britain
by Amazon

50409917R00182